DON PENDLETON'S

STONY

AMERICA'S ULTRA-COVERT INTELLIGENCE AGENCY

MAN®

PERILOUS SKIES

A GOLD EAGLE BOOK FROM

W🌐RLDWIDE®

TORONTO • NEW YORK • LONDON
AMSTERDAM • PARIS • SYDNEY • HAMBURG
STOCKHOLM • ATHENS • TOKYO • MILAN
MADRID • WARSAW • BUDAPEST • AUCKLAND

Recycling programs
for this product may
not exist in your area.

First edition February 2013

ISBN-13: 978-0-373-80437-5

PERILOUS SKIES

Special thanks and acknowledgment to
Timothy Somheil for his contribution to this work.

Printed in U.S.A.

PERILOUS SKIES

CHAPTER ONE

Adelmo Valdes searched the ocean horizon around the speck of Bahamian sand called Glass Key and saw nothing but empty water. The skies were just vast blue emptiness punctuated by a few pure white clouds.

Glass Key was little more than a sand dune in the Caribbean. The island occasionally broke through the surface to become a streak of sparkling white sand. It was the perfect beach, but like all good things, it didn't last. Glass Key would emerge from the water for no more than a few days at a time, when the tides were just right.

Valdes didn't even know why anyone had bothered to give it a name. The place had no value and no purpose for anyone, anywhere—except for him. To him it had a unique and special function.

Also of special use to him was an acquaintance in the U.S. Coast Guard. This acquaintance had some very special secrets, and Valdes knew what they were. He had a vivid piece of video shot from one of those nifty new smartphones with exceptional optics, which made the video all the more interesting. The special optics made the faces on the video quite distinct and recognizable.

Adelmo Valdes was not one to break his promises. He would dispose of that video once his friend in the Coast Guard did him this one favor. It was a big favor, but it would be over soon and the acquaintance in the U.S. Coast Guard would be free to get on with his life. Valdes, if the U.S. Coast Guard acquaintance kept his part of the bargain, would be free to spend his millions.

It was a high-stakes undertaking involving many millions of dollars' worth of cocaine going into the United States in one large shipment. It would be the equivalent of several months of smaller-scale shipments, such as Valdes's family was accustomed to sending. But sending small shipments meant sending more shipments, which meant more possibility for mistakes and more opportunity for carelessness. And more would be lost to seizure by the U.S. Drug Enforcement Administration.

But carefully planning to send in a single large-scale shipment every few months, with more careful preparation and oversight, would inevitably lead to more successful shipments. Valdes was absolutely certain of this.

He was banking his future, and the future of the family, on it. After the irresponsible actions of his brother, product and revenues had been wasted and lost on a massive scale. The family had seen its fortunes crumble in a matter of weeks.

Those had been the worst weeks of Adelmo Valdes's life.

He had been the one left with the obligation to inform his sickly father about Pyo's actions. But informing his father had been a mistake. The shock was so great it caused another final and fatal heart attack. The old man died cursing Pyo for what he had done to the family and cursing Adelmo for being the messenger of such ruinous tidings.

His mother was no better. She had been screaming

at him about Pyo for days. As if Adelmo could control what Pyo did. As if Adelmo was somehow responsible for Pyo's carelessness and his mistakes and his rebellion.

It had been their father who was at fault. Old Roberto was the one who'd given Pyo control over the business. Adelmo had begged him not to. Adelmo had tried to convince their father that Pyo was simply too headstrong and too foolhardy to run the business.

Out of respect for his mother, Adelmo had held his tongue in the presence of the rest of the family. But then his father died, right there in the upstairs bedroom of the huge house that the family business had paid for. And then his mother was screaming at him like a madwoman for hours at a time, sobbing uncontrollably and then screaming again. Finally Adelmo had screamed back at her. He'd screamed about his father, and how he had made a mistake and had given Pyo the means to destroy the family.

Unable to withstand any more of her hysteria, Adelmo had backhanded her viciously. She was flat on the floor in the vast kitchen of the family home. The servants froze in horror, then gathered around her and carried her up to one of the other bedrooms and put her to bed. That was two months ago. She had lived her life in that tight little suite of rooms from that day forward.

But his own act of violence had stilled any indecision in Adelmo's mind. He became calm and confident. His course of action was clear.

Pyo, he the elder brother or not, was entirely unfit to run the family business. With his father dead and Pyo obviously incompetent, it fell to Adelmo to take control of this business.

Pyo, conveniently, was nowhere to be found. He would disappear for days at a time, drinking and whoring. His absence gave Adelmo plenty of time to act.

Adelmo had considered this course of action before, in the first few months when Pyo had been given control of the business, when their father had first become bedridden. He had seen even then that his brother was on a ruinous path. He should have acted then. But even thinking of taking control then had felt like betrayal.

Now it felt appropriate—the correct thing to do.

The takeover had happened calmly and with only words. He gathered what was left of his father's people on the family estate and he announced his intentions. He was calm and reasonable, and laid out the rationale for his decision. His father's people didn't protest or even disagree. They, too, were fed up with Pyo's impulsive acts and the horrible cost in lives and money of those mistakes.

"We are starting over," Adelmo announced to the gathering. "Pyo has lost most of the cash, including most of the money in our bank accounts. What is left to us is only this house, and whatever property we retain, and our current shipment. We must make the most of our next sale to provide the seed money needed to get us back into full-scale business. We can do this if we approach it intelligently, with a real strategy. That is how I intend to do business. I will not be a cowboy that my brother seems to think he is. I will plan carefully, and do what I can to keep this family business out of sight and out of mind of those who would put a stop to us. My way of running the family business will not be as exciting as my brother's. If you want excitement, I will not give it to you. But you can be assured that I will not lead our people into disaster as Pyo has."

Then he asked the people in his father's house, "Will you join me, and support me as the leader of this family, even when Pyo returns to confront me on it?"

Again, there was no protest and no disagreement. His father's people had been decimated by Pyo's carelessness. They wanted nothing more to do with the elder brother. They immediately agreed to support Adelmo as the leader of the family.

The work began. The planning was careful and extensive. The preparation work for this one shipment had been beyond anything that his father's people had ever seen before.

But the people saw how Adelmo made his own connections in the United States, and they saw how this would open the door for this single all-important shipment to reach the United States. Adelmo was running the drug-smuggling operation like a careful and intelligent businessman, just as he had promised he would do.

And then Pyo returned. He looked like hell. He claimed he had paid to be freed from a Mexican prison. He had paid with his family's money—from a bank account Adelmo had not even known existed. And now it was gone.

The men who had gone with Pyo were now in a Mexican jail in Juarez. The local police who held them had identified Pyo and the men as members of a criminal organization. If this local police force turned them over to the federal police they would get nothing. But they would free them to Pyo for a hefty ransom—a ransom they called a "bail." But there was nothing legal about the payoff.

Pyo claimed that he intended to go back to free all his men. In a loud and very public altercation, Pyo demanded Adelmo surrender the cash. He loudly decried Adelmo's assumption of leadership of the family. He demanded that Adelmo turn over access to his father's bank accounts. There was just one family bank account with any real sum of money left in it. It was less than four million dollars, a fraction of the family's previous wealth.

Pyo was flabbergasted when he realized that his father's men had indeed given their loyalty to Adelmo. But after ranting for some time, he calmed himself and became thoughtful—and claimed he would accept Adelmo as the leader of the family business.

Adelmo did not believe or trust his brother, but when Pyo claimed he needed the money to free the last few men still held by the police in Juarez, Adelmo had to give it to him. If there was a chance of getting those men out of jail, he must take that chance. Only Pyo knew which individual would be able to free these men—for the specified bail.

Pyo, quite predictably, disappeared with the money and had not been heard from in weeks.

Adelmo would not let the betrayal distract him. Not today. Today, when this operation was successful, the family business would have a new start and the family bank accounts would begin to fill again with cash.

But he could not escape the heaviness in his heart that had come from all this. He mourned the loss of his father, now in the ground, and the loss of his mother, who had shut herself away from the world and from her family—but he could not mourn the loss of his brother. Pyo had been, in truth, lost for years. He had gone crazy as a teenager; he'd suffered an overdose when he was fifteen and was never quite right after that. From then on he was impulsive and wild and destructive. And careless in his work for the family—no matter how many times their father had tried to beat the carelessness out of him.

RIGHT ON TIME, THE LUXURY motor yacht appeared on the blue sea, heading swiftly toward Glass Key. She was a seventy-foot luxury catamaran named the *Great Escape,* with expansive deck space and luxury interior appointments. She had been leased out of Key West three days ago by a trio of freshly graduated law students. The students were all studying for the bar—about to begin button-down lives, with big-time careers as corporate lawyers in St. Louis. Before they took that step, they wanted a little bit of excitement on the high seas. Young Americans, with promising futures, who wanted to have one really wild story to tell their closest friends in their future years.

Adelmo Valdes had made contact with them through some of his own old acquaintances at St. Louis University. He had flown up to meet them and give them the hard sell. He promised them an adventure they'd never forget. They'd get the private luxury cruise, fully stocked with food and liquor. Entertainment would be provided in the form of a half-dozen University of South Florida sophomore coeds, while the yacht itself would be manned by a professional crew hired by Valdes. All they had to do was to lease the boat under their own names, pay for it themselves, with cash, which Valdes provided, and enjoy themselves. Get drunk and get laid and get the boat to Glass Key within forty-eight hours—

and, most importantly, be on hand to meet the Coast Guard if the yacht should be stopped.

Boys like this, with a believable story to tell and with fathers with political connections, were the safest possible bet should the *Great Escape* be stopped by the Coast Guard or the DEA.

The three American boys and their six hired sophomore playmates would spend an afternoon playing on the beautiful white sands of Glass Key, while Valdes and his men loaded up the *Great Escape* with the shipment. The American boys would turn around and head back to Florida. They would have another forty-eight to seventy-two hours to get drunk and screw the coeds from the University of South Florida, do some deep-sea fishing and generally just enjoy themselves.

Valdes guaranteed that they would be met by a Coast Guard ship with which he had made special arrangements. The *Great Escape* would not be searched. He assured them that they would return to Florida unmolested.

With their family connections and their family wealth, nobody was going to pester these boys too much. If there was an official record of their getting searched once, nobody could search them again.

The carefully engineered scenario had its own built-in series of checks and balances. The status of the three young soon-to-be lawyers made them unlikely suspects by the DEA, particularly with their high-profile activities and the extreme expense of their rental boat. Regardless, these boys could be watched. But there would be no suspicious activity during the cruise that would alert the DEA, even if they were staring down on the *Great Escape* night and day with their spy drones.

The shipment had been brought to the Glass Key days ago, in several small sailboats, and sunk on the site. That was one of the most significant risks of the entire operation—and it was a huge risk to leave the valuable, irreplaceable cargo in the middle of nowhere, unguarded for days.

But it was also key. The DEA didn't tend to stop boats that never stopped themselves. Smugglers needed to stop to transfer cargo but the drop-off boats never did. Just dumped their stuff over the side in their special submergible containers and kept going.

Creating an erroneous perception was key. The actors in this play had to not behave like drug smugglers— even when viewed on radar or on the digital feeds from a DEA patrol drone.

The well-staged play would continue even when the *Great Escape* came to Glass Key. There would be nothing more than a few fishermen already on the stretch of sand. The fisherman's open boat would not raise the suspicions of the DEA, even if it stopped by.

Valdes was dressed for the part. He looked like some low-wage Bahamian fisherman. Their boat was an old tub that cost them a hundredth of the lease cost on the *Great Escape*. But it was just as important to the operation.

Everything looked *right*. Everything would work correctly. Valdes had thought through every aspect of this operation, looking for flaws, looking for potential problems. As the *Great Escape* headed for Glass Key, he grew more confident. This was going to work out the way it was supposed to. There would be no surprises.

And then a shadow flitted over the sand. Valdes thought it was a bird and dismissed it from his mind almost immediately. Then his mind replayed the image of the shadow. The wings of the birds seemed too stiff. He was not alarmed yet, but he did turn to check out the bird.

Instead he saw an aircraft zipping at two hundred feet above the surface of the Caribbean Sea. It was off-white, almost gray, and it almost seemed to absorb the color of the sky around it. It was an almost angelic-looking little craft, with strange curves. Valdes found it difficult to lock his eyes on it, as if it was every second on the verge of fading into the blue sky behind it.

And it was *silent*. It was a glider or some such…

But that wasn't true, either. As it banked and lined up on the long, narrow stretch of sand, Valdes heard the gentle purr of a jet engine. The aircraft almost disappeared from his vision again, now that he was staring straight down the nose.

One of his men cursed.

"What is that?" Valdes demanded.

"I don't know."

Valdes wanted to say more, but he became aware that the thing was closing in on them very fast. It was coming in for a landing on the sand. He found himself wondering if it was a big toy—because it moved too easily in the breeze, as if it didn't have enough mass to be a real, human-size aircraft.

No, it was manned. There was a wide-aspect glass windshield mounted over the cockpit and there was a man at the controls.

Small or not, there was no way it was going to have enough room to land on this tiny stretch of beach. Valdes kept thinking the pilot must be about to pull up— but the little jet seemed to be aiming right at him.

His men began to shout, and they scattered away from the center of the Key, while Valdes stared the thing down. He didn't like this development. He didn't understand it. He had not accounted for it in his planning— how could he have? He wanted to raise his gun and shoot that plane out of the sky simply for being an anomaly.

Instead he hurried into the waist-deep waters of the Caribbean to escape being run down. The aircraft became louder as it hissed past him, settled on the sand and taxied almost gently for just a few hundred feet, throwing up sand and a fine mist of water.

THE AIRCRAFT HAD COME upon them so quickly that they had not even had time to consider making a run for it. As Valdes watched the aircraft slow to a halt and make a nimble U-turn on the sand, he again got the impression of a toy plane, with very little mass. The belly of the aircraft seemed to reflect and absorb the color of the beach sand, while the upper fuselage, seen against the Caribbean sky, seemed to absorb the blue.

It taxied in his direction. Even close, the two small engines mounted alongside the tail made no more noise than a well-tuned SUV. Adelmo wondered if it could possibly be DEA—but then he realized that there were no numbers on the tail. No markings anywhere.

The pilot waved, and even with the sun glaring off the glass Adelmo recognized his brother.

"It's Pyo," he snapped angrily.

The other men lowered the weapons they had brought to bear on the strange little plane.

"Since when is he a pilot?" one of his men asked.

"Since never," Adelmo declared. Pyo would never

have had the self-discipline needed to take flying lessons, and certainly not the aptitude. But as far as Adelmo could tell he was the only one at the controls of the small jet.

Adelmo glanced at the *Great Escape,* sailing smoothly to the still waters inside the other sandbars that protected Glass Key.

"So what's he doing here?"

"I don't know that, either," Adelmo said, and he did not like his own answer. He had planned this operation meticulously. Leave it to Pyo to screw it up. Adelmo realized suddenly that he hated his brother.

He also realized that only one of his men had been demanding answers. His second man was hanging back, silent. And Jorge was a man who was not often silent. Adelmo wanted to turn on Jorge and question him, but he controlled himself.

He *must* regain control of this situation—whatever direction this situation took.

Adelmo's mind was burning with questions about the aircraft and about Pyo's ability to fly it—but he wouldn't give Pyo that satisfaction.

"What the hell are you doing here?" Adelmo demanded.

Pyo gesticulated ridiculously at his head, indicating he couldn't hear what Adelmo was saying. Then he flipped a switch on his dashboard and spoke, and his voice was played loudly over an external speaker somewhere on the aircraft.

"Like it?"

"What are you doing here, Pyo?" Adelmo asked.

"Taking what's mine," Pyo said. He adjusted something and snapped another switch on his dashboard, and gunfire cracked from under the nose of the small jet. The man alongside Adelmo slumped to the sand, one knee shot out.

The man screamed and grabbed his bloody knee, and Adelmo cursed, took a step back and thrust his gun at his brother in the seat of the aircraft.

"You *fucker*."

"Stop, Adelmo," Jorge said. He was now holding his automatic weapon on Adelmo from five paces away.

Over the loudspeaker, Pyo laughed.

Adelmo regarded Jorge—a man he had trusted.

"I am sorry, Adelmo," Jorge said. "Pyo promised to give me back my own brother if I would help him."

"And you believe him? You are as big an idiot as he is."

"An idiot?" Pyo asked over the loudspeaker. "You're the one who'll look like a fool, Adelmo, when this is all done. I'm going to see to it. Whatever sweet words you used to talk father's men into serving you are going to be undone by this time tomorrow. You watch and see."

Pyo wanted Adelmo to demand answers. He waited for Adelmo to argue. Adelmo knew his brother—knew he became irritated when someone showed no interest in his secrets. It was little-boy behavior they had never grown out of.

Pyo demanded attention, and Adelmo refused to give it to him.

"Well? Don't you care how I'm going to do it?"

"No," Adelmo said.

Pyo hissed and snapped, "Get him to work."

The gun that was pointed at his stomach waved slightly at the sand where the anchored containers would be buried. Made of plastic and steel, they would protect the cargo.

In the days since they were dropped, the containers had been buried in a foot of the shifting tidal sands.

"Start shoveling," Pyo ordered from inside the aircraft.

It only took a few minutes for Adelmo to shovel off enough sand to access the top of the containers. He pulled out the packages and was directed to drag them alongside a hatch in the side of the aircraft.

By then, the *Great Escape* captain had radioed, demanding an explanation. He wanted to know why there was an aircraft on the stretch of sand where they were making their rendezvous.

Adelmo's guard, Jorge, radioed back. "Everything is okay," he said. "Go ahead and anchor."

Adelmo wondered what was in store for the occupants of the *Great Escape*. He cared nothing for the rich young men and he cared nothing for their college whores, but he cared for the three men who served as crew on that yacht. They were men he had hired, men who had been associated with his family on and off for thirty years.

He also wondered if those men would be smart enough to smell a trap. Certainly the young college men would not be.

Adelmo could see his brother, behind the glare of the sun on the windshield of the strange little airplane. His brother was keeping an eye on the approaching *Great Escape*. He did not seem to be concerned by the fact that the *Great Escape* had cut its engine too early and was drifting offshore, and the powerful-looking man on deck was watching the activity on shore through binoculars.

Clearly Adelmo's men on that boat would recognize him and would see the gun being held upon Adelmo. He heard them demand attention through the radio on Jorge's belt. Jorge did not answer it. He just shifted on his feet. It must be uncomfortable for him to be stabbing these men in the back, even if it was an unnecessary price to get his brother back.

Of course, Adelmo knew, Pyo would not give Jorge back his brother. The entire story was a fabrication. The brother was almost certainly dead.

It was foolish to expect the men on the watercraft to effect a rescue. There was more firepower on this little stretch of sand than in the *Great Escape*. Certainly more manpower, considering that the young college students from America could probably not even shoot a gun and would probably go running to hide in the closets if shooting started.

The traitor—the one who thought that Pyo was going to give him back his brother—spoke to the airplane.

"They are calling somebody about this," Jorge said.

"Who will they call?" Pyo snapped. "Our mother? It's afternoon. She is deep in the grape by now. There is no one there who can help. There are no favors they can call in. Do you hear me, Adelmo? There is no help coming for you."

"What is it you want, Pyo?" Adelmo demanded.

"That should be pretty obvious. I want what is mine—the family business—and I'm taking it today. I'm taking over, and I will run this business the way it should be run. And it will be the proper family business again. Only it will be better than before."

Adelmo stood. "I am not going to help you."

Pyo stepped out of the aircraft and stood in the sand in bare feet, with the door held between himself and Adelmo.

"Put Adelmo in shackles. He goes in the rear, with the shipment."

Jorge pulled a fistful of rolled plastic cuffs from his back pocket and approached Adelmo timidly. Adelmo stood straight and stared the man in the face, but held his wrists out in front of him. If he would be chained like a dog, he would be chained with dignity. It would be the one putting the bonds on his hands who would feel the shame. And Jorge felt it. He would not look Adelmo in the face. He slid the plastic loop around one wrist, but before he could loop the second wrist Pyo snapped at him again.

"Behind his back," he said.

Jorge growled under his breath. "Turn around." He tried to make it sound gruff, but instead he sounded like a frightened boy on the playground.

Adelmo saw no profit in resistance or fighting. He had little doubt that if he began to resist, he would be shot in knees like the man bleeding to death at his side. If he tried to run, he would be shot in the back before he could make it to the water's edge.

Yes, Pyo would shoot him in the back without a second thought.

By now, the *Great Escape* was rumbling quietly away from the strip of sand, and in the glaring sun there was no one left visible on deck. Adelmo felt abandoned.

So he let the cuffs tighten on his wrist. More were looped into his belt and between the wrist cuffs. He was walked to the belly of the aircraft, shoved to the sand, and his ankles were cuffed, as well.

The hatch on the aircraft opened to reveal an unexpectedly large storage space. The shipment was wedged inside, leaving a tiny, cramped space for himself. He was lifted and folded into that tight space, and the hatch was closed around him.

He did not quite understand what was going on. It made sense to him that Pyo would feel unfairly used by the turn of events. Pyo was always the victim. But when had his brother learned to fly an aircraft? And what did he hope to do with the shipment now that he had it?

More important, Adelmo realized, was what Pyo would do with him.

The space in which he was wedged was impossibly tight. His knees were against his chest, and his head rested against the interior of the storage space. Still, there was light coming in, and when he craned his neck he could see a tiny window above and behind him. It was just a few inches long, but when he turned his head, he found another, just off the floor, that allowed him to see the sand below the aircraft. Stretching his body into a position to see out either of these windows was incredibly painful, but it was something for him to rest his eyes on.

There was an identically shaped window in the wall that separated the storage compartment from the cabin. He looked through it and could see the back of his brother's head. In the tiny aircraft, he was just inches away from the man. If Adelmo had had a gun, it would have been a can't-miss shot. If the wall was not there and if his hands were not bound, he would not have had to reach far to get his hands around his brother's throat.

He could see that the bulkhead he was against was not even a permanent fixture of the aircraft interior. It seemed to be bolted into place, but the bolts were on the other side of the wall, and the wall was sturdy enough to keep shifting cargo from breaking through into the cabin. Adelmo did not think he was going to find a way to break down the wall to get to his brother.

He felt movement. He looked through the front hatch and saw Jorge seating himself inside the cabin. He closed the door but ignored the seat belt, and Pyo touched a button that brought a loud hum from the engines of the aircraft.

They were leaving the wounded man there on the sand. The man was not even dead. His legs were ruined and he would never walk again but he was not dead. And yet they were going to just leave him here, until he did finally bleed to death, was cooked in the sun or the ocean came up and swallowed him.

It was a reprehensible act, but it was an act that Adelmo understood. It made sense for his brother to do such a thing. What did not fit into Adelmo's view of the world was Pyo's ability to control this aircraft. Pyo was a rough man who muscled his way through any challenge, battered his way through any fight and shouted his way through any argument. Finesse was not his style. He had never been skilled—at anything. And yet he was deftly handling the controls of the aircraft as if it was one of his favorite old Hummers.

Something else wasn't right. The aircraft was making almost no sound. The engines were rushing, they sounded like a big fan, not like a jet.

And how was this thing going to take off from a short stretch of soft Caribbean sand anyway?

He didn't know much about aircraft, but he didn't think that this was something aircraft were supposed to do.

Pyo's plane nosed to the far end of Glass Key, dipped its front wheels in the ocean and spun in a one-eighty. Now it pointed to the far end of the island, which was not that far away. And still, the engines were as quiet as a well-tuned BMW. Adelmo began to wonder if the aircraft could even get off the ground under these circumstances.

His back and his knees and his head were strained but he kept himself pulled up high enough to watch as Pyo went through the takeoff procedure, which was deceptively simple and short. He switched a panel gear to a mode that he wanted, then he pulled back on the throttle and the quiet little aircraft sprinted across the sand. Adelmo was knocked off balance, and by the time he had maneuvered himself to see out the front window again, they were in the air. Indistinct, through the front windows, Adelmo could see the Caribbean Sea speeding underneath them.

Pyo reached up behind him and slid open the tiny hatch window.

"Hey, Adelmo, you have got to see what this thing can do."

Adelmo's ankles were screaming at him from the strain of holding his position, but he held it as the small aircraft descended and leveled out, until it was cruising fast just a few feet off the surface of the Caribbean. The absence of a loud engine noise made it seem dreamlike, but within seconds he recognized the shape on the surface of the ocean, and they were coming up on it fast.

Adelmo remembered how quiet the aircraft had been

approaching the Glass Key. His men aboard the *Great Escape,* with their own engines likely now pushing them along as fast as possible, might not even hear the aircraft closing in on them.

It took seconds for the small jet to reach the *Great Escape.* Even from his uncomfortable perch in the cargo compartment, Adelmo witnessed two of his men scramble to the deck of the boat at the last moment and raise their weapons to fire. But they never got the chance. Pyo grabbed a trigger stick and Adelmo heard—and felt—machine guns firing from under the nose of the jet. They cut down the two men. Then the *Great Escape* was underneath them and behind them.

Pyo pulled back slightly, raising the aircraft gently to less than fifty feet and turned it in a sharp bank that allowed them to line up again on the *Great Escape.* There were two men on deck lying in pools of blood. As Pyo swooped down on the *Great Escape* again, another man burst from the cabin firing a combat shotgun. Pyo should have been expecting it, but he was startled and he jerked back, sending the aircraft into side-by-side warbling. For a second it felt as if he was going to lose control of the aircraft, but he pulled back on the wheel and the throttle, and nosed the aircraft into a controlled ascent.

"Son of a bitch," Pyo grumbled. He turned the aircraft again and swooped down on the *Great Escape.* It was a diving attack, something straight out of a World War II movie. The small-caliber rounds of the machine gun stitched across the deck and slammed through the cabin exterior. Adelmo's last man stepped into the open again, leaped across the deck, twisted in midair to face upward and blast the underbelly of the aircraft at the very last moment. Adelmo heard the rain of pellets against the exterior of the aircraft. He heard his brother laugh. "He might scratch my paint job!"

The traitor in the seat beside Pyo said nothing.

Pyo turned the aircraft again and swooped down on the boat for a third time. The shotgunner was already a nonproblem. He must've taken rounds before he even made his last desperate act. He lay where he had landed, with the bodies of his two companions not far from him and a pair of red blossoms on his chest.

As Pyo made lazy, wide circles around the *Great Escape,* the three college boys and their female companions emerged on deck, hands in the air, ready to surrender. Pyo ordered the man in the copilot seat to make a phone call. The traitor phoned up the United States Coast Guard on the satellite phone. He called in a mayday and gave the *Great Escape*'s GPS coordinates.

They waited for an hour, idly circling the *Great Escape.* Once, when the college boys got the smart idea of starting the engines and trying to get the hell away from there, Pyo swooped in on them, machine gun peppering the deck and inadvertently tagging one of the coeds in the foot. Her screeches could be heard even in the aircraft as they sped away. But the boys got the message. They didn't try to motor away again. They didn't even try to go belowdecks. They wrapped the coed's shattered foot in a dirty shirt, then pretty much ignored her. None of them seemed to notice that she'd gone into shock.

Abruptly Pyo broke off and headed northeast. On the boat they heard no more than a loud hush as it accelerated and vanished in seconds, the self-camouflaging fuselage fading into the light blue Caribbean sky.

The would-be lawyers waited five minutes, just to be sure that the aircraft was not going to return, then started the engine on the *Great Escape*. They had traveled less than five miles, and were still deep in a frantic argument as to the best way to dispose of the bodies of the dead crew, when another aircraft appeared. It was not quiet; it made a thunderous racket as it descended on the *Great Escape*, and the command from the Coast Guard came simultaneously through their radio. They were to prepare to be boarded.

HOURS LATER, ADELMO FELT the aircraft landing. By then, his hands and his feet were screaming in pain. His entire skeleton ached from being stuffed into the miserable compartment, where the shifting containers had split up against him and half crushed his body, and as the hours went on he had less and less strength to shove them away.

He certainly did not have the strength to turn and crane his neck to look out the little windows. He didn't think it would have done him any good. They were on the ground for no more than fifteen minutes, taking fuel. He heard the clunk of the nozzle going into a space above his head. He heard the curious sound of aircraft fuel trickling down through the fuselage all around him. The fuel piping and tanks seemed to be built into the walls and the belly of the aircraft.

He heard his brother and the traitor conversing briefly outside the cargo hatch. It seemed that the traitor wanted to let Adelmo out to stretch his legs and take water.

"He can have a glass of water when we get to Colombia," Pyo argued.

Adelmo's heart sank. They were going to travel all the way to Colombia in this aircraft? He didn't think he would survive it. His hands and his feet had swollen, and the circulation was all but cut off; his limbs would be dead if he didn't get these cuffs off in another few hours. And he really wanted a drink of water.

But he didn't get one.

It was dark when Pyo took the plane down to land on a pebbly, rough stretch of asphalt. The air became stifling hot and thick, and it smelled like a swamp. Not, Adelmo thought, like Colombia.

The hatch opened. The heat intensified. Adelmo was instantly swarmed by little biting bugs. A sweaty, greasy man began offloading the cocaine without giving Adelmo much more than a glance.

"Want some water for your friend?" the man asked. He spoke English. He sounded like one of those white men from the rural parts of South Florida. That's where this must be, Adelmo thought. Florida.

But flying an aircraft unnoticed into the United States was virtually impossible now. They used drones to patrol the airspace. They tracked every flight by GPS and became very suspicious of strange behavior—and Pyo had landed on a street, of all places. The swamp was close on either side of the crumbling road—it must be an abandoned swamp road.

"He's fine," Pyo answered.

It took all Adelmo's will to not break down and beg his brother for a sip of water.

He entertained himself with the fantasy of rolling out of the cargo hatch and across the pavement for a few feet until he splashed into the black, murky slime of the swamp. If he did that, would Pyo fish him out again or let him drown?

Pyo, Adelmo knew, would fish him out. Pyo wasn't done tormenting him yet.

The drug buyer got in his vehicle and drove away. Pyo waved a stack of bills in Adelmo's face. "You were getting, what, five million? Here is ten. And I did not pay for any stupid gang of college kids to smuggle this into the United States for me. And I never would have had to make a ridiculous exchange on some Caribbean island. I could fly it directly here, to the United States, and get my money and turn around and fly right home, like I will right now. And you know what, Adelmo, this is the proof—proof that I will run the operation better than you. Safer, and with more profit and less overhead. And less risk. See?"

Adelmo said nothing.

"I am better, see?" Pyo insisted.

Adelmo did not look at him.

"*Fuck* you! *Fuck* you!" Pyo shouted in his face. "We'll see how you feel when we get back. You can just stay in your ties until then."

Adelmo went into a place of endless agony. Now he had the cargo hatch all to himself, and found himself crashing into the walls when the aircraft changed position. His hands had gone numb, and he was sure they were dead. His tongue was swollen in his mouth.

They landed finally in Colombia and the cargo hatch was opened. Adelmo flopped onto the pavement, barely conscious. He heard his mother scream.

Pyo must have lured her out of her damned bedroom. First time in weeks.

"What did you do to him?" his mother demanded.

Adelmo heard Pyo speak. "Less than he deserved. Should've killed him for what he did to this family. He's a traitor."

Adelmo's mother was in hysterics. "You are the traitor!"

Adelmo opened his eyes with great effort, just in time to see Pyo backhand their mother. The richly dressed woman crumpled. And now she has been struck by both her sons, Adelmo thought.

But Pyo was holding up his precious stack of cash, and the family's top men—what was left of them—were gathering around him and congratulating him. Even the traitor Jorge was all smiles now. And their mother—when she saw that money—it was as if her madness evaporated. And she had nothing but smiles for her eldest son, Pyo.

Adelmo could feel the poison from his gangrenous hands seeping into his bloodstream and he thought it would be acceptable to die soon. But from his pathetic broken body he looked and saw that the aircraft was parked on the football fields on the grounds of the family mansion. Adelmo and Pyo had played soccer here, together, when they were boys, before they hated each other.

Now the professionally maintained turf was gouged by the presence of equipment. A fuel truck and several of the family Hummers. And another one of those small, camouflaged jet aircraft was rolling over the grass in their direction. One of the family's top men was practicing driving it around the grounds.

Pyo seemed to be assembling his own little air force.

CHAPTER TWO

Even a country as poor as Bolivia had its well-to-do population. Even in the city like La Paz, where most of the population was destitute, there were a handful of those who were affluent. And there were always businesses to cater to the affluent. Jewelry stores selling million-dollar baubles. Restaurants serving hundred-dollar plates accompanied by thousand-dollar bottles of wine. Hotels with spacious suites, fine furnishings, twenty-four-hour concierge service and, for the truly ostentatious, gold-plated plumbing fixtures.

The Hotel Europa was one such business—a high-class lodging operation in one of the newest high-rises in the city center. The hotel occupied the top fifteen stories of the thirty-story building, and it included a vast diamond-shaped glass window at a steep angle that served as the upper roof.

Behind that window on the twenty-eighth floor was one of the most expensive restaurants in Bolivia, where a dinner for two cost as much as most Bolivian families made in the year.

Behind that window on the twenty-ninth floor was a chic little spa that offered yoga classes, massages and specialty beauty treatments. A complete makeover at the spa could cost as much as one thousand U.S. dollars, and in La Paz the dollar was the preferred currency. The spa also sold designer clothing for both men and women. If desired, a couple could arrive at the spa and have a complete makeover over a two-hour period, including a complete new outfit suited for their body type.

In the late afternoon the spa closed for an hour, the merchandise and fixtures were cleared away and new fixtures brought from storage to transform the spa into a chic club.

The idea was that wealthy clients could lunch at the restaurant, come to the spa to have a complete makeover and to acquire a new wardrobe, have dinner at the restaurant and return to the spa location to find it an ideal spot for an evening's entertainment.

It was therefore possible, the hotel literature claimed, to experience the best of Bolivia without ever leaving the Hotel Europa.

Behind the window on the thirtieth floor was the presidential suite and penthouse. An extremely wealthy couple, after their day of spa treatments and fine dining in the floors below, could make love in a fifteen-foot-wide master bed and look directly out through the top of the diamond window onto the city of La Paz and the high mountain plains in which she was nestled.

From thirty stories up, even the greasy cook fires in the hillside La Paz slums looked like twinkling stars.

THIS NIGHT, THE TOP STORY of the Hotel Europa was exceptionally busy and crowded. The penthouse suite had been dedicated to a single event, along with the penthouse courtyard facility, which was an airy, open outdoor social area with enough plantings to make it feel like a garden.

Renting out the entire top floor of the Hotel Europa was a huge expense—unless one owned the hotel. Adan

Neruda was the majority owner in the Hotel Europa and he had acquired it primarily for the purpose of staging his annual birthday party. He used the entire top floor space to create a number of party spaces so that all his guests, old and young, millionaires and almost-billionaires, would be comfortable and, most importantly, impressed.

There was no lovemaking happening in the vast master bed this night. A mound of rich brocade pillows filled the center of it, turning the edges of the bed into a long, luxurious cushioned bench. The bedroom itself was transformed into a very classy and elegant lounge area, with a bar and a small stand for a Bolivian classical guitarist.

Truth be told, there would be lovemaking in that bed this evening—later, when the guests loosened up. Adan Neruda had spread rumors that at past parties the hippest young people would surreptitiously burrow into the great mound of pillows and have quick sex, just a few feet away from other guests sitting on the bed and enjoying their cocktails.

It was the kind of story that turned a party into an event. It stoked people's expectations of the party. It made the party into one of the can't-miss events on the upper-crust La Paz social calendar.

If anybody had once thought it was odd that Adan Neruda threw his own birthday party, they got over it years ago. The party wasn't even about him, really. He didn't make a star of himself at these events; the parties were about his guests. No expense spared.

He could afford it. He was one of the wealthiest men in the country, in fact in all of South America. It had been a hard road to get here. His life had been one struggle after another, constantly battling for another measure of control, always fleeing from one enemy or another, until finally power consolidated around him and the enemies became afraid to approach him. When all the pegs fell into their holes, he was transformed from a man on the run and scrabbling for funds to a power broker with a steady flow of revenue from hundreds of sources. Gas interests. Land interests. Distribution of almost any product that came into and left Bolivia. And the drugs. Of course, much of his income came from the drug trade. He was a franchise-holder of many lucrative distribution rings, and that's where the real cash came from.

Adan Neruda was himself somewhat surprised when his years of ambition began to pay off so handsomely. But he knew how to consolidate and hold his power. To retain power, one must have the support of the powerful. Support the powerful, and the support of Bolivia, just as in any other nation in the world, was easily purchased.

When Neruda began the annual tradition of throwing himself a birthday party, and inviting the most important people in the country to come out and celebrate, there were some mutterings of derision. Now it looked like a work of genius.

Everything about the event was appealing to the self-important and power-hungry. Neruda would fly in chefs from Europe and America and from Rio, and bring in rare specialty foods that even the wealthy didn't often get their hands on. The wine was always special. Each year he would buy a complete wine collection, usually worth a million or more, and open up the complete inventory to his party guests. Sommeliers came from France and New York to serve it. Neruda had artisans craft hundreds of special gifts, and ensured that every guest left with a valuable and unique memento of the event.

It was a chance for even the aristocrats of Bolivia to sample rare and unexpected luxuries. And everyone went home with a priceless little gem of a party favor.

After several years, it had become a status symbol to have attended an Adan Neruda birthday party. Even the wealthiest members of Bolivian society went to great lengths to display their Adan Neruda party favors in their homes.

It also became politically or socially ruinous in some circles to be snubbed.

Every year, as a result, there were those who attempted to get on the list. Party invitations had been forged. Neruda had been offered as much as one million dollars a ticket. He didn't take money, although he had been known to take favors. Those who were left out often felt that their careers, as well as their social lives, were at an end. As a result, at least three suicides had been attributed in past years to an Adan Neruda birthday party snub.

The suicides, Adan Neruda decided, were the best possible publicity that his parties could get. They generated word-of-mouth that enhanced his reputation the way that no ten-thousand-dollar knickknack could.

But the ten-thousand-dollar knickknacks were strategically important, as well. This year he had commissioned a team of Chinese artists to create one hundred root carvings. Each of them was made by hand, carved from hundred-year-old pieces of mangrove root wood, all with the Chinese longevity character but also with something extra—a special symbol or totem dictated by the shape of the root and the imagination of the artist. This meant they were all unique, enhancing their value even more. Expertly carved, and beautifully stained and lacquered and hand polished, and each set with a single perfect gemstone in a star carved as part of the symbol. Some were set with emeralds, some with rubies and some with diamonds. All the stones were as near to perfect as possible. Adan Neruda had let it be known, indirectly through a gossip leak, that each little piece of art would indeed have an international collector's value of upward of ten thousand U.S. dollars.

Tonight's earliest entertainment came in the form of two teams of chefs, one from France and one from Japan, and they would have a secret-ingredient cook-off battle. He had provided them with some of the freshest food and produce that the world had to offer. Never mind he had to charter a jet from Alaska to bring in crab, and from Hawaii to bring him tuna.

Adan Neruda never bothered to worry about the cost of his party anymore, because the party always paid for itself in his own enhanced security, in new connections, in new obligations by the guests. It made him someone that everyone wanted to be friends with, and that was a kind of power that money couldn't buy.

It was barely 7:00 p.m. and Adan Neruda had already determined that this would be his best success yet. The guests had oohed and aahed over the display of artworks that officially started the party. They were all eager to get their hands on their own party favor to see which gemstone had been chosen for them. They were all eager to try the special blend of Scotch whisky that had been commissioned and barreled more than a year ago, specifically for this party. Adan Neruda had informed his guests that only enough of the special blend had been made to serve at the party tonight, plus an extra half-dozen bottles, which would be awarded as special prizes.

The only thing Neruda was worried about now was how he would top this party in another year.

He never dreamed that this party was already almost over, and that there would never be a Neruda party in La Paz again.

HE STROLLED THROUGH the penthouse library, which had been transformed into a tasting room for the finer liquors imported for the event. He glad-handed with several business leaders, clinked glasses with two of the power brokers in the national government and shook hands with a visitor from Brazil—one of the biggest crime bosses in Latin America.

They all seemed happy to see him. They all had complimentary words for his booze and his women.

A more raucous bar has been set up in the adjacent parlor. Here several acrobatic bartenders were tossing bottles and spinning glasses as they mixed colorful drinks, mostly for the wives and daughters of the invited guests. In another room, a dance floor was set up and a German techno group, apparently one with several major hits in Europe and Japan, was playing to a packed crowd of forty or fifty young people.

He emerged through an open archway and crossed a small garden, leaving what was technically the presidential suite of the hotel and entering the courtyard. Here half the roof was removed at this time of year to admit the mild nighttime air. The banks of plants turned the courtyard into a true garden, and here the real mingling took place. Tuxedoed waiters brought drinks, and small knots of the most powerful people in the country talked and joked comfortably. A quartet, hidden behind a display of planters, played just loud enough to entertain, but not so loud as to interfere with conversation.

Enthusiasm was running high, as it always did at the start of the party, and by the time it wore itself down in the next hour and a half, the dinner entertainment would start. The two chefs would go head-to-head with the secret ingredient that would be unveiled by Adan Neruda personally, only at the last moment. Then the two chefs and their teams would have an hour to create culinary masterpieces. It was a grand contest that mimicked an American television show, and every party guest would get to taste the dishes and help serve as judge by voting for their favorite. Adan had in fact tipped off the cooking teams to what their secret ingredient would be, just so that they would be able to plan in advance and produce the best possible dishes. It wouldn't do to have one of them crack under the pressure and put out something subpar. Not at Adan Neruda's party. So he had let them know, secretly, that he had flown in several hundred pounds of Norwegian Ruby Red Trout, which would be live in holding tanks when he unveiled it as the secret ingredient. A live ingredient was always more dramatic than a bunch of protein on ice.

In fact, the Norwegian trout would still be alive at midnight. There would be no one around at that point to prepare them.

AS QUIET AS THE QUARTET behind the planters was playing, it was still loud enough to mask the noise of the attack aircraft. It was only when the players ended a song, several conversations stalled and a momentary lull fell across much of the open-air garden that the rush of the engines was heard. Several guests glanced up, curious, not yet alarmed—until they saw the aircraft diving on the rooftop.

It was a small, barely visible jet flying low in the thin air over the city and apparently headed directly at the Hotel Europa. A few women screamed. Adan Neruda turned to see what the commotion was about. For a fraction of a second he was thinking that the screams were delight over some part of his entertainment. Then he saw the aircraft.

The aircraft was clearly a jet, but it was small and slow, moving at the speed of a single-engine plane and with almost no noise at all. It passed low over the top of the Hotel Europa, so close that Adan Neruda could've hit the thing with a rock if only he'd had time to grab one from the decorative planters. A hatch opened near the tail and tiny objects rained down on the party. Several partygoers panicked and ran for cover with their hands over their heads. Adan Neruda glared at the objects as they tumbled end over end and clattered to the floor of the garden.

He snatched one of the objects before it even stopped moving on the stone tile. It was a piece of varnished bamboo, just a few inches long, hollow, with no markings. He was mystified until he realized that there was a roll of paper inside. He tapped it out quickly and unrolled it. It was printed with a brief message.

Party's over, Adan,
and payback is a bitch.

Your old friend,
Soros

Adan Neruda shook his head in disbelief. He'd once known a man named Soros. He'd ended the man's career twenty years ago. The man had been a nothing, nobody, a local Bolivian official with grandiose dreams of power. His ambition and his intelligence had taken him far, moving him up the ladder quickly, consolidating power in much the same way Adan Neruda was consolidating power. Adan Neruda was smarter, and more aggressive, and Soros had put himself in Neruda's way. Neruda attempted to come to terms with Soros, but Soros balked at compromising his own career for the sake of Neruda's. So Neruda ended Soros's career, creatively framing the man for murder and extortion.

In Bolivia, a public official commonly got away with murder and extortion, unless the people he murdered or the people he tried to extort were more powerful than he was. Neruda had made it look as if Soros had killed family members of a local governor, and made it look as if Soros had attempted to extort money from the same governor. Soros's career had gone down in flames. Adan Neruda heard years later that Soros had joined the drug trade and made a reasonably good living at it—in southern Brazil. So everything worked out in the end.

But now it appeared that Soros held a grudge and was about to do something about it.

But that seemed impossible. It was too long ago. Soros was too weak to touch Adan Neruda now. He was too dim-witted to have held a grudge for that long. At least that's what Adan Neruda had thought...

Because now he could see another jet, a twin to the

first, which had been following behind the first and was now diving toward the penthouse courtyard of the Hotel Europa.

Neruda watched, fascinated, for all of five seconds. This one was moving much faster than the first, its engines hissing angrily, aggressively. Neruda knew he was in trouble and broke out of his fugue and bolted for cover. But the aircraft opened up. There was a clatter of angry machine-gun fire and flashes from the nose of the jet, the rounds slamming into the stone tile of the penthouse garden.

Adan Neruda crouched behind a column, breathing hard, his attention drawn suddenly to a grunt and a thump. A staggering man fell to his face, with half his shoulder missing. He'd taken a machine-gun round in the upper body and was now dying on the broken stone tiles. A woman dressed in lace and bling grabbed his hand, shouting at him, and tried to drag him to cover, and then froze. She dropped his hand. She stared at the man, now seeming to realize that it was only a body. She shrieked and fled.

There were others running all over the rooftop. They all went in different directions; none of them seemed to know where they were headed. It was chaos.

There were angry shouts and a desperate pounding. When Neruda bolted inside, he spotted men scrabbling frantically at the elevator. They were jamming their fingernails in the seam and trying to drag the doors open. The indicator above the elevator was flashing red.

The attack was planned well enough. Their first targets were the exterior elevator shafts. They were pretty, but they were also vulnerable to the outside. It would only have taken a quick barrage to crack open the glass and damage the components inside, which would put the thing into emergency shutdown.

They were thirty floors up. It was a long walk down. That would keep victims on hand in case they wanted to attack again.

And Neruda knew that they were going to attack again. His quick assessment of the courtyard had showed five or six bodies, and maybe fifteen injuries. If the attacker really was his old friend Soros, and he really wanted his revenge, he would want to do a lot better than that.

He was playing with Neruda. He was determined to make him suffer for a while.

Adan Neruda had no intention of sticking around to be audience to whatever theatrics Soros had in mind. He headed for the nearest emergency exit, to the stairs. There were already others streaming through the steel fire doors, but he moved quickly among them, descending half a floor when he heard cries from above. "They're coming back! Move fast."

"No!" somebody else shouted. "They're trying to cut us off."

Neruda didn't like the sound of that, but he was already at the doors to the twenty-ninth floor. He looked through the doors. The spa/nightclub was dark tonight in deference to the Neruda party. Neruda had no line of sight to the outside. And those planes were so damn quiet—they could be attacking at this moment and he wouldn't even know it until the barrage began.

There was a scream from up above, and he tried to make sense of the words, but then the barrage did begin again. Heavy machine-gun fire ripped through the walls around him, as if seeking him out. As if somehow the pilots of those planes knew where to target him. That was impossible, and he realized that they were in fact simply trying to cut off escape routes.

They had not counted on how fast Adan Neruda could make his escape. He scrambled down the next flight of stairs, and the next, and panicking hotel guests were flooding into the stairs along with the party guests. Neruda shouldered all of them out of his way, until the crowd became too dense to penetrate. A large man in a bellhop uniform turned on him with a glare when Neruda tried to get past. The bellhop elbowed him in the jaw. It was powerful, and Neruda nearly lost consciousness—but it convinced him to stay in line with the rest of the crowd.

But not before he had memorized the face of the bell-hop. When this was over he would have the man fired, and then he would have the man killed.

If he could manage to avoid being killed himself. He tried to make sense of the chatter of the panicking guests around him, but nobody seemed to know what was going on. There were distant crashes. Windows were breaking on the twenty-ninth and twenty-eighth floors above. But the escaping crowds were in fact leaving the devastation behind.

Already, as his sense of security returned, he was thinking ahead. Once he extricated himself from this herd of cows, and once his safety was assured, he would dedicate all his resources to a new project: hunt down Soros and ruin him utterly.

There was a heavy thump that shook the building. It seemed nearby—as if one of the tiny planes had flown itself into the building at Neruda's level. Women began to scream again around him. Neruda stopped and grabbed on to the handrail and would move no further, despite the curses and shoves of the people around him desperately streaming down the stairs.

He dragged on the handrail, pulling himself upstream against the descending crowds.

Suddenly he was second-guessing himself. And he was a man who never second-guessed himself. He was proud of his ability to make a decision and stick to it and trust it was the *right* decision. But not now. And now he was making the most important decisions he had ever made. The decisions that might or might not save his life.

His mind spun with the realization that these attacks were aimed at humiliating him, but ultimately, certainly, to kill him. He had to think about that. He had to decide what his attackers had in mind. What they would assume he would *do* once the attack started. He would have to deduce their strategy and come up with an effective counterstrategy, and he had only seconds to do it.

He assumed that they would be certain of killing him by killing everyone in the building.

The only way to accomplish that was to be certain that no one in the building escaped. At least no one who was attending his party.

Even to a man who had murdered casually, the thought of wiping out so many people at once—so many important, high-ranking, wealthy people—was staggering. Who could do it and live with themselves? Who would risk that kind of political blowback?

It didn't matter, he firmly insisted to himself. He could consider such matters later. If he lived, he would have plenty of time to think about what had happened, why it had happened and what rationale had been used by this forgotten enemy.

This man Soros. Neruda could not remember enough about him. Could not remember what he was like, or how he had behaved, or what motivated him. He could not remember if the man was meticulous in his planning, or impulsive, or foolish, or intelligent.

That was twenty years ago. And he had considered himself disposed of that problem. The details had been filed away long ago.

He must assume that the planes would continue their waves of attack, and would strike the lower floors, far down enough that they could be assured of damaging the building and trapping all the partygoers in the floors above. That would be the only way to trap them, keep them in place—keep him specifically in place—then they could wipe everyone out.

That is what he would do, if he were making this attack. If he had planes such as these, if he had guts enough to commit mass murder on this scale, all for the sake of petty vengeance, all to settle scores that had been forgotten in the 1990s.

The crowds were in a panic, and when he looked into the eyes of the people streaming down the stairs, he saw glassy gazes and people who moved with a lack of focus. Scared stupid.

He found himself face-to-face with the mayor of the small town where one of his companies was building a retreat. It was something of a combination resort and guesthouse, and was costing him millions. He expected the payback to be ten times the construction costs. He would have his own golf course, world-class, where he could entertain dignitaries and businessmen from all over the world. The mayor of this town had been personally installed by Neruda to help him get the cooperation of the town, to get everything he needed to make his guesthouse a reality. This man was becoming wealthy because of his association with Neruda, but now the man's eyes were rolling white and unfocused, and he barely recognized Neruda when they came face-to-face.

"My God, where are you going?" the man demanded, and he grabbed Neruda's sleeve to pull him with the crowd toward escape.

"Come on, you have got to get out of this building!" the mayor exclaimed.

Neruda didn't answer him. He felt disdain for the man, for his horrified stupidity. The tide of people dragged the mayor away, and Neruda held on to the handrail with a death grip. Let the mayor get dragged down to the lower floors, and see what good it did him. Neruda knew what was coming. Logic told him what the enemy would do. The enemy would hit the building hard, maybe at the twentieth floor. That would be enough to stop the people from escaping. Only then would they unleash their killing weapon. The weapon that would exterminate everyone on these top floors. In that way they could assure themselves that they had wiped out Neruda along with everybody else.

He exited into the near-empty twenty-seventh floor and didn't know where to go next. He heard a thump and another rattle of showering glass. The long shower of the breaking windows started up one side of the building, maybe two floors down, and he could hear the sound travel across the entire floor, unbelievably slowly considering that it was the result of gunfire from the jet.

And how amazing was it that the jet was not only

flying so slowly but was flying so quietly that some of the glass and the sound of the machine-gun fire itself completely masked the sounds of the aircraft engines.

Neruda recalled hearing about these stealth aircraft being sold around the world, illegally, to smugglers and gun-running crime families. It seemed like a strange joke to him that there be a need for such hardware. What good could they do? What benefit would they offer?

Obviously Soros did not see it that way. Soros had taken advantage of this new technology. He'd bought himself a couple.

These things were cheap by aircraft standards—less than one million dollars each. If a man could come up with two million dollars to buy two of these aircraft, surely he was doing well enough that he didn't need to take revenge on such a magnificent scale against Adan Neruda. Why would he go to such lengths? You cannot kill seventy-five or one hundred of the top power players in a South American country and expect to get away with it. If Soros had a power base now, it would come crashing down when the government and the rich families of Bolivia discovered who it was that had wiped out so many of their people.

Then a new picture popped into Neruda's head.

Soros was out for revenge, but Soros probably wasn't insane—and not insane enough to wipe out everyone at Adan Neruda's party. He would know the repercussions. He wouldn't risk that—unless he was insane.

So maybe Soros had no intention of wiping out everyone at the party or even of killing Adan Neruda. What he was doing was *ruining* Adan Neruda. Neruda, who had carefully and methodically built, brick by brick, his foundation of power, for all these years, might not survive a blow to his power base like the one that was being delivered this very moment.

HE FELT HIS PHONE VIBRATE against his chest. He snatched it out of his jacket pocket. It was a number he didn't recognize.

He answered the call.

"Yes?"

"Happy day, Adan."

"Is this Soros?" Neruda demanded.

"Soros died thirteen years ago, Adan."

Of course! Neruda saw it now. Whoever was behind these attacks would not be stupid enough to leave his calling card in the form of hundreds of little taunting messages dropped on the rooftop party. It was a red herring.

"So who is this, then?" Neruda demanded

"It's your old friend Encina."

Yes. Nicolas Encina. That *did* make sense, and Adan Neruda felt almost relieved. It had been too mystifying that an old adversary from two decades ago had come after him in such a ludicrous and ostentatious fashion. It didn't make sense. It didn't fit into what he knew and understood about how people operated.

But this did make sense. It was Encina. Encina had framed an old, minor adversary named Soros for the chaos and the killing. And when the people of Bolivia, the power players of La Paz, discovered that Soros was long-ago dead, there would be no one to blame except Neruda himself.

"Are you still with me, Adan?" Encina demanded.

"Still here."

"You are destroyed," Encina declared matter-of-factly.

Adan Neruda could not argue with that. "You are a pathetic coward," Neruda snarled.

"Call me what you wish," Encina responded. "You are the one who's going to look like a coward by tomorrow morning. The coward or the most hated man in the country. All your money cannot save you from the downfall that is coming to you. You will have no more parties, no more women, no more real estate. All of that will be gone. You know what they will do to you? They will arrest you, they will humiliate you, they will confiscate your holdings, strip you of everything you own and you'll have nothing left. You will be hated and feared and reviled. If I were you, I would flee the country tonight. Right now."

"Is that what you want me to do? Flee down the stairs, where your aircraft can get their sights on me and cut me down?"

"Don't you understand, Neruda? I could've killed you a long time ago. My new toys give me access wherever I want. I've had your car bugged with a GPS tracker for months. Anytime I wanted, I could've flown one of my planes over, while you're on Mountain Road, on your weekly Tuesday dalliance with the whore at the beach house, and taken you out. I could've cut you down while you were talking on the phone in front of your apartment picture windows while meeting with Perez. Or on your trips to the lake. I could've got you at any time I wanted. But that is too good for you. Dead would be unsatisfying. Ruined, that will make me happy. To see you utterly ruined."

Neruda wondered if his old rival was finished. "So what in the hell do you want from me?" he asked.

He was feeling desperate—an emotion he was unfamiliar with.

"I want you to show the world what a coward you are. I want to see you humiliated and brought as low as you can possibly go," Encina said. "And you're going to do it for me. You see, that is part of the fun. You have to do it for yourself."

"Do what?" Neruda demanded

"Run away like a coward," Encina snapped back with a hearty laugh. "Flee and leave all your wealth and possessions behind. Or kill yourself. Which is really the same thing. Whatever you do, you have to do it yourself."

"I'd rather take my chances with the planes."

But even as he said the words, Adan Neruda became aware of the quiet. The hotel was silent. The rattling gunfire and the crashes of glass and the thumps of explosives hitting the building had all stopped. He ran down the stairs, quickly catching up to the descending crowds. He pushed and shoved his way through strangers and acquaintances and business partners and people he had called friends, and eventually found himself emerging on the ground floor.

There were ambulances and army and police gathered around the Hotel Europa. They didn't seem to know what to do with themselves, other than care for a few wounded victims. Most of the people streaming out of the building were simply shaken up.

The casualties had been amazingly light considering the spectacular attack. And that, Neruda did not doubt, was exactly what Encina had wanted.

Men were shouting at the military commanders on the scene. Demanding action. Demanding explanation. Soon enough their anger would turn on Neruda. It was his party, it was his building, and there would be little doubt that the attackers were after him.

Neruda had been trying to come up with an alternative explanation, one that would wash, one that the people La Paz would accept. But he knew how this crowd behaved. He knew they would not accept a crime without a perpetrator. The strange messages signed "Soros" would only perplex them and exacerbate their anger. They would surely turn their anger to Neruda soon enough.

There was no way he was going to talk his way out of this.

As much as it galled him, Neruda was going to have to take the exact steps that Encina had mapped out for him. Kill himself or flee the country. And he would not kill himself. He was not a weak man. He was not a stupid man, either.

He could assume that all his property and probably his entire fortune that was in-country would be forfeit. His vast Bolivian assets would be frozen within hours.

But he had other assets, in Swiss and in Caribbean banks, untouchable by outsiders. It was a only a fraction of his total net worth but enough to keep him living very well for the rest of his life.

There were soldiers already taking up positions in the parking tower alongside Hotel Europa. Adan Neruda strolled on by and headed into the small, expensive shopping district adjacent to the hotel. He wasn't going to risk trying to get by those soldiers. And he had other cars. A five-minute walk took him to a building where he kept an office suite, along with the headquarters of one of his shipping businesses. He observed the front entrance of that building from a distance, and found more soldiers taking up positions at the entrances. These soldiers were attracting the attention of the agitated city people, who had already heard about the aerial attacks at the hotel.

Neruda was getting a sinking feeling that Encina had orchestrated more than he had let on.

Neruda got on his smartphone and pulled up a Bolivian news app. They were unusually quick to update: there was already information being posted about the attacks at the hotel.

One of the bullet items told him that the military counterterrorist task force was thought to be mobilizing.

He scanned the item for less than ten seconds before he found out what he needed to know. The military had been alerted more than a day ago that a well-known and well-placed Bolivian businessman had been funding and equipping a terrorist organization. But the businessman had double-crossed the organization, and terrorists were planning payback.

The army, the news item said, didn't get enough actionable information, and had been forced to sit and wait—for a full day—for the attack to happen.

And now it had happened. The target told the Bolivian antiterrorist investigators exactly who the "well-known and well-placed Bolivian businessman" was. Adan Neruda was the man who had been funding and equipping terrorists.

Neruda ducked into a high-end clothing store and quickly bought a ridiculous sun hat and an oversize jacket. He paid cash, pulled on the jacket and jammed the hat on his head, getting strange looks from the young woman behind the counter.

They would eventually come and question everyone on this street, and they would question this clerk, and she would remember him. If Neruda had a gun he would've shot her in the chest. But he was unarmed, and there were thirty people within sight, on the street outside. There was no way he could cover his tracks.

The best he could do was get out of La Paz and out of Bolivia as fast as possible. He walked six blocks, trying to keep himself from hurrying, trying to look unexceptional among the agitated city folk. Even as he was keeping his eyes peeled for unwanted attention from the military, his mind was spinning, trying to come up with an exit strategy.

The army certainly had been ready for something to happen. They had covered the city with uncharacteristic efficiency. Small groups of men, army and police both, were taking up positions on every street corner, each with a plainclothes commander. All they had been waiting for was the name of the traitor. And now they had it—and it was *him*. They would waste no time in locking down Adan Neruda's homes, apartments and offices. He couldn't return to any of it. Not ever. It was all taken away from him.

He should've put anonymous transportation in place for himself. But he'd simply never felt vulnerable enough, not in all these years. And now it was too late. That didn't mean he couldn't find himself a ride.

He strolled into the deteriorating sections of the city and found himself in front of an auto repair shop. It had been there for years, the grounds crowded with rusting hulks.

He was surprised to see someone on duty this late in the evening. The mechanic had black, broken fingernails and filthy clothes and his hair was matted with oil. He was watching the stranger standing outside his shop, and he was getting suspicious. He stepped away from the door and returned with a wrench, which he pretended to wipe with a filthy rag.

Neruda headed in.

The man had already determined that Neruda had not come to have his oil changed. The mechanic was stiff and ready for trouble. Neruda gave him a smile, but it wasn't a good one, and the mechanic was not put at ease. The mechanic was an old, scrawny man who wheezed with every breath. Half the people in La Paz had breathing problems. The air was thin up here.

"I need to buy a car."

"I don't sell cars."

Neruda pulled out his wallet and began counting bills onto the workbench. The mechanic's attitude changed dramatically. All of a sudden, he did have a car to sell. It wasn't a pretty one.

"Will it get me to Cusco?" Neruda demanded.

"Yes. It runs pretty good. It will get you pretty far. I take good care of it."

"Good," Neruda said. He was not headed to Cusco. He was headed for the coast, which was not as far.

"Got an extra shirt?"

The mechanic was slightly bewildered.

Neruda put more money down on the counter.

The mechanic sold him a shirt. It was not a clean shirt. Neruda took off his thousand-dollar suit jacket and his three-hundred-dollar shirt, his T-shirt, and put on the old mechanic shirt. There were places where the dirty oil stains were so thick they soaked through the shirt and clung to his skin.

There was no way that this mechanic was going to fail to remember Adan Neruda, his strange purchase of a car and a shirt and his huge wad of cash. He'd have a lot to tell the army, as soon as they came asking questions on this street.

But Neruda knew exactly what to do about that.

Adan Neruda was younger and stronger, and as they strolled to the back drive he satisfied himself that there was no one else in the shop tonight.

The car, a twenty-one-year-old Ford with rusting body panels, belonged to the mechanic himself.

"You sure this will get me to Cusco? These tires look pretty thin."

"It'll get you there."

"Is there a spare?"

Adan Neruda took the keys from the mechanic and opened the trunk and sorted through some trash, then pulled back the fabric flap. He unscrewed the brace on the spare tire, pulled it out and bounced it on the floor.

"It's good," the mechanic insisted, holding on to his pants, on to the wad of cash in his front pocket.

"Yeah, it's fine," Adan Neruda agreed as he shoved the tire back into the trunk, screwed the brace back into place, then snatched up the crowbar and bashed the mechanic's skull as hard as he could. The mechanic's head seemed to collapse, and Neruda grabbed him by the shoulders and steered his falling body behind a heap of cast-off auto parts.

Neruda took back his cash, prying it from the mechanic's hand, and took the mechanic's driving license and ratty leather wallet. Then Neruda bashed the old man in the head a few more times, just be sure.

Then he got behind the wheel of the old Ford and pulled out onto the street.

AS HE DROVE THROUGH La Paz he wiped his hands on the greasy shirt and wiped the grease onto his face and into his hair. He appraised himself in the rearview mirror. It hadn't taken long to make himself look like street rabble. He certainly didn't look like one of the most powerful men in Bolivia anymore.

Despite the occasional patrol of military men, Adan Neruda managed to get out of the city without being stopped.

He drove through the night.

At Villazon he detoured to the west, crossing the border without incident at Piscuno, where there was little more than a shack and a pair of bored border guards on duty.

He was soon inside Argentina. His first instinct had been to get to the coast, in Chile—but there was a good reason to go to Argentina instead.

It was because of the way that his enemy, Encina, had buzzed his *L* slightly when he pronounced the word *kill*. It was the way that Encina had used the pronoun *vos*. These were speech elements indicative of Argentinean Spanish-speakers.

Encina must have come to Argentina after being forced to flee Bolivia.

Now Neruda turned back east and finally stopped to sleep in the small Argentinean town of Pueblo Viejo. In a dirty little bus stop he paid two dollars for a filthy cot and a plate of runny eggs and pork gristle. The food tasted like heaven. The bed felt like heaven.

But he did not go to sleep at once. First he stared at the stained ceiling in the back room of the bus stop and made a quick oath, almost like a prayer. He would track down Encina, here in Argentina.

His business with Encina was not yet done.

CHAPTER THREE

The Texan crouched behind the ancient Mayan wall, his back to the moldy stone, and stared at the patch of jungle. He'd been staring at the same patch of jungle for two hours.

This was not the kind of work he enjoyed.

"This is stupid."

"You'll not get any argument from me."

Standing next to him was a black man with an M-16 draped over one shoulder. The two men weren't on guard so much as they were in wait-and-see mode. The ruin of the wall had been interesting to look at for something like ten minutes. The jungle had been interesting for five. The remaining hour and forty-five minutes were monotonous.

The King's Wall was all that was left of the once-massive Structure 33, a stone temple or king's chamber. The lower walls were plain and unadorned, but the upper walls were honeycombs, the stones laid to form alcoves more than two yards square. There were six rows of these alcoves, and in most of them were the crumbling remains of ancient statuary. At one point, every one of the alcoves had been home to beautifully carved, life-size human figures.

Now the upper walls on three sides had collapsed, and most of the roof was gone. Only the front-facing

wall remained, looking out into the central acropolis
of the Chilan ruins.

The brochure said that the Structure 33 was a masterpiece of stonework that dated back to 750 A.D. It had
been built by one of the first kings of Chilan, and may
have served as its central temple. A dramatic stairway
led down the front of the extant wall into the grand
plaza.

The jungle of southern Mexico came close behind
Structure 33, but throughout the remainder of the plaza
the jungle had been chopped away. The Mexican government had an ambitious schedule for opening these
ruins to tourists.

The Chilan ruins had been big news when Mexico
began to unearth the structures. Although their existence had been known for decades, no one had fully understood the extent of the ruins. The dig had uncovered
one of the largest archaeological sites in Mexico, with
some of the best-preserved interior frescoes.

After years of negative publicity over growing drug
violence, Mexico's tourist industry was suffering and
needed to lure people to come take their vacations in
the country again.

Interest in the Mayans had been growing for years,
fueled by the misinterpreted warnings in the Mayan
calendar regarding the end of 2012. The Mexican government was banking on that interest continuing—even
though the 2012 Armageddon had failed to materialize.
The world hadn't ended. The truth was, the Mayans had
never said the world would end over Christmas vacation of 2012.

The Mexican government hoped to cash in on this re-
vived interest in all things Mayan. Jungles around Chi-

lan had been cleared with amazing speed, tearing away the dank shadow of jungle and revealing a magnificent series of buildings that once served as the home of one of the most powerful kingdoms in the Mayan world.

The idea was to bring in tourists even as archaeology continued. New frescoes were being uncovered on an almost weekly basis, the site promoters intended to create touring areas of the working sites.

It was an approach that was already starting to pay off. A boat-in tour group had been on hand when a team of diggers opened up an entirely new room. The tourists had been permitted to come to the entrance of the new room. In fact, the group was among the very first people in the world to see a chamber that had been closed off for more than a thousand years.

The permanent on-site reporting team had recorded it all, and the news around the world picked it up. Members of that first team of tourists had been treated like celebrities. They did talk shows and appeared in *People* magazine. It was unbelievably good publicity for the Chilan site.

It was exactly what the Mexican tourism promoters wanted.

And it was exactly why Chilan was being targeted now.

"What's the certainty that these guys will even show up?" the young Texan asked.

"Pretty damned good, I guess," said the black man at the moment that a shadow emerged over the top of the jungle canopy and momentarily shaded their sunlight.

The young Texan, Thomas Jackson Hawkins, leaped to his feet and pulled his own M-16 off his shoulder, taking aim at the sky. The plane had sailed over the top of the wall and was drifting low over the campus of ancient Mayan ruins.

Calvin James, the black commando, tapped his headset.

"The bird just arrived, and boy is she quiet. We didn't even hear it when it was overhead."

"I don't even think the damned engines were on," Hawkins said under his breath.

James was still for a moment, listening. He looked through the square window in the wall. The small gray aircraft seem to be floating over the ground, and his ears picked up a faint rush from the engines.

"She's on—I guess," he said into his headset. "I can hear engines running. Coming your way, Manning."

GARY MANNING, A HULKING, square-jawed figure, was camping out in a building at the opposite end of the central plaza. An unobstructed view of the long, flat plaza stretched between himself and, in the distance, Structure 33, where T. J. Hawkins and Calvin James were holed up.

Manning's building, Structure 30, was one of the best-preserved buildings in the Chilan site. Structure 30 had three broad doorways that faced out onto the central plaza, each door entering into one of three parallel chambers that made up Structure 30. Above Manning's head was a series of impressively engineered stone support beams. There were twelve of them. Manning knew this because he had been standing here looking at them for the past two hours, with nothing better to do, and had counted them over and over, wondering if that number had significance. He finally decided that the number of support beams in the ceiling had no significance whatsoever. It was just a convenient number. Like 2012 was a convenient number.

But Manning was certain that if he ever came back to this place and took the regular tour he would hear the tour guides speculate that the number of vaults in the ceiling signified some great prophecy.

But sometimes a number was just a number—even if it was the Mayans who came up with it.

All this concentration on the supposed mystical aspects of the Mayans ignored the culture's true accomplishments. The vaulted ceiling in Structure 30 at the end of the central plaza was a real triumph of structural engineering. Despite the ravages of time and the destructive attack of the jungle, the roof of Structure 30 was intact, even after thirteen hundred years.

Structure 30 was one of the few structures that had already been completely cleared of overgrowth at the Chilan site. Also cleared was the central plaza, which had been completely overgrown by jungle. In the past two years the developers had cut down and dug up all the trees and undergrowth that had made their home there since the departure of the Mayans in something like 900 A.D. They had cleared off the long plaza and covered it with gravel, making of it a staging area for the heavy equipment that had been working here until very recently. Heavy equipment to continue the deforestation and the building of new structures.

The new structures were not as well engineered as Structure 31. Instead of stone, they were made mostly out of cheap lumber and drywall. Instead of being used for religious ceremonies, their intended functions was to sell tacos and coconut ice cream and Coca-Cola to the mass influx of tourists expected to begin arriving at Chilan within a year.

Of course, that depended on how quickly the road was done. The Mexican government had moved its heavy equipment to the jungle and begun to clear more trees to provide space for a new highway that would bring in tourist buses—only to discover more ruins. They had moved the equipment two hundred feet to the west and begun to clear again. More ruins. It happened a third time. Manning suspected that the developers would normally have plowed over any such ruins and denied they ever existed. This was where the developers' own publicity worked against them. The constant media attention on the site made every discovery news on some scale, and made it impossible to conveniently ignore ancient sites that were in the way of fresh asphalt.

There had even been talk about providing access points through Guatemala, which was about four hundred feet away from where Manning now stood, on the other side of the Usumacinta River. But the whole point of this development was to bring tourist dollars into Mexico. They weren't letting any of it leak into Guatemala if they could help it.

Manning's boredom evaporated when his eyes spotted the small aircraft drifting over the jungle. The thing seemed to be moving too slowly even to stay in the air, and he heard no sound. It had simply popped into existence over the jungle and floated over the heads of Calvin James and T. J. Hawkins in Structure 33, and floated down over the central plaza. Now Manning could hear some noise coming from the thing, a rush of turbulent air like a fan. He heard the radio message from Calvin James and it occurred to him that the tiny jet was moving pretty quickly after all—and wondered at the wisdom of stationing himself in Structure 30, at the far end of the plaza.

The small jet was using the central plaza as a landing strip. Manning knew for a fact that this aircraft was untested at best, and it seemed like an awfully short distance to bring a jet of any size to a halt.

Manning's forehead creased as he watched the jet touch down, throwing up dust and gravel. If that aircraft was incapable of making the ridiculously abrupt landing it was supposed to be capable of, it was going to barrel directly into Structure 30. It would be a shame to smash a jet into this archaeological marvel. But mostly, he thought, it would be a shame to smash a jet into Gary Manning.

He could hear the gravel under the wheels. That distracted him momentarily. A jet, even a small one, should be making enough noise that he wouldn't be able to hear the gravel under the wheels as it landed.

It lost momentum quickly, and when the pilot stepped on the brake, the back end fishtailed slightly, throwing up more gravel as the aircraft did a neat one-eighty. The ass end of the small jet, and the hot breeze from the twin tail-mounted engines, were pointed at Gary Manning. The jet pulled off the gravel and into the grass. The pilot parked it under the shade of a nearby tree— one of the few jungle giants that had been left standing along the gravel plaza.

A cloud of dust drifted away.

Manning touched his headset and said quietly, "Everybody seeing this?"

"Seeing it, mate," answered a male voice with a British accent. "I thought for a second that it was going to mow you over."

"Yeah, me, too," Manning said. "You ever hear a jet like that? Came in like a glider."

"My bathroom fan is louder," the Briton answered.

Manning was quietly getting himself settled in to position with the sniper rifle, covering the small, gray-camouflaged jet, which seemed to absorb the shadow of the great tree and disappear. The way it absorbed colors had a camouflage effect.

In a moment, he had another surprise. The hatch opened and the man he presumed was the pilot stepped out. Followed by a copilot. Followed by three more men, one after another, each of them carrying heavy packs. All of them were armed with automatic weapons.

"Christ," Manning said under his breath, then he touched his headset. "It's a damned clown car."

One more man had stepped out of the jet, also armed, also carrying a heavy pack. There had been six men with packs inside that little plane.

Manning heard the voice of T. J. Hawkins come through his earpiece.

"Correct me if I'm wrong, but from down here it looked like six guys piled out of that little toy plane."

"You got that right," Manning replied, then went silent as the men began to disperse in pairs. Two went left, west, cutting across the open plaza and heading for the acropolis, which included Structures 19, 20 and 21. The partially rebuilt acropolis was positioned to face the rising sun, and it was one of the most impressive piles of rock on the site. Once restored, it would be magnificent.

A second pair headed directly up the center of the

open plaza, toward the huge honeycomb wall, where
Calvin James and T. J. Hawkins were waiting for them.

But the last pair headed directly toward Gary Manning, in the impressively vaulted Structure 30.

"Manning?" asked David McCarter, the Briton, over
the headset.

Manning responded quietly. "Changing position,"
he said.

"Coming to help you out, friend," another voice announced in a low growl.

Manning did not respond. The pair from the tiny jet
were hustling up the short flight of stairs, and would
be entering one of the three doors momentarily. Manning had, of course, planned for such a contingency. He
shouldered the sniper rifle, snatched up the automatic
rifle that he had leaned against the wall, and moved
quickly to the rear of the center room. At the rear was
a hallway that connected all three rooms together. In
one of those alcoves was a niche formed by the crumbling of rotting rock, and leaving a tight, dark niche that
barely fit a man as big as Gary Manning. He stepped
into it, maneuvered his body for an unrestricted position and waited in blackness.

ALL THAT WAS LEFT NOW of the small Structure 14 was
a pile of broken rock, and the stocky Cuban had convinced himself it was the remains of an ancient mystical
Mayan outhouse. There was no place to hide in it, so he
crouched behind it and even that was hardly adequate.
But Rafael Encizo had gone unseen by the six—count
them, *six*—occupants of that little jet.

The Cuban-born commando didn't want to think

what it was like inside that little plane with six guys. And all of their cargo.

He crept up alongside Structure 30 as the pair entered, and he was keeping an eye on the other two pairs. The two across the plaza disappeared inside Structure 21, on the south side of the acropolis. The final pair was headed up the central plaza, in plain sight, and Encizo was going to have to chance that they would not turn around and glimpse him. He stepped up the stone stairs and slipped into door one. The pair from the jet had gone through the central door, door two, so Encizo had room one all to himself. He and Manning had scoped out the structure carefully, and Encizo was confident that he knew what he was doing.

The bright morning Mexican sun gave way to the cool, dark interior of room one. Encizo followed the route he had already mapped out, and walked carefully, making his way against the wall, allowing his eyes to adjust to the dim light, and listening. He could hear the voices of the pair from the jet. They were not trying to be quiet. They assumed they had this site completely to themselves.

Encizo heard the noise of flimsy metal being manipulated—the intruders were making use of one of the aluminum ladders stacked in the central room, left over from the archaeological staff, which had still been rushing accumulated dust from the ceiling just a few days ago.

Encizo came to the corner, and peered into the alcove at the back end of the room. He saw the figure of Gary Manning ensconced in his dark niche. Manning gave him a brief wave. Encizo waited.

IN STRUCTURE 15 THE British commando named David McCarter was the commander of the team called Phoenix Force.

It might seem unusual to have a British national commanding a commando group from the United States—but that wasn't the most unusual aspect of Phoenix Force. Phoenix was one of the enforcement arms of the highly secretive Sensitive Operations Group, which was headquartered at Stony Man Farm in Virginia.

Team commander McCarter had made Structure 15 his headquarters. It was small but solidly built, and had survived the centuries far better than most of the other buildings at the Chilan site. The building was accessed via a steep stairway and was high enough to give the Phoenix Force commander a good view up and down the central plaza, and all of the major structures of the Chilan site.

Despite the strangeness of this probe, it appeared that Stony Man Farm instincts had been on target. They had guessed that the site would be a target to vandals—if not total destruction. A drug lord's way of paying back the Mexican government for enforcing its laws too vigorously, which had a direct impact on the drug lord's bottom line.

A bloody shame to see the site damaged, yes, but it wasn't McCarter's job to stop the vandalism or even to apprehend the vandals; the real goal of Phoenix Force today was to take possession of the vandals' little toy plane.

McCarter had deduced that the vandals would target the acropolis, with its impressive trio of structures, as well as Structure 33, the distinctive honeycomb wall at the far end of the plaza. He had also guessed they might go after the bridge foundation, almost eight hundred feet away from his current position and on the shore of the Usumacinta River. The government had been busily restoring part of the bridge foundation. There were even plans to rebuild the entire Mayan suspension bridge. The government was promising that it would show just how impressive and ahead of their time the rare, large-scale Mayan suspension bridges actually were.

But McCarter had been mistaken about the bridge. Instead of heading for the suspension bridge foundation, the last pair of vandals were headed into Manning's building, Structure 30. Encizo and Manning could handle that situation quite well.

McCarter waited until the final pair had made its way inside Structure 33, where T. J. Hawkins and Calvin James awaited. Then McCarter stepped out of building 15. He moved down to the edge of the central plaza and covered the entrance to the acropolis from a distance.

"Take action, mates," he ordered.

FINALLY, THOUGHT GARY Manning. He stepped out of his niche and into the alcove that opened into the central room. Room two. He saw what he had expected to see. One of the men had climbed onto one of the aluminum ladders and was hammering nails into the crevices of the rock near the ceiling.

The second man was holding the pack and standing at the bottom of the ladder. It was just Manning's luck the one on the ladder was looking in his direction at the moment he stepped inside. The man gave a shout.

Gary Manning could have very easily cut both of them down in the moment it took them to get their bearings, but that wasn't what this probe was about. He hit both men with their secret weapon: in the darkness of the ancient stone building, the brilliant bluish-white LED flashlight stabbed them in the eyes and blinded them momentarily. That was long enough for Gary Manning to cross to them and deliver a savage kick to the legs of the wobbly aluminum ladder. It collapsed, sending its occupant plummeting on top of his companion.

Rafael Encizo had materialized in the room and knocked the radio away from the man with the pack—but he wondered if it was too late. A signal may already have been sent. The radio clattered across the stone floor as Gary Manning struck the man with the pack. Manning's pal bounced the man's head into the stone floor and the man went limp. The man from the ladder was trying desperately to roll himself over. He got some help. Gary Manning snatched him off the floor, twisted him savagely and sent him back to the floor face-first. The impact was enough to knock the wind out of the vandal. His consciousness wavered and he groaned feebly as his hands were twisted behind him and bound in plastic cuffs.

The unconscious man was similarly secured, and then Gary Manning patted them down. He disposed of their handguns, sending them across the room without their magazines, and the job was done.

Encizo was talking to David McCarter.

"They made some noise and they had a radio. See any sign of alert?"

THERE WERE THREE ANCIENT jungle trees that had been spared during the clearing of the central plaza, and

David McCarter had taken up a position behind one. In the quiet, hot Mexico morning, the sound of the brief battle in Structure 30 had reached him. It seemed unlikely that the pair that had entered the acropolis buildings would have heard it. But maybe. Even if they didn't get the message over the radio.

McCarter triggered his mike. "T.J.? Cal? Talk to me."

WITH ONLY A SMALL SECTION of the roof intact, and with three walls missing, Structure 33 offered no dark alcoves for hiding commandos, but there were other kinds of hiding places. Hawkins and James had identified it as the perfect place to go unseen if needed. Many of the alcoves that made the wall so dramatic still contained life-size stone statues, presumably the kings and the heroes of the ancient city state of Chilan. Most of the statues had disintegrated over the years, but a few were virtually intact.

The first row of alcoves above ground level contained the best-preserved statues. Calvin James took a position directly above the entrance from the plaza. He was standing maybe fifteen feet above the spot where the vandals would enter the building, if they did indeed come up the stairs. Hawkins found a good niche on the same level, maybe twenty feet to the west of James's position.

James had exploited the easy hand- and footholds in the decaying rock face and now stood in an alcove behind the statue of a king. The statue had big hooded eyes and seemed to be holding a chunk of something in one hand and a sort of a block with holes and pegs in the other. To James it looked like a snack and a game board. But he wasn't an archaeological expert like the scientists who made the *Ancient Aliens* TV show. They would probably determine with a high level of confidence that the figure was holding a remote control and a ray gun.

Whoever the figure was, he was a barrel-chested character, built broad enough to make easy cover for Calvin James. He stood behind the king's statue and peered around the king's space helmet to watch the figures make the long march of the central plaza. He could have taken them both out and they never would have seen him. It would've been easy to wipe those two off the face of the earth.

And Calvin James would have liked to have done it. These men were high-value drug runners. Dope peddlers on a continental scale. They worked for one of the biggest coke-running organizations in Mexico. They kidnapped innocent tourists, they corrupted the government and they would not hesitate to murder civilians in the interest of furthering their business interests.

But he wasn't supposed to be doing that. Not today. This was not about stopping the drug trade.

Today their job was to get their hands on that aircraft.

That need was the currency by which this pair was buying their lives. This pair seemed pretty confident that they were alone. They should be. There was a small security force employed at the Chilan site, but they'd been scared off or lured away. Or maybe they were dead in the jungle. Calvin James and his companions had found no evidence of the security team on-site. The guard shack had been empty. The pot of coffee on the low electric cooktop was half full and just barely warm when they'd arrived.

The pair of vandals was going to make it easy on Calvin James. They came to the top of the stairs and ensconced themselves in the entrance almost directly below James's feet. They began to work, unzipping their pack and removing the contents. Those would be explosives, and they would be timed to go off in an hour or so. Or perhaps be remotely detonated. The blast would take out the stones and bring the entire wall down—an interesting method of payback against the Mexican government that had been too meddlesome in the business of drug running lately. The destruction would send a very clear message: you meddle in our profit-making initiatives and we will meddle in yours. If the Mexican government was so determined to stop the drug trade, then the drug trade would stop the business of the Mexican government. And right now, after years of negative publicity, with tourist revenues in the toilet, Mexico needed every good vacation draw it could come up with. The new archaeological site at Chilan was going to be the star attraction of the coming winter travel season. Mexico hoped to bring in wannabe Indiana Joneses from the United States by the thousands.

But that certainly wouldn't happen if there was violence in Chilan. That certainly wouldn't happen if the magnificent king's wall was turned into rubble.

Calvin James intended to give the vandals a few more minutes to become absorbed in their work, then he and T.J. would step down and take them out.

Then the plans changed.

"Trouble, mates," said David McCarter in James's headset. "The alert might've gone out."

Sure enough, James detected a change in the pace of the work below. It seemed as if something had been dropped; he heard the clank as a steel tool hit the ground. There were quiet discussions. Calvin James looked down at the entranceway below him and saw one of the men emerge, scanning the rubble that had once been Structure 33's missing three walls. He then scanned the jungle, covering it with his automatic weapon and hissing words that James could not understand.

James stepped around the statue of the king and looked out the front of the building. There was another man there, also with an automatic weapon, glaring out at the central plaza and peering into the distance at Structure 30. There was nothing to see. David McCarter was out there somewhere, but he was hidden from view. The man took a radio off his belt and spoke into it quickly. He got the answer he expected. He radioed again; it was some sort of a brief response. That must be the pair in the acropolis.

The man touched the radio with his thumb and talked again. He got an answer—again. That didn't seem right to Calvin James. With the Structure 30 vandals out of commission, who could he be communicating with?

James saw the faintest movement of a shadow off to his right and peered over to where Hawkins could just barely be discerned in his own alcove, looking down at the man with the radio.

This section of Mexican jungle was eerily quiet. The jungle stilled the wind, there was no machinery or electricity or buildings to create an electronic hum. Calvin James could not even risk speaking into his own headset without fear of being overheard by the gunmen below. Maybe it was time to take them out....

There was movement at the far end of the central

plaza. The pair of gunners burst out of Structure 21 on the acropolis, found cover behind the remains of a stone statue, then jutted out simultaneously to look for signs of trouble, covering the plaza with automatic weapons. There was nothing for them to see. One gunner turned to face Structure 33. By then, Calvin James had taken his place again behind the statue of the king and he went unseen. He assumed Hawkins would've done the same. The man below them spoke into his radio. It was in Spanish, but the tone of voice told Calvin James that he was reporting no sign of trouble.

The second man at the acropolis, still scanning the plaza, dropped his gun, lifted one leg and toppled over. His cry echoed up and down the plaza, bouncing off the buildings of Chilan. He rolled off the rock and collapsed in the grass at the foot of the statue, leaving a bloody red streak on the rock. He was wiggling and holding his bloody ankle.

The man just below Calvin James shouted into his radio, but the second man at the statue ignored him, jumped on top of the statue and fired wildly into the plaza. His bursts of gunfire kicked up dust and rock and thudded into stone ruins, filling Chilan with more noise than it had heard all day.

DAVID MCCARTER WAS impressed with the bulky suppressor provided to him by his good friend "Cowboy" Kissinger. The Stony Man armorer knew a thing or two about weapons—how to build them, how to improve them, how to make them more deadly and even how to make them quieter. He couldn't make them silent— a "silenced" firearm was a movie myth. The best you could do was muffle the bang. But John Kissinger's improved suppressor for the Heckler & Koch MP-5 did the job better than David McCarter would have thought possible. He had fired it while the two men were busy talking on the radio and they never knew they were being shot at until one was pegged in the leg.

McCarter could have circled around to get a clean shot at the second man at the acropolis, but didn't want to expose himself to the pair at Structure 33. He would wait it out.

"Cal?" he radioed. "Proceed as is convenient."

GARY MANNING HEARD the ruckus out front and moved to the front door to see a wounded man screaming at the base of the statue. Hearing the comment from David McCarter, he ducked back into the blackness.

"I can get a clean shot at number two from the upper level if you need me to take him out," he told McCarter.

"Negative," McCarter responded. "We want to keep these guys alive, remember?"

"All of them?" Manning asked. "Isn't that overkill, so to speak?"

"Just following orders, mate. But wouldn't hurt for you to be in position, just in case."

"Understood," Manning said, snatching at his sniper rifle and nodding to Rafael Encizo as he headed up. A small gap in the collapsed wall at the rear had created an irregular but easy stairway to the upper level. The second level had also been roofed in, but the roof had largely disintegrated over the centuries, collapsing onto the floor. Manning picked his way quickly through the rubble and took up a position looking down onto the central plaza of Chilan. His sniper rifle gave him enough power to take potshots at the kings in the honeycomb wall at the far end of the plaza, and easily take out the man crouching behind the statue not a stone's throw away.

It was an easy shot. One pull of the trigger, Gary Manning thought, and one less piece of slime kid killer in the world. One round. They could take it out of his salary....

He didn't do it. There was a good reason not to. But he really, really would have liked to.

AT STRUCTURE 33, under the gaze of dozens of ancient Mayan kings, the two vandals were now stationed at the front, together, taking some efforts to stay behind the rock wall but unclear as to how to proceed. One of them radioed, and the man at the acropolis—the one who wasn't screaming and writhing on the ground— answered them. Conversation was brief, but the result was that the pair at Structure 33 stayed where they were.

T. J. Hawkins went unnoticed by the distracted pair as he crept across the easy foot- and handholds along the back side of the wall and emerged into the alcove to stand elbow to elbow with Calvin James.

One of the men below spoke harshly. There was a brief argument, then the second man moved back under the entranceway.

T. J. Hawkins understood enough Spanish to translate.

"He told him to get back to work," he said to James.

"Is it my imagination, or was he radioing somebody else earlier?" James asked.

Hawkins looked a little blank. "I couldn't overhear all that they were saying."

More radio conversation came from below. Calvin

James squinted at the man at the acropolis, to see if he responded. It didn't look like he did.

"There," James whispered. "I don't think he's talking to that dude."

"I don't think so," Hawkins agreed. "Hard to understand what he's saying."

There was hammering going on directly below them and Calvin James judged that he could contact McCarter without being overheard. He touched his headset.

"I think there's a fourth party listening in," he said.

"Structure 30 is secure. The only two left are at the acropolis," McCarter responded. "The guy on the ground and the one behind the statue."

Calvin James felt uneasy about that conclusion. "Could there possibly be somebody else inside that aircraft?"

Hawkins made a sound of disbelief. McCarter sounded similarly doubtful. "Even six guys inside of that thing seemed impossible. I can't imagine that they could have one more person in there," McCarter stated. "Let's prepare to take out the rest of them and wrap this up."

"Understood," Calvin James said, although he still didn't feel easy about it.

Hawkins was enjoying himself climbing around on the big wall of kings of Structure 33. Now, this was the kind of tourist activity he could enjoy. He had a feeling that the Mexican government wasn't about to open up the ruins to climbers.

He made his way down hand over hand and touched the ground in under a half minute, then he edged along the rock wall to the main entrance and turned the corner. He held the barrel of his weapon at gut level, not two paces away.

The working man raised his head to see that he was covered with the business end of an M-16 aimed at his gut. It was too close to miss, but not so close that he could have grabbed for it. Hawkins nodded to the ceiling, and the man dropped his hammer with a clang and raised his hands in the air. He opened his mouth, started to speak, but when Hawkins shook his head, the man closed his mouth again and was silent.

Calvin James had found a large chunk of loose stone. It was more or less round, and more or less solid. It was heavy. He dropped it.

"Hey," he shouted.

The man with the gun turned fast, saw his partner a few steps away with his hands in the air, realized that the shout had come from above him and looked up just in time to see the massive stone home in on his head. He didn't have time to move or to make a noise before it cracked against his skull and broke it.

His weapon fell to the ground and he fell alongside it. The huge hunk of stone came to a rest, face up at Calvin James.

Only then did Calvin James realize that the head-size hunk of stone was actually a head. A head of one of the other statues had found its way into the alcove of the king James had been spending time with.

It looked undamaged by the fall. Still—oops.

T. J. Hawkins had his own prisoner trussed up, wrists behind his back, and threw him to the ground alongside his limp companion. Calvin James made it to the ground and checked for a pulse on the one with the cracked cranium. He was still alive, and James had his wrists bound in seconds.

"Really, Cal?" Hawkins said, nodding at the angry-looking face of the Mayan king. "That's got to be really bad karma."

"I just thought it was a piece of rock," James said apologetically.

The radio made a questioning noise, and Hawkins snatched it off the belt of his prisoner. He could see the man now. He appeared to be hiding behind his stone pile in a crouch.

"I think he saw that, boys," McCarter said through the headset. "You all secure?"

"We're fine," James responded. "Let's get on with this."

The prisoners' radio squawked again. It was the voice of the man hiding behind the pile of rubble up at the acropolis. He obviously assumed that his companions were incapacitated at Structure 33 and at Structure 30. But he was talking to somebody.

James knew he'd been right.

"McCarter, dammit, there's somebody else around here," he affirmed. "He's not reporting to home base. He's talking to another party."

"No signs of life in the aircraft," McCarter replied.

From the ruined roof of Structure 30, Gary Manning added, "Our friend at the acropolis has his eyes on the skies. He's watching for another aircraft. I'd say we've got another one coming."

DAVID MCCARTER SWORE under his breath, and touched his headset again. "Stony!"

"Here, Phoenix," Barbara Price said, her voice calm

and in control. Price was the Stony Man Farm mission controller. Naturally, the Farm had been monitoring all of their communications, but the nature of the probe made it advisable that the Farm not interfere with the activities of the commandos on the ground at Chilan.

But now Stony Man Farm's input was needed.

"Stony, we have another damn airplane in the area," McCarter said.

"We are not seeing anything, Phoenix," Price responded.

"Did you see the first one?"

"Negative. No radar. No reliable satellite."

"So there could be thirty of those things flying around over the treetops right now?"

"Unfortunately there could be, Phoenix," Price confirmed.

"Christ," McCarter growled. "We're not calling in G-Force for pickup if we've got another one of those planes flying around here unseen and undetected."

"We need to get him on-site as soon as feasible, Phoenix," Price said. "We need time to get the stealth jet secured for airlift."

"I'm not gonna get Jack shot down by some asshole drug runner in a plastic plane!"

"Understood, Phoenix," said Stony Man Farm's mission controller.

McCarter could now hear the urgent voice of the man at the acropolis. He was still shouting into his radio.

"Rafe?" he said into his mike. "What's he saying?"

ENCIZO WAS STANDING just inside door three of Structure 30—the door on the west side of the building, closest to the acropolis. Inside the foot-deep lintel he was out of the line of sight of the guy behind the statue, but he could hear the men shouting.

"He needs a pickup," Encizo told McCarter.

The wounded man at the base of the statue tried to stand, but his ankle bent sideways and he collapsed again. There was a grotesque gargle and fresh screaming.

The man with the radio spoke more urgently.

"He would like to be picked up very soon," Encizo said in a dry deadpan. "Everybody is dead except him and Perez, and he is going to shoot Perez dead himself if Perez doesn't stop wailing like a little girl. Everything has gone to defecation. Someone's mother is a prostitute and that person had better come and pick him up at once or he is going to hunt down the other man's prostitute mother and kill her and then engage in sexual relations with her. I'm cleaning up the language a little."

"Yeah, thanks," McCarter said. "Does it sound like he's talking about one airplane or thirty?"

"I can't tell," Encizo said. "There's nothing to indicate that there's more than one."

"That's not helpful," McCarter snapped.

"Hold on," Encizo said.

The man on the radio had lowered his voice. The wounded man at the base of the statue had stopped crying and was simply moaning quietly. For a moment the city of Chilan had gone silent again. Which was likely what the Mayan kings wanted—for everyone to just shut up and leave them alone.

"They're giving him an ETA," Encizo advised. "Twenty seconds."

BLOODY HELL, MCCARTER said in his own head, and stepped out from his cover behind the trunk of the plaza tree to search the skies. He scanned the jungle above Structure 33, which was where the first little stealth jet had emerged from. He saw nothing. He looked in the other direction, over Structure 30, across the Usumacinta River, across the vast tracts of jungle on the other side of the border in Guatemala. He saw nothing. Of course, he heard nothing.

He contacted Encizo. "Where from?"

"Unknown," Encizo said.

CALVIN JAMES JOGGED through the entranceway at the bottom of the King's Wall and stared out over the tops of the trees again. There was one tall upper canopy tree, and the first plane had flown in almost directly over it. There had been less than thirty feet of daylight between the upper branches and the belly of that aircraft when it came in. But now there was nothing. He clambered up the King's Wall until he stood in the alcove of his old friend the extraterrestrial king again. Here he could see over the canopy for a mile or more.

The morning heat of southern Mexico was cooking the jungle and raising steam. The tiny stealth jet was colored like a hazy sky, and was made invisible. At first James thought he saw movement, decided it was only heat haze and then changed his mind again.

"Incoming!" he announced into his headset.

Rafael Encizo bellowed in response, "Cal, get the fuck—!"

"I SEE THEM! I SEE THEM!" said the man at the acropolis into his radio. "They are at the King's Wall. Shoot just as you clear the trees! Kill those fuckers!"

Encizo got it—the man was telling the pilot where to

target Calvin James and T. J. Hawkins. Encizo shouted into his mike again, "Cal, get the fuck—"

That was as far as he got before he heard the rattle of heavy machine-gun fire and saw the starlight twinkle of heavy rounds firing from above the jungle canopy. He then witnessed the shape of the small stealth jet materialize, a hazy gray against the hazy gray in the sky, and there was an explosion of stone from the King's Wall of Structure 33.

GARY MANNING WAS HORRIFIED for a half heartbeat. The aircraft-mounted machine gun unleashed on the King's Wall. The shower of stones thrown off by the heavy rounds. The plummeting body of a black man, in the same camos he was wearing now. His friend. Calvin James. Crashing to the stone steps leading up to Structure 33.

Manning swore savagely to himself. He should have killed that little son of a bitch the moment he had him in his sights. Orders or no orders, he should've just gunned that little prick down. And then he wouldn't have been able to radio to that goddamned plane where to target their machine guns, and maybe he wouldn't have just had to witness his friend Calvin James getting shot out of that goddamned wall.

Order or no orders— "Hey, asshole!" Gary Manning shouted at the drug dealer not a stone's throw away. The man spun and faced him. Gary Manning triggered the sniper rifle, felt the kick into his shoulder and watched the man at the acropolis open up at the neckline. Blood splashed in a dark puddle behind him. The man collapsed into it.

"Take cover," ordered McCarter from far down the central plaza.

Gary Manning realized that for a moment he'd actually forgotten about the aircraft. It was not coming in for a landing; it strafed down the center of Chilan, the heavy machine-gun fire stitching all the way down the main plaza and homing in on Structure 30. Gary Manning was lying prone, with no roof to protect him, amid the rubble of stone, and would be highly visible. The jet, slow as it was, was already on top of him and he heard the fanlike rush of the engines and the rattle of the guns, and he propelled himself off the surface and flipped to the side as the trail of rounds cut into the stone where he had been lying.

Then it was gone, rushing across the river and into the jungles of Guatemala. For a moment, the roof of Structure 30 was silent.

Then Gary Manning struggled to his feet, his body screaming at him. It was not a gunshot. If one of those large-caliber rounds had slammed into him it would've ripped off a good chunk of flesh—at least—and he probably would've bled to death in seconds. No, he had landed on a carved corner piece of fallen rock, which had stabbed into his lower back. He would be bruised as hell.

Which was better than being shot. He snatched up the sniper rifle and nearly collided with Rafael Encizo, who grabbed him by the shoulders.

"You okay?" Encizo demanded.

"I'll live. What about Cal?"

CALVIN JAMES WAS FACE-DOWN on the stone steps, limp and bloodied.

"Talk to me, buddy," Hawkins ordered.

But when James pushed his eyes open the first thing he saw was the head of the Mayan king not two feet away from his own. The king looked—satisfied.

"Payback is a bitch," James said, and pushed himself onto his hands and knees, then turned to sit on his rear. The great King's Wall, out of which he had just fallen, tilted alarmingly to the right, straightened, then leaned to the left, like some cheap special effect in an earthquake movie out of the 1970s.

But it was all in his head, which, James now realized, hurt like hell.

He could feel blood covering his face. Chips of stone had flown at him when the large-caliber rounds cracked into the wall. He had thrown himself off just in time to avoid being stitched open. Now the world was pretty unstable but getting better by the second.

"Just let me sit here for minute," he complained to Hawkins.

Hawkins's eyes traveled over James's head, saw something in the distance, and he said, "A minute you don't have. We're out of here."

Calvin James understood vaguely that the aircraft must be coming in for another strafing run. But that fast? Hadn't he just fallen off the wall a moment ago— or had he gone unconscious for some period of time?

Those slow-moving stealth jets couldn't line up for a new attack *that* fast, could they?

Hawkins dragged James to his feet, and James fought to remain upright in the unstable world. His head hurt with every movement, but he allowed Hawkins to steer him down the steps, in search of cover.

"CAL IS OKAY," HAWKINS announced, "but that aircraft is making another run at us."

Manning felt great relief. In his head he could still see Calvin James taking a dive off that stupid wall. It must've been a hell of a hard landing.

His body was still screaming from his own mishap, and he hoped he hadn't damaged some internal organs when that corner of stone thrust deep into his back, but right now he had other things to worry about. He hustled alongside Encizo through the interior of Structure 30, past wriggling prisoners, and stood at the front entrance. The aircraft would be coming up from behind them, they assumed, and buried inside this house of stone, they would probably not even hear it.

They wouldn't know what was coming until it popped into view directly over their heads.

But that wasn't true, either. The aircraft made itself known by firing its machine guns long before it flew over Structure 30 again. It was still looking for Gary Manning on the roof. Then the small gray jet materialized in the sky above them, with maybe thirty feet of clearance between it and the ruined structure. Manning had the sniper rifle at his shoulder.

JAMES FOUND HIMSELF falling again, only this time Hawkins had shoved him. He landed in the grass behind a partially rebuilt short wall, containing a stelea of some sort. Mayan words carved in stone thirteen centuries ago were obliterated in a second by a torrent of large-caliber machine-gun fire from the aircraft. James and Hawkins were on the move again as soon as the aircraft had passed above them, then it was gone over the top of the jungle again. It would be back soon.

"There," James said, indicating another small nearby building. Structure 27. The back wall was completely missing, but the vaulted ceiling was solid and complete. The gunner in the aircraft would never see them in there, and even if he did, that thick stone would stand up to his ordnance.

Hawkins jogged across the corner of the central plaza, and slowed to grab James by the sleeve of his BDUs and drag him along. James was moving slow, but his wits were coming back. Still, it was an immense relief to sink to the ground under the safety of Structure 27.

DAVID MCCARTER ASSURED himself that Hawkins and James were under cover. He ordered Manning and Encizo to stay out of sight when the jet came back. It was going to be coming straight toward them this time. It was too risky to stand in the doorway and attempt to gun the thing down from head-on.

It would also be too risky for McCarter to try to shoot at it from the middle of the plaza. If he was successful, he could bring the aircraft crashing down right into Structure 30. Right on top of Encizo and Manning.

He jogged up the plaza and ducked alongside the outer wall of Structure 30 and took up a position behind the structure. He climbed a pile of rock so that he was peering out over the room and roof of the structure, where he could see the aircraft but it would have a hard time seeing him.

From here, he would have an opportunity to take a few clear shots at the belly of the aircraft as it passed overhead.

Whether a few rounds from a submachine gun would bring it down was another question.

It was coming. He witnessed the materialization of

the craft over the canopy of the jungle again. The near-translucent body hid it amazingly well against the daylight sky.

But it was behaving differently. It was flying at a higher altitude and gaining speed. It did not look like it was coming in for landing or even for an attack this time. Maybe it was just an inspection flyover. At that height, McCarter had almost no chance of doing it significant damage from the ground. Not that he wasn't going to try. It was still gaining altitude as it passed over Structure 30 and McCarter felt foolish when he sent several rounds from his submachine gun chasing after the thing. The little jet ignored him and flew away.

Then something burst apart nearby. David McCarter raced around Structure 30 and found the first aircraft, parked under the old tree, engulfed in flames. That was the reason for the final flyover. They were destroying their own aircraft. He watched the thing become a ball of white-and-orange flame, which quickly reached out to the tree and began to burn it. He saw the plastic wings dripping. He saw a flood of liquid gush out of the belly, and turn the fire.

It took less than five minutes for the flames to reduce the aircraft to a flaming unrecognizable pile.

CHAPTER FOUR

Halifax, Nova Scotia, Canada

Halifax was not a place where Carl Lyons expected to find terrorist violence. But in the twenty-first century, nowhere in the world was immune from terrorism. But Lyons, leader of Able Team, a covert trio of counterterrorism specialists, was relentless in his pursuit of terrorists.

And Halifax had invited in the elements that might attract violence. Like it or not, casinos brought with them the elements of vice. The elements of vice could sometimes attract the elements of organized crime. And now the line was blurring between the crime organizations and the terrorists.

Blackrock Island Resort and Casino had been built specifically for travelers who did not want the Vegas experience. It couldn't have been in a more geologically different part of North America. The island was in Halifax Harbour, a mile from the Seaport Market. Here the railroad lines fanned out into the great shipping and logistical center at the port of Halifax. The lines were less heavily used than they had once been, and one of the old lines had been rebuilt and rededicated for transporting vacationers to Blackrock Resort. A light-rail line had been extended from Halifax Stanfield International Airport for visitors arriving by air, and intersected with the dedicated station for the resort train. Other visitors took long rail trips in the well-appointed railcars, turning their Blackrock visit into the final stop of an old-fashioned rail tour of northeast Canada.

It was even possible for travelers to take a transcontinental rail trip, starting on the West Coast of North America in Vancouver. The Via Rail line out of Vancouver was equipped with some of the same overnight railcars with expensive sleeping berths. The route took the train to Edmonton, then across Canada through Saskatoon and Winnipeg, through Sudbury and finally to Toronto. Here, travelers had no need to change train cars. The special luxury travel cars were transferred to a different engine for the short jump from Toronto to Montreal, where they linked up with the line to Halifax.

A great deal of attention had been paid to the luxury cars when they were commissioned two years before, and to their old-fashioned, luxurious amenities, offered at what was a price more reasonable than a regular hotel. The trains garnered a lot of attention from the media, and continued to spur more publicity. It seemed that every time a local in a small town decided to take the trip on the Blackrock Island Transcontinental Railway, they became minor celebrities. They would get write-ups in their local papers or be interviewed on local news when they returned from their great adventure. Occasionally those stories would get picked up and run as fillers across North America.

It was a public relations boon for Blackrock Island Casino, and that was the entire point—to focus the attention on the climactic endpoint of a Blackrock Island railroad car trip. The implication was that if getting there was such a grand experience, then being there, at the luxurious casino on its own island off Halifax, Nova Scotia, must be even better.

It seemed to be a successful advertising campaign. Despite the vast cost to build the casino and essentially remake Blackrock Island from a deserted, private nature preserve into a multifaceted vacation destination, the business seemed to be thriving.

And now it was potentially in danger.

Carl Lyons was bothered by this setup. He felt exposed and unprepared, not knowing how the attack would come, or even where precisely the attack would be targeted. Blackrock Island was a large enough piece of land to support a sprawling resort, golf course, even biking and walking trails and outdoor event spaces. It sat off Point Pleasant Park in the waters of what was technically Purcell's Cove.

It seemed unlikely that an attack would be coming from the direction of McNabb's Island, a mile over the water. Nor from the waters that stretched to the southeast and eventually crossed an invisible line that put them in Halifax Harbour. Keep going, and the water opened into the North Atlantic.

To the west was Purcell's Island, and little land development. Just the occasional house and a few inns sitting out on the water's edge. It was awfully peaceful-looking.

The problem was, the attack could come from any direction. Even in the light of day, it could come fast, quiet and unseen until the very last moment.

Hermann "Gadgets" Schwarz seemed to be reading his thoughts.

"Christ, they could come from anywhere. And the weather isn't helping."

"No, it's not," Lyons growled. The sky was gray and heavy, and the lapping of the cold waters and the wet blanket of the sky seemed to muffle the sounds of the afternoon in Halifax. A ship passing a few hundred yards to the north was almost unheard.

A near-silent aircraft could sneak up on them like a cat.

They were sitting in the waters in their own boat, which had been docked for them at Purcell's Cove. It looked like one of the local pleasure boats—a robust, well-insulated piece of work meant to endure the harsh climate of the east coast of Canada. But a pleasure craft all the same.

Carl Lyons was the leader of the tight, three-man commando outfit called Able Team. It was a fairly innocuous name. The members of the team were anything but. Lyons himself was formerly a detective in Los Angeles, and he had gone up against one of the most infamous and dangerous vigilantes in U.S. history: Mack Bolan. Very few men antagonized Mack Bolan and lived to tell the tale.

Eventually Carl Lyons's perspective had shifted and he found himself fighting alongside Bolan.

Lyons, like the two other members of Able Team, was recruited to the team by Bolan.

The other two were Hermann Schwarz, a gizmo guru who sometimes went by the nickname "Gadgets," and Rosario Blancanales, the member of the trio whose people skills had earned him the nickname "Politician."

Schwarz and Blancanales were a pleasant pair, considering what they had been through.

At some point the United States federal government essentially gave up on its efforts to stop Mack Bolan and instead decided to harness his energy. Hal Brognola, the Justice Department official who had been coordinating the effort to bring in Bolan, instead became Bolan's partner in the development of a new and highly secret anticrime-antiterror organization that was based in a well-funded facility within sight of Stony Man Mountain, a four-thousand-foot peak in Shenandoah National Park. Operations had started in the farmhouse of a working farm and eventually expanded to larger belowground facilities. From the base at Stony Man Farm the mostly international commando team Phoenix Force was deployed, as well as Able Team, which primarily worked in North America. It served as Bolan's base, as well, sometimes—when it suited him. He had never allowed himself to be controlled by the government. To this day his efforts remained essentially those of a vigilante.

Able Team had gone through hell, time and again, for the good of the country and the peace of its people. And sometimes the three men found themselves doing other people's jobs.

"Tell me again why there are no Canadians out here keeping an eye on the place." Rosario Blancanales leaned on the rail of the boat and glared at Blackrock Island.

Lyons shook his head. "Beats the hell out of me."

"Couldn't have a bunch of armed Mounties loitering around the place. It would make the gamblers feel insecure," Schwarz said. "Hard to relax on your vacation if you think you're about to be attacked."

Lyons nodded grimly. "Yeah."

The fact was, there probably were Canadian security forces of some type in the vicinity. They'd been alerted to the possibility of an attack on this location. But tourist destinations were always at risk. They were always a target to terrorists. Governments were constantly forced into the position of having to decide which threats to address and which to ignore—a constant struggle to balance security and ongoing, uninterrupted operation.

And right now, what was *not* a target of the stealth planes? No one knew how many of them were out there, and no one knew who had them. So there was no way of knowing what they would be used for. And so far, they seemed to have been used for just about every dirty deed you could think of. Revenge. Smuggling. Robbery. And worse.

And always, they had the advantage of the stealthy approach. There seemed to be no place in the world where they couldn't perpetrate damage. No place was safe. No radar seemed capable of spotting them. You never heard them coming. They seemed to have chameleon skin that absorbed the color around them, making them difficult to spot. They seemed highly maneuverable—and they were deadly.

Most of the aircraft were mounted with .50-caliber machine guns under the nose. A stealth plane in Italy had attacked a Mafia motorcade with at least two weapons blazing—5.56 mm NATO rounds were recovered later. The survivors of the battle claimed the weapons were being shot from armored slots in the belly of the aircraft.

In Turkey, a series of attacks in Kurd-claimed regions had relied on jettisoned incendiary devices.

Several of the attacks had even used flamethrowers, and curiously, in most of these cases, the aircraft had crashed and burned themselves. What was left was mystifying—mostly melted plastic and badly burned components. Whatever was being used for flame-thrower fuel must have been deadly.

Only now, after a full two weeks of worldwide attacks, was a picture of the aircraft starting to come into focus. It could be that the entire aircraft was itself highly flammable and triggered to self-destruct—or to easily be destroyed from a distance. This was the lesson that Phoenix Force had learned in southern Mexico just hours before.

And now, if the warnings were correct, another attack was planned for this place. Its cause was unrelated to the attack in Mexico, and to every other known attack around the world. Likewise, the perpetrators were not known to have a link to any other stealth plane perpetrator in the world.

That was the real problem. These planes were everywhere, in the hands of all kinds of despicable people. A new tool with which to right wrongs, exert influence, solve disputes and kill innocent people.

The death toll was in the hundreds and climbing. It had to be stopped.

But first they had to actually get their hands on one of those planes so it could be dismantled, studied, and so they could trace back to its source.

But could three men in a fishing boat hope to actually bring down one of those aircraft?

"It would take one hundred Mounties to cover that island," Blancanales observed. "You would have to have them in the hotel, tucked in the bushes on the golf courses, hanging out in the wedding gazebo, everywhere."

"Even that wouldn't do any good," Schwarz said. "Not unless they had antiaircraft hardware."

"So how do we protect this place?" Blancanales demanded.

"We don't," Lyons said. "It's not our job. We're here to take down and take out whoever attacks this place. Find out where they came from. Find out where they got their planes. And then follow the trail back."

"Yeah," Blancanales said. "And why do we think they're not going to attack the rail first?"

"We don't. It's just an assumption. We had a little bit of intelligence, and what it indicated was that Blackrock would be targeted in some way."

"That's kind of general," Blancanales said. "Doesn't rule out the rail. My inclination would be to lump that in as part of the resort."

Lyons nodded shortly. "Me, too."

Hermann Schwarz turned away from the water and looked behind him as if there was something to see there, then opened one of the compartments and pulled out a glossy brochure for the Blackrock Resort. He examined the map in the middle and looked over the top at the distant mainland of Halifax.

"Let's head that way," Schwarz said, "deeper into Purcell's Cove."

Blancanales sat behind the wheel. "Okay," he said. "Let's go there."

Lyons looked over Schwarz's shoulder at the tourist map. It showed visitor-friendly destinations. Point Pleasant Park. The Public Gardens. The Commons.

"You want to move us away from Blackrock Island?"

"Yeah," Schwarz said, tapping a spot on the tourist map. "Here."

Lyons leaned in. "Atlantic School of Theology?"

"Not exactly," Schwarz said. "Here. The railroad line runs pretty close to the water. I'm thinking that almost anybody who decides they're going to come after that train, no matter how much stealth they've got on their side, is still going to want to make a low-profile approach. They can't do that outside the city limits to the west, where there's a lot of traffic to and from the airport. So they're going to do it by coming in this way, or this way."

He indicated two routes on the map.

"The first one comes in over mostly low population areas, including these two chain lakes. Then they follow this road. St. Margaret's Bay Road. Or another lake, Chocolate Lake it's called, and then they fly up the length of the cove, where they're essentially running parallel to the rail tracks. They can swerve overland to the train anytime they feel like it, if they time their approach correctly. But I don't think that's the way they would come."

"I don't think so, either," Lyons said. "It would be only slightly less high profile than if they flew right into the city itself. I don't think they would get any secrecy that way. The only real advantage is the proximity to the tracks."

"Right," Schwarz said. "So this way."

With a slash of his finger across the page he indicated the second approach route. It came in from the southeast, over largely undeveloped land.

"If they come in from the ocean, and they cut over Herring Cove, they've got several miles of almost empty land to fly over before they make a quick bank to the northeast, when they're within just a mile of the tracks.

If their timing is good, they'll find themselves on top of the train as it makes the turn in the same direction, and at that point the train is already slowing down on approach to the station in Point Pleasant."

"Easy pickings," Blancanales said.

"Yeah," Lyons agreed. He glanced at the GPS map on his tablet computer. Blancanales was bringing them at a leisurely pace to the point in Purcell's Cove where the railroad made that turn, and he thought he could even glimpse the tracks beyond some of the large homes and university buildings on the waterfront. He turned to look behind him at the wooded lands on the other side of the cove.

"That way. That's where they'll come from, if you're right, Gadgets."

"It's just a guess," Schwarz said. "I'm not married to the idea."

Lyons nodded. "Good enough for me. Let's keep a kind of patrol going back and forth from this point to offshore of the island itself. We'll keep it slow and casual."

Lyons touched his headset and updated the mission controller at Stony Man Farm

"There is no indication that the attack is going to be on the train," Barbara Price reminded him.

"But our intelligence is pretty damned vague on this," Lyons responded.

"Agreed," Price said. "There are several shuttle trains that make the run from the airport to the resort dock throughout the day. It depends on the arrival schedule. But if I were going to attack the train, I'd want to go after the vacationers who come in on the run from Toronto. Much more high profile."

Even as she was speaking, Lyons spotted the movement of a train a mile away from where they sat on the water. It was moving at a slow pace through the mostly high-end residential district of the city, and slowed further to take the turn away from the water. It was a short train. A small engine and a single passenger car emblazoned with the logo of the Blackrock Resort.

"We're seeing one of those shuttles now," Lyons reported. "What time's the Toronto train expected?"

"Rail traffic control says it's already in queue on the tracks, maybe five miles from your position," Price confirmed. "I guess it's a couple of minutes early. It has slowed to five miles an hour outside Windsor. That's a standard practice. Railroad traffic control's usually very skilled at juggling trains to make the most efficient use of high-traffic lines. It should hit the junction in twenty-five minutes. By then the shuttle that you see now will have offloaded its passengers and be clear about the final leg of the track."

When Barbara Price described the train staging itself by slowing to five miles per hour outside Windsor, a small town to the northwest, Lyons felt some alarm. He exchanged glances with Blancanales and Schwarz as he enabled the conference mode on his headset.

"Sounds like an ideal opportunity for the attackers," Lyons said.

"Maybe," Price said. "Maybe not. It's well wooded in the vicinity. That would deter a close-proximity aircraft approach."

"Not really," Schwarz said. "Rail lines keep a good margin of cleared land alongside their tracks. From what we know about these aircraft and their maneuverability, they could get in and make their strike without a problem."

"We're keeping an eye on it," Price said. She wasn't reassuring.

"We'll keep listening," Lyons snapped. He was irritated. For a man like him, who preferred to find a target and strike it hard and fast, all this sitting around was maddening.

"We can't be in two places at once," Blancanales said.

"Somebody sure the hell should've been there," Lyons said.

Their headsets came to life every few minutes with the voice of Barbara Price reporting no activity. Everything normal with the incoming passenger train from Toronto. Blancanales allowed their pleasure craft to drift slowly on the lapping waters of Purcell's Cove until they ceased their back-and-forth circuits. They didn't want to look like they were on patrol. They took up station offshore of the track turn, and quiet tension grew on the boat.

Lyons found himself gritting his teeth, anticipating an attack to come that his team would be unable to stop. They were not equipped to take down aircraft or to protect passenger rail—or, if the attack bypassed the railroad entirely, to protect an entire island and three hundred visiting vacationers.

Able Team was good, but they weren't miracle workers.

The airport shuttle rolled into view, took the curve and vanished behind the large houses, then accelerated slightly until it was gone from central Halifax. Over their headsets, Price reported that the Quebec passenger train had switched track at the junction and was now headed into the city.

They saw another train, and Lyons knew it was not the train in question.

"Cargo train," Schwarz reported. "On the adjacent rails. Heading to the seaport."

Listening in, Price confirmed, "We see it on the rail traffic control system. Strictly cargo. It won't impact the running of the passenger train. They run on more or less independent rail logistics once they reach the city congestion."

Lyons felt the tension in his brow. Information from Price didn't seem to tell him much of anything, but there was something in his gut that made him more alert. What little intelligence they had said that the target was the resort. They'd only assumed that the resort's passenger line might be a target. It was a reach as it was. It seemed unreasonable to expect a convenient cargo train to be involved.

"There's the passenger train," Blancanales said, almost mumbling.

Lyons could see the second train moving at an easy pace along the tracks, alongside the slower-moving, more heavily burdened cargo train. It always seemed somehow reckless to see two massive trains running alongside each other with just a few feet of clearance between them. These two had an arm's length of distance between them, but at their slow speeds, moving in essentially the same direction, there seemed to be no danger.

So what was he worried about?

Carl Lyons was, he realized, worried about something.

And so was Blancanales.

And Schwarz was pacing now, in the tight quarters of the deck of the pleasure craft, watching the pair of trains moving at an almost leisurely pace around the perimeter of Halifax. Turning his head, he watched the other shore, where his own theories had suggested that an attack stealth plane might emerge. And he looked up Purcell's Cove, the alternate route. And then he looked back at the trains.

He saw nothing. His agitation only seemed to grow.

Lyons knew exactly how he was feeling. "Stony?" he barked.

"Yes, Able?" Price responded.

"What's going on?"

"Nothing. No sign of alert or alarms. Anything on your end, Able?" she asked, an inquisitive note in her voice, as if she could read something of their mood.

Lyons was on his feet. He was doing Schwarz's routine now—looking at the trains, across the cove, up the waterway.

"There's something," he said.

"The island?" Price asked.

Blancanales was keeping an eye on the island through a pair of field glasses. "Nothing."

Lyons's mind was spinning. There were hundreds of people on the island. There was security staff there. If the attack came on the island, there would be plenty of people to sound an instant alarm.

Why did he think the aircraft would come here? he demanded of himself. When had he even come to the conclusion that the target was the train?

The long snake of the cargo train had started around the corner at a near crawl. The passenger train was moving slightly quicker, still meandering down the long length of the cargo train. He could make out the Blackrock logo on the passenger cars in the rear. They looked polished and new against the faded paint on the old tank cars of the cargo train.

"Stony," Lyons snapped. "The cargo train's pulling a lot of damned fuel. How come it's not going to the Imperial oil center across the water?"

"There are a lot of reasons they could need fuel on this side of the water," Schwarz suggested.

"I'm pulling up the manifest," Price responded. "Heating oil, diesel, nothing exceptional. Not a special order. This is a scheduled delivery for the seaport."

"Scheduled," Lyons said.

"Yeah," Blancanales said, turning his binoculars to the sky low over the opposite shore. Then he spun to look up the waterway. There was *nothing*.

And then, there it was. The small aircraft seemed to float peacefully out from over the trees on the opposite shore of Purcell's Cove. It came from the southeast, just as Schwarz had predicted it would. It came out at under a hundred feet, so low it agitated the treetops, and was on top of them even as Carl Lyons got the first words out of his mouth.

"Incoming, Stony. They're targeting the fuel."

The small white jet took no notice of Able Team or any of the craft on the water. It banked sharply and the pilot seemed to hit the brakes, causing it to wobble over the water and almost flutter over the treetops of the Maplewood Estates on the Halifax shore. Lyons thought for a moment that he was going to see this thing flop to the ground. Somehow the pilot kept the plane in the sky, or maybe it was the sophisticated electronics that controlled its operations. The low-flying jet managed to line itself up on the same trajectory as the rail lines after they made their curve and headed to the ports.

As careless as the flying looked, it also looked to Carl Lyons as if the timing had been perfect. As it slowed above the side-by-side trains, something flashed from the belly of the plane and slammed into the ground not a yard away from the tracks. It burst apart, caving in the steel tank car with a flash of fire. Clear liquid burst from the tank car, and then it was lost behind buildings.

"Get us there," Lyons snapped at Blancanales.

Before he could finish speaking, the pleasure craft jumped forward and Lyons had to grab on to a rail to keep from tumbling to the deck. His eyes remained locked on the place where the burst tank car would be. He expected at any moment to see a flash of light and billowing smoke. There was nothing, and the small, quiet plane had zipped away and out of sight.

"It tagged a tank car on the cargo train," he reported quickly to Price.

"Stony, they knew the passenger train and the cargo train were coming in at the same time. They're going to take out the passenger train by blowing the fuel on the cargo train."

"Understood," Price responded.

"We lost the plane. It doesn't look like their first attack scored the way they wanted it to. No signs of an explosion."

"They will come back," Blancanales said.

"Can you get a fix on them?" Lyons demanded.

"Nothing yet," Price said. "We're trying to pin them down."

Lyons's grip on the handrail tightened as Blancanales

steered their pleasure craft at a private dock in front of a large old home facing the water's edge. Blancanales kept the throttle down until the last moment, then cut the engines and twisted the wheel, sending up a massive spray of water as the craft lurched broadside. It was enough to slow it down before slamming into the dock—almost. The dock tipped and some wooden parts cracked noisily, and the members of Able Team were already leaping onto the planks and hustling to the shore.

They sprinted across the dense, dark green lawn, and one of the several back doors of the mansion flew open. A towering figure in a suit jacket and a perfectly knotted tie stormed across a large brick patio, waving a telephone. Lyons and Blancanales ignored him, but Schwarz chose that moment to free the hardware strapped on his back. The well-dressed man with the telephone took one look at the bulky, high-tech-looking weapon and changed his attitude in a hurry. He was backing up with his hands in the air as Schwarz followed the others around the side of the mansion.

They ran across the front lawn and across a road that took them to the tracks, where the huge, snakelike cargo train was still moving slowly. Lyons had no difficulty stepping up onto one of the boxcar ladders, hardly feeling the change in acceleration. The thing was moving at just a couple of miles an hour. Maybe it was already coming to a stop. The others clambered onto the boxcar roof alongside him, peering ahead with binoculars.

A hundred yards ahead they could see the broken shell of the tank car. There was no sign of fire.

Through his field glasses Lyons could read the legend on the broken tank car. "Blended chemicals?" he read aloud.

Schwarz cursed. "That could be anything."

He sniffed the air. A laboratory-like pungency had just enveloped them.

"Smells like shit," Schwarz said.

"At least it's not flammable," Blancanales responded.

"Maybe not, but those are," Lyons said, training his field glasses on a long line of nearly identical tank cars coming up behind them. "Ethanol." He redirected his binoculars to the front. "Ethanol and diesel. Most of those tanks look flammable. We got lucky the first time."

The voice of Barbara Price came through their headsets. "Able Team, any sign of our plane?"

"Yes," Blancanales said. "They're heading in for another attack. Coming in over Halifax Harbour. Heading south-southwest. They're lined up on the trains, Stony. They're going to try to hit the tanks in front and take out the resort train at the same time."

Lyons had spotted the gray glimmer of the incoming stealth jet and had come to the same conclusion. The plane had done a three-sixty out over the water, passed dangerously close over the tops of the loading cranes at Ocean Terminal Pier 23, and was drifting down to treetop level for another close-proximity strike at the freight car tankers. Lyons blinked behind his binoculars, trying to get a read on the thing. It was almost invisible against the cloudy sky, and watching it come from head-on meant he couldn't even judge the speed. But he knew exactly where it would strike. One hundred and fifty yards ahead of them, a large cluster of black tankers traveled alongside the polished wooden passenger cars of the Blackrock train.

His mind flirted for an instant with the possibility of

striking the plane before it could attack the train again, but there was no way.

All three of them were lining up their weapons on the incoming stealth jet. Carl Lyons acquired his target and held it there. He saw the burst of rounds from the belly of the jet. He saw them strike the ground alongside the freight train tanks, and he heard the crack of opening metal. Suddenly the stealth jet became brilliantly contrasted against an ugly orange ball of rising fire and black smoke.

Carl Lyons exhaled and allowed that new reality to flow away from him.

In another moment he would be able to process that information. In a moment he would think about an explosion of tank cars ripping apart the train he was standing on. In a few more seconds he would allow himself to consider what might have happened to the passenger train cars that had been adjacent to the explosion and allow himself to consider the consequences to this part of the city of Halifax if there was a chain reaction of exploding ethanol tanks.

But now he had a target that he would not fail to tag. The jet was gaining altitude away from the explosion, but it was still moving slow and low by jet standards, and Lyons thought he just might get it.

He triggered the M-203. The round sped across open air and passed twenty feet below the suddenly banking aircraft.

He'd missed.

"Fuck!" Lyons exploded. "Gadgets!"

Schwarz was already firing.

And he wasn't missing.

THE U.S. ARMY DESIGNATED it the XM-25 Counter Defi-
lade Target Engagement. They shortened it to CDTE.
Even that was too much of a mouthful. The Special
Forces soldiers in Afghanistan who fielded the weapon
for the first time called it simply the Punisher. It was the
first "smart" weapon made for the average grunt. It was
a shoulder-fired grenade rifle with a laser range finder
to acquire the target. The gun's computer also sensed
temperature and air pressure, factored in the ballistic
of the grenade and fed the data into a microchip inside
the 25 mm round itself. The result was a weapon that
could fire as far as seventy meters and find a stationary target with uncanny precision.

All of which helped Hermann Schwarz not at all
when targeting a fast-moving aircraft, which was why
he was using point-detonating rounds. Schwarz triggered the CDTE and watched the 25 mm high-explosive
antitank round zip underneath the ascending jet.

Schwarz adjusted his aim but was distracted by the
trajectory of the first round. The weapon was powerful and fast, and they were using live fire in a metropolitan area. The heat round was supposed to be smart
enough to know that it had missed its target and blow
itself up after a certain distance traveled. The rounds
had worked as expected during test firing at Stony Man
Farm. For some reason, Schwarz had a feeling in his
gut that this time around the CDTE would do what it
was supposed to do.

His hands were frozen on the trigger. He couldn't
make himself shoot a second round at the city of Halifax, knowing that he might miss again, knowing that
the round just might not self-destruct in time.

"Blow," he whispered.

The 25 mm HEAT burst apart, high in the air, its outward force flying into the conflagration bursting from the train. That was all Schwarz needed to see. He triggered his second round, his mind suddenly blank and calm. He wasn't acting "smart," either, but rather with the instincts of the seasoned warrior. Even without the experience of having fired this specific new sort of grenade launcher at a small jet aircraft, aiming became suddenly easy. The second round homed in on the ascending jet as if it were laser-guided. It hit the belly of the aircraft and cracked it open. The aircraft bounced as if it had gone over a speed bump, and large chunks of plastic and metal spiraled away from it. There seemed to be very little fire, but fuel spilled out of the gaps in the broken hull.

And then the jet seemed to level out and continue its ascent. Schwarz fired again. A round hit the aircraft broadside and cracked open the hull just in front of the twin rear-mounted engines. It was precisely on target, right where Schwarz wanted it to be. And then metal shrapnel from the grenade and the explosion of scrap plastic and metal from the aircraft itself swirled into the uptake of the turbo fans. The engines immediately smoked and one began to scream in protest. The aircraft leveled out and for a moment the turbo fan cleared the smoke. The screaming of distressed machinery coughed and became quiet.

Hermann Schwarz was momentarily convinced that the jet was actually going to shake off two hits by 25 mm antitank rounds and survive.

But then the turbo fan belched black smoke and pieces of itself, and the jet arced gracefully out of the sky. It was going into the waters of Purcell's Cove.

It must've been shallow where the small jet hit, because it shattered into a thousand plastic pieces without even submerging.

At that moment Schwarz remembered the blaze coming from the front of the train. His mind shouted at him. Ethanol fire. He didn't get a chance to see it before Carl Lyons slammed into him and sent him flying off the boxcar.

Hermann Schwarz was thinking, for a fraction of a second, that it was going to be a long way to the ground.

It was.

He hit hard, felt the breath knocked out of him, felt both elbows crack against gravel and weeds. He forced his stunned body to roll through the impact and dissipate the energy.

He launched himself to his feet, trying to assess by feel whatever damage had been done by the ungraceful impact, and found himself crumpling to the earth again. Still he was looking at the tongue of fire that had rolled over the tops of the train cars—including the one where they had been standing.

Blancanales was there, bending over him, squeezing his limbs.

"Ouch, damn!" Schwarz said. Blancanales was merciless, testing Schwarz's arms, then his legs.

"Is he broken?" Lyons demanded, keeping a close eye on the nearby conflagration.

"Just black-and-blue," Schwarz said.

"Stony," Lyons said into his mike, "do we have emergency personnel on the way?"

Price responded over the headset. "It's coming, Carl. How big is it?"

Lyons shook his head. "Getting bigger."

As if to reinforce his point another of the tank cars ahead blew apart, and Lyons turned his back to it, riding out the fierce hot breeze that swept over them.

"Carl," Price said. "You okay?"

Lyons was glaring at the ball of yellow-orange fire that had come just a little closer to them. The heat of the flames was intense. It was going to break through the steel shell of the tanks and work its way down. Every time one of those tanks blew, the intensity would grow. The spread of the killing flames would be wider. There were at least eight more tank cars up ahead, then a dozen or so boxcars. Then a long, long chain of tankers. Diesel. Ethanol. Gasoline, for Christ's sake. Weren't there regulations against pulling this much flammable shit through a metropolitan area?

"Stony, we're going to try to mitigate some of this damage before it happens."

Barbara Price sounded even more calm than usual. "Able Team, I don't think that's a good idea. Those tanks are going to start blowing in more rapid succession. You're not going to be able to get away when a chain reaction starts."

"Neither is anybody else. We're in a goddamned residential area, Stony. Gadgets, start hiking out. We'll catch up with you in a minute."

"I'm fine, Ironman," Schwarz said. "What's your plan?"

"Go!" Lyons said, and then jogged forward, making a quick examination of the couplers between the boxcars, then going flat to the ground and examining under the train cars. Their forward motion had now stopped completely—then came another heavy thump as a tank car ahead of them cracked open. The air seemed to suck itself away from them, the gray afternoon gave way to momentary harsh brilliance and another heavy, super-heated wall of wind swept over them. Lyons covered his head with his arms, face in the gravel, allowing it to rush over him. It dissipated only slightly. The line of train cars jerked and rattled. Lyons sprang to his feet and pulled out an AN-M14. He jogged forward and ducked in between the next two boxcars.

Lyons felt intense discomfort and realized he was not breathing. The air was torrid, and it would be dangerous to stay here for more than a few seconds. He made a quick assessment of the coupler between the two cars. It was an AAR Type F—the same coupler as on a million train cars around the world. So tough and well engineered it would keep the train cars coupled even in many derailment scenarios. With the couplers under tension, there was no way Lyons was going to separate them. He wedged the bottom end of the incendiary grenade into the coupler knuckles, slipped the pin and got the hell out.

Blancanales was jogging toward him, coming to offer assistance.

"Other way," Lyons said quickly. They both sprinted alongside a flat edge of the train cars, and Lyons tried not to gag on the noxious hot air that he had accidentally inhaled. He saw a glimmer of light that came from behind him, but the rush of the fire almost completely masked the detonation of the incendiary grenade.

Schwarz was moving awkwardly, staggering like a horror movie zombie over a low berm alongside the tracks. Lyons on one side and Blancanales on the other grabbed him and dragged him to the ground as another harsh crack indicated another tank car had blown.

"That was too soon," Lyons shouted above the rush of noise. "I don't know if it worked."

Lyons poked his head over the top of the grassy berm and witnessed the chain reaction—the explosion sent one train car slamming into the next. Then burning wind rushed over them and they dropped back down. Lyons could swear he saw streaks of yellow fire in the air around him.

He gave the firewater a moment to weaken, then peeked over the berm again.

"Ironman," Blancanales complained, "you'll fry your eyeballs."

Lyons pulled back down even as another explosion erupted at the front of the train. He could hear the crash of a train car being shoved violently into the car behind it, followed by the next and the next. Finally he could restrain himself no more and he glanced briefly out over the top of the berm. It was akin to thrusting his head into a blazing furnace, and he fought to keep his eyes open for only a second, and that was enough. His grenade had done its job. The powerful coupler melted in the extreme heat of the grenade and the explosions had created a violent impact that jolted from car to car—until his boxcar was shoved away from the rear of the train. It was separating itself at a snail's pace from the exploding train.

A feeble effort, at best, Lyons thought as he sank down behind the protection of the berm. His skin was on fire and his eyeballs felt as if they had been roasted in their sockets, but he had seen what he had come to see.

"Let's go," he ordered, and rose onto all fours to begin a quick crawl away from the berm and the burn, only to be dragged down again by Blancanales as another tank car burst behind them. When Lyons glanced up, he saw a sky filled with pale yellow flame.

The next explosion just might send a tidal wave of burning fuel to engulf them. And explosions were coming in more rapid succession. Lyons allowed them just seconds of wait time, but as soon as the wall of fire began to diminish he shouted at the others.

"Move out now."

He had a firm grip on Schwarz's BDUs and thrust himself to his feet. Blancanales was dragging Schwarz by the other arm. Schwarz was complaining vigorously. They could talk about it later. Not now. Who knew how long it would be before the next tanker blew.

How long turned out to be less than six steps. Lyons heard the crack, sensed the rush of igniting fuel.

But now they were behind one of the houses. The big old building shielded them from the flame. The residents were already fleeing the fire, running along the water's edge.

Able Team hustled to the dock.

Lyons touched his headset. "Stony, there's an extremely hazardous situation here." Quickly he briefed Barbara Price on the events of the past ninety seconds.

"Carl, are you getting out of there?" Price asked.

"Yeah. We're in the boat."

"How's Hermann?"

"Hermann is fine," Schwarz declared. He stepped off the dock into their watercraft, landing on both feet with a belligerent thunk. At that moment there was another explosion, louder than all the bursts that had come before. It was a staccato crack, followed by a heavy clank.

The three of them sank low and waited for any shrapnel from the blast to sail past them.

"That sounded like an explosive charge," Blancanales said.

"Or something else on that train," Lyons added. "Some cargo we don't know about. Something even more dangerous than ethanol and oil."

"Look," Schwarz said.

The last blast had accomplished Lyons's goal. The clank had been the powerful collision of the train cars being slammed together by the percussive force of the blast. The last car had rocketed off the tracks, flown six feet and slammed into the loose train cars behind it. It was powerful enough to nudge the line of cars away.

Blancanales muscled Schwarz out from behind the wheel and he steered them away from land. They watched the fascinating, horrific sight of the tank cars exploding down the line, one by one.

Price was watching it happen, as well, over Lyons's lipstick cam.

"It's working, Ironman," she said to Lyons.

Carl Lyons wasn't so confident. He watched the slow-motion escape of the back line of train cars race the approaching explosions from the tank cars still attached to the main train. The final tank blew, cracking open and releasing a mushroom cloud of orange fire and black smoke. The ball of flame rose over the burning cars and fiery tongues reached out in all directions. They licked at the first car in the slow-moving line of escaping cars. There had to be twenty more tanks back there, that Lyons could see. If the first one blew, the whole train might blow. If the whole train blew, it would burn down this entire section of the city.

The flames pulled back, and the first tank car rolling away showed no signs that it had even been singed. Still Lyons watched, glaring at the car that seemed to be moving almost at its leisure away from the catastrophe.

"It worked, Carl," Barbara Price said confidently.

Lyons laughed without joy. "That is not exactly what I had in mind, Stony. It wasn't my rounds that blew the train back. It was strictly dumb luck."

"It was your rounds that separated that section of the train so that it could be pushed back," Price responded. "Give yourself some credit, Ironman."

"Stony, what the hell is the problem with the Canadians? Why the hell aren't they out here minding their own goddamned store?"

"They are on their way now, Able."

"A lot of good it will do now. The damage is done."

"Transport is on its way, Able," Price said.

"The resort itself is still vulnerable," Lyons said. "We're going ashore at Blackrock."

"No way. The Canadians are finally taking your advice, Carl. There are a hundred troops on their way to Blackrock Island, in addition to the hazmat firefighters moving in to the train. They'll take care of the situation now."

Lyons could see large Canadian troop transport helicopters already on the horizon, over the mainland, coming from beyond Dartmouth.

They had been staged, waiting for something to happen. The Canadians had been just sitting there waiting for this to happen. They could've had their own people on the ground keeping it from happening.

One hundred troops, and some serious firepower, might have prevented this from happening at all.

CHAPTER FIVE

Stony Man Farm, Virginia

The attractive blonde, blue-eyed woman was in an embroidered cowboy shirt and a pair of well-worn, snug-fitting jeans. She wouldn't have looked out of place on a ranch. In fact, Barbara Price was the Stony Man Farm mission controller, which meant she had operational responsibility for two of the most successful commando teams that had ever been fielded by the United States.

Barbara Price answered only to the director of the Sensitive Operations Group. The director in turn answered only to the President of the United States. The SOG antiterrorist organization was so secret that its existence was unknown—in theory—to anyone outside of the President and the SOG itself.

The director of the SOG, the man who served as the liaison between Stony Man Farm and the President, was Hal Brognola, a Justice Department official with an office in Washington, D.C., that gave him a view of the Potomac River.

In the Stony Man Farm War Room, Barbara Price touched the controls to bring up a video feed of Brognola from his D.C. office. The big Fed loomed even bigger than life on the large plasma screen that dominated one end of the War Room. A secondary screen showed the image of a burning stealth plane under a burning tree.

When the camera image pulled back, it was revealed that the aircraft and tree were burning amid a campus of South American ruins.

"I take it we are not going to get any useful information out of that plane," growled Brognola.

Brognola was seeing the video feed at the same time as Barbara Price. It was showing on one of the auxiliary monitors in his office in D.C.

"We didn't even try," Price said. "Jack took one look at it and said it wasn't worth the danger. Phoenix would have to stay on-site for hours before the thing would be cooled down enough to even start poking around in the leftovers."

Brognola nodded. "What about prisoners?"

"Early results from our questioning were not promising. We don't think they know anything about the plane's origin. We'll keep working on them. Who knows?"

"Give me an update," Brognola said, "on the scope of this problem."

Barbara Price nodded, knowing that she had come to the part of this conversation that was going to cause Brognola some true consternation.

"We are up to 124 suspected incidents with the stealth aircraft, worldwide, in twenty-four days."

The oversize image of Harold Brognola looked directly at Barbara Price from the office in D.C.

"Did you say 124?"

"I did. Up from seventeen incidents one week ago."

"Where?" Brognola asked.

Price summoned a map of the American continents on an auxiliary screen. Mexico and South America were covered with yellow dots. There were dots in the Caribbean and in Florida, and along the border between the United States and Mexico. There was a sprinkling of dots across Europe, just a few in the Middle East, and more large groupings in Indonesia, Malaysia, China and other Southeast Asian nations.

"Most of these were simply sightings. Some were attacks. In Mexico there was much drug gang violence— one Mexican gang against another."

"But all using stealth jet technology?" Brognola insisted.

"Most of the ones shown are confirmed stealth jet attacks," Price said. "There's been a rash of attacks in Vincente. It's a small town fifteen miles outside of Juarez in northern Mexico. The Vincente family is well established there. They've been running drugs into the United States for eight years. This after displacing the Querol family. The Querol family was driven out of the area, into central Mexico, and has apparently been trying to reconstitute their organization. Three days ago, attacks began against the town of Vincente in Mexico, and the Vincente family homes were destroyed. Safe to assume the Querol family has taken possession of a couple of the stealth jets and is using them to quell the competition and get back into the family business. They even targeted the livestock. Vincente family horses and cattle were slaughtered in the field. Gunned down or burned."

"Burned?" Brognola asked.

"Get this," Price said. "Eyewitness reports said that they were throwing Molotov cocktails out of the windows of the aircraft."

Brognola shook his head. "None of this makes any sense. How come you got all these people, all over the world, suddenly getting their hands on this unbelievably sophisticated stealth technology, and then using that technology to attack with burning beer bottles of gasoline? What's wrong with this picture? Why am I not understanding this?"

Barbara Price shrugged. "I don't have the answers."

"How did you get a lead on the Mexico attack?" Brognola asked.

"CIA," Price said. "An agent in Mexico picked up rumors that there would be a payback attempt at one of the new high-profile Mexican tourist sites in the southern part of the country. The rumor said they'd be attacking one of the sites that wasn't accessible by car yet. That had to mean Chilan."

"And the rationale behind the attack? Payback for heavy-handed drug enforcement by the Mexican government?"

"Exactly," Price said. "One of the drug gangs in Mexico passed the word. They didn't like how heavily the Mexican government was coming down on their business practices. They wanted to make it clear that if the Mexican government was going to hurt their revenues, they were going to hurt the revenues of the government. That meant sabotaging Mexico's big tourism promotion push. Mexico's lost billions from the slowdown in tourism over the last few years."

"Never mind that the reason people are staying away is because they're afraid of the drug violence," Brognola growled. "We have a line on which one of the drug gangs carried out the attack?"

"We will," Price said, "once we process the prisoners. We're taking them to a safehouse in Mexico City. They'll be questioned by Mexican-born operatives.

We'll get their identification. I'm not too hopeful, however, that we will get any useful information about the source of the aircraft."

"What have we learned from this, and from Able's mess in Canada?"

Price frowned at Brognola's referring to the mess as "Able's," as if they had caused it.

"Able reported that fuel leaked from the aircraft fuselage when it was compromised by a grenade," Price said. "If they store fuel in the fuselage, it may make the aircraft extremely flammable, and that would explain why all the crashes we know of have resulted in nothing but melted plastic and burned components."

"Flammable aircraft?"

Pryce shrugged again. "Maybe."

She could tell that Brognola didn't like what he was hearing. She was giving him a report that included a lot of incidents spread across a vast area, but she was not giving him any indication of progress. There were, at the very least, dozens of these small stealth aircraft in existence. They had come out of nowhere over a period of several days, perpetrating violence worldwide, invisible to radar, untraceable by any of the United States's best technology. It was the kind of technology gap that the U.S. military did not like to have. And the United States was not accustomed to competing for military technology with South American drug gangs.

"We have got to get our hands on one of these damned planes," Brognola complained.

"Able Team," Price said, "is en route to Florida. There has been a surge of UFO reports, of all things, in Glades County, and that prompted some local investigation by the FBI. They believe that there has been stealth plane activity in the area—but no reports of attacks. If the planes are there, it is safe to assume they're bringing in drugs."

"They'd be perfect for it," Brognola complained. "All but invisible. Quiet. Even the DEA drones haven't been able to spot one."

"Able's going on-site. They're going to try to track down one of the shipments and take control of the aircraft while it's on the ground offloading cargo." Price met Brognola's eyes through their video feed. "It's a long shot."

"Fine," Brognola said. "Anything else? Do you have any solid information that I can relay to the Man? The President's asking for a report and I'd really like to be able to give him *something*."

"You've got what I've got, Hal," Price said.

"All right. Thanks, Barb."

The plasma screen went dark.

CHAPTER SIX

Palenque, Mexico

The transport aircraft sat on the tarmac at Palenque airport. Inside, Jack Grimaldi was standing in front of the flat screen, as if watching the video from just a few feet away would help him understand it better. But he gave a shrug and sat at the conference table.

"I've seen this video twenty times and I still can't believe it," Grimaldi said. "It's like the thing is made to burn up."

Jack Grimaldi was the lead pilot for Stony Man Farm. He had flown almost every aircraft in existence, but these strange little jets had him baffled. He had been asked to join this conference call with Stony Man Farm. They were on board the Phoenix Force transport jet; once this meeting was concluded, Grimaldi would be piloting it back to the United States.

A second display showed the War Room at Stony Man Farm. Barbara Price sat at the conference table, along with Aaron Kurtzman, a powerful-looking man in a wheelchair. There were others working in various terminals in the room, among them a big, older black man in a suit and tie. A young Japanese man was pounding keys on a terminal in the corner with his right hand while his left hand worked, seemingly independently, on a second terminal on a portable cart.

On the main screen the three-minute video of the burning aircraft came to an end and restarted.

"Now look at this," Jack Grimaldi said. "Right at the start, you see that the wings are dripping. The plastic is melting and dripping off, and it is burning."

"I used to burn my G.I. Joe's in the backyard, and they would melt like that," T. J. Hawkins said. "It was kind of cool. Of course, when the show was over, you didn't have a G.I. Joe anymore."

"Yeah," Grimaldi said, "but your G.I. Joe was made of thermoplastic. Cheap, easily moldable, flammable thermoplastic. You're not supposed to make aircraft out of flammable material."

"You don't think that it was the self-destruct medium that was burning?" Price suggested.

"No. There's too much of it. I wish I'd got there in time to witness it myself. By the time I came to pick up the boys, this thing was just a slag heap. But I'm telling you, it's the plastic that's burning. See the volume of material that is dripping off—that's the actual wing, melting and turning to goo and burning up. That black smoke is what you get when you burn thermoplastic. Now watch what happens at 1 minute, 15 seconds."

As the time marker reached 1 minutes and 15 seconds, something else began to pour out of the belly of the aircraft. It was another liquid, but it had the viscosity of water and it streamed on the ground, burning brightly.

"That, to me, looks like fuel."

"Fuel tanks in the belly of the aircraft?" asked the big man in the wheelchair.

"Would that be more dangerous or less dangerous

than making the entire aircraft flammable in the first place?" asked David McCarter.

"Now wait," said Jack Grimaldi, watching the time marker again. "Okay, watch this right wing at this section here, along the roofline. Watch what happens."

From the steady burning of the plastic erupted a tiny jet of bright flame that dripped to the ground. It came from the seam that Grimaldi had indicated in the wing. Another jet erupted on the roofline, and the bright yellow flame seemed to trickle along the burning body of the aircraft.

Grimaldi turned to his Phoenix Force audience. "Did you see that?"

"I saw, Jack," Price said from the Farm. "Can you explain what it was?"

"Fuel. More fuel. If I didn't know better I would say that there are fuel leaks coming not only from the belly of the aircraft but from the roofline and from the wings."

"Whoa. There's got to be aircraft-design best practices that say you don't surround the passengers with fuel," Calvin James commented.

"You bet there is," Grimaldi said.

"It does correlate with the report from Able Team," Price asked. "But why design an aircraft like that?"

"Save space, maybe?" Grimaldi suggested. "I'm just guessing here. But what else could be spitting out of the roof of the plane, of all places. You don't keep any hydraulic fluid up there. If you're smart you're using fire-resistant hydraulic fluids, regardless. Phosphate esters. It's stable and has a long performance life."

Aaron Kurtzman was still glaring at the screen. Jack Grimaldi was certainly the most expert among when it came to aircraft engineering. Still, it seemed outlandish to suggest that this stealth aircraft was built to be a flying fuel tank.

"I assume that an attempt was made to track the second jet when it buggered out of Chilan," McCarter said.

"Yes. For what good it did," Kurtzman said. "We didn't get a blip. Nothing. We looked at commercial air traffic control radar and they saw nothing. Our military monitoring saw nothing. It's as though those aircraft were not even there."

"How is that possible?" McCarter demanded.

There was no response from Grimaldi or from the conference table at Stony Man Farm.

Finally Kurtzman said, "We really need to get our hands on one of these things."

"I've been told," Barbara Price said.

DAVID MCCARTER HAD BARELY settled into his seat in the transport jet before he felt the change in direction. They had taken off from the small airfield outside Palenque in southern Mexico, disgruntled at their lack of success, and were heading north, back to the United States. And then, less than fifteen minutes into the flight, the plane banked. The aircraft was turning around.

McCarter poked his head into the cockpit. Jack Grimaldi was just straightening out the aircraft on its new heading. Alongside him was a U.S. Air Force copilot, currently serving a stint at Stony Man Farm. Like all the military and intelligence staff who served rotations at the Farm, he was sworn to absolute secrecy. Revealing anything about his time at the Farm—even to high-level commanding officers, at any time in the future—would be considered a crime worthy of immediate demotion and dismissal.

As Grimaldi handed the controls over to the Air Force pilot he turned to McCarter.

"We forget something?" McCarter asked.

"Just got word from the boss lady. She said forget D.C., head for Córdoba."

McCarter thought for a second. "Argentina? Something new must have happened in the last half hour."

"She said she'll give you a call in a few to discuss it."

In fact, as McCarter returned to the cabin he found the other four members of Phoenix Force gathering around a central monitor, and Barbara Price herself was on the screen.

"Afternoon, again, Phoenix," she said. "I've just given Jack instructions to change course to Argentina. You are headed for the Córdoba province. We might have a line on two more of those aircraft."

"That's good news," McCarter said.

"Emphasis on *might*," Price warned. "It's little better than a rumor at this point. I'm inserting you in the middle of what might be a transnational South American gang war. I hope you are okay with that?"

"Better than okay. We love transnational South American gang wars," Rafael Encizo said. "Especially if it gives us another chance to snatch a plastic plane."

"Specifically, I need you to be on hand to deal with a kidnapping. We think some of the players involved are the parties who shot up the hotel in La Paz."

"Really?" Hawkins said. "That was a real ballsy move. I saw a network news animation of how it must have happened."

"That attack had brought the existences of the stealth

aircraft to the attention of the public worldwide," Price said. "It's causing some panic. No thanks to the news networks outlets speculating pretty wildly about the supposed capabilities of these aircraft. They have the people convinced these things can fly silent and invisible anywhere they want—and crash into any buildings they want."

T. J. Hawkins looked across the table at the others. Encizo had the same expression on his face. They'd seen these planes. They didn't think what Price had just said qualified as "wild speculation" at all. It was pretty close to accurate.

"They're also beginning to piece together a list of attacks worldwide," Price continued. "The number of attacks has escalated quickly in recent days. You should also know that we've just received word of another suspected stealth jet crash. This one in Thailand. Local news is claiming it was armed for an attack on the People's Republic of China, but that's likely just speculation."

"I don't suppose there's anything left of that jet?" McCarter asked.

"No," Price said. "The news is describing the remains as a puddle."

"So where are we headed?" McCarter said.

The image of the pretty blonde mission commander faded and on the screen was a picture of a vast, flat, white desert plain, with mountains in the distance—and row after row of neat piles of white rock.

"Oh. It's the Salinas Grandes," T. J. Hawkins said. "The salt mines."

"Yes," said the voice of Barbara Price. "The Salinas Grandes is a salt desert in central Argentina. The desert as a whole is bigger than Delaware, smaller than Connecticut, and it's the site for numerous mining operations. Most just salt, but also potassium and even lithium. This particular salt flat scraping operation happens to be the agreed-upon handover site in the kidnapping case."

"How'd this bit of intelligence come to us, Barb?" McCarter asked.

"Hal relayed it. Apparently he got it from one of his contacts in the CIA. It has come a long way from a phone call in a case related to the attacks on the highrise in La Paz, Bolivia. It seems the CIA became interested in the disappearance of the man who was presumably the target of the attack. He was Adan Neruda, an industrialist and real-estate mogul in Bolivia, but he's got his fingers in all kinds of narcotics distribution, as well. He was quite a financial success, but never quite corrupt enough to get himself in trouble with the government of Bolivia or with the CIA. Langley's been keeping tabs on him, however."

She explained that a South American CIA task force became intrigued by the attacks on the Neruda celebration at the Hotel Europa. It took them totally by surprise, and the CIA task force became worried that there was more to this Neruda than they had ever suspected. They examined one of the calling cards left at the party—ridiculous little bamboo tubes containing a message from someone Neruda had backstabbed decades before. The only problem was that the man was long dead. There was also a warning sent to the Bolivian government, claiming one of the wealthiest men in the country was about to be revealed as an international terrorist. Despite the government's fast response to the

attacks on the hotel, Neruda had slipped away and disappeared from Bolivia within the hour.

"But traces run on his cell phone records show that
he received calls during the attack," Price continued.
"It took some work to trace the caller, but it appears to
come from a man named Encina—a man who actually had some serious run-ins with Neruda years before. Whatever the conflict was, Encina was forced to
flee Bolivia. He moved to Argentina and managed to
make a success of himself by moving drugs, a large-
scale fencing operation and in gambling."

"So what is the connection between Encina and Adan
Neruda now?" McCarter asked.

"None, as far as we can tell," Price said. "There's
no evidence that they have communicated in a decade.
And yet Encina struck out at Adan Neruda."

"So is this just some long-simmering resentment?"
Encizo asked.

"It looks like it," Price said. "And I think we're starting to see a pattern in this. These aircraft are giving a
power boost to a lot of marginalized, midlevel crimi-
nals, smugglers and other gangs. It gives them leverage they never dreamed of having. A longer reach. And
they're using it in just this way. To settle old scores, to
right perceived wrongs. There are a lot of feuds that
are apparently being addressed with these aircraft. At
least that's the pattern we believe is emerging. And that
would fit this time.

"If this man Encina has been stewing over his betrayal at the hands of Adan Neruda for all these years,
and he finally gets a tool that will allow him to get
revenge, why not use it? So he attacked Neruda during his party, killed several VIPs from within business

and government and essentially left Neruda responsible for the whole mess by default. Everything that Neruda owned in Bolivia has been confiscated by the government and courts. Even if he was somehow cleared of all wrongdoing and then mounted a legal battle for return of his property, the power players and Bolivia's court system would string him along for years or decades. Regardless, yesterday the CIA traced a call going out from Adan Neruda's cell phone. He was calling back the number of the person who called him during the attack. They did a listen-in. They heard someone they believed to be Adan Neruda contacting this Encina and telling him that he had kidnapped his sister. He even transmitted a photo, taken with his phone, to Encina. Unfortunately, the CIA got only the voice."

"I can imagine the response from Encina," McCarter said.

"He flew off the handle. It was pretty clear that he did believe Neruda had his sister in custody. Encina went into somewhat of a rage."

McCarter shook his head. "Yeah, I can see that. The guy has been festering about getting payback against this Neruda for years and years, and he finally gets it in spectacular fashion, but his victory lasts only a few days before the guy is stabbing him in the back again. I would be a little ticked off myself."

"Neruda was already in-country. In Argentina," Price said. "His sister lives in the Córdoba region. She's not involved in any of her brother's illegal businesses— she's a schoolteacher, and the conversation between Encina and Neruda made it sound as if she distanced herself from her brother a long time ago. But Encina said he'd pay."

"What is the ransom?" McCarter asked.

"Five million U.S. dollars," Price said. "Neruda claims that he wants enough money to live on for the rest of his life. He named the place for the exchange."

"Neruda did?" Hawkins said. "He picked the salt flats, not Encina? It's the perfect place for Encina to use his stealth jets."

"And Neruda must know it," McCarter added. "He's baiting Encina further. He wants to humiliate him somehow."

"Clearly, there's more to this than meets the eye," Price said. "We can assume that Neruda will have some built-in insurance. Something that will give him safe passage out of Argentina, if in fact he does get the five million dollars. On the other hand, we can assume that Encina is not going to make the exchange and let Neruda just walk away."

"Can't wait to see what happens when this pair of losers try to give each other the shank," Hawkins said.

"Yeah," Encizo said. "I'm sure it'll be a real hoot. Now let's talk about how we can keep the innocent schoolmarm from getting killed."

"And how we can grab one of those stealth planes for ourselves," McCarter added.

CHAPTER SEVEN

Salinas Grandes, Argentina

The exchange of ransom for prisoner was scheduled for six o'clock in the morning. Phoenix Force was on-site before four, only to discover that Adan Neruda had beaten them to it. He'd come, deposited his prisoner and then hidden himself away somewhere.

The salt deposits had been scraped and piled in neat rows, thousands of them, in a field two miles across and a full four miles long. The work had been completed and then the field left, to sit there untended until it was needed. There was no weather that would disturb the prepped salt. There was no reason any human would make the trip into the desert to steal it.

The only dot on the vast desert floor, other than the rows of salt piles, was a tiny plywood shack that had served the supervisory staff when the salt-scraping operation was under way. Now it was empty and musty. Phoenix Force had arrived in a single vehicle, driving dark for the last several miles, and appropriated the shack for their own use. From his lookout on the roof, as soon as the sky began to lighten, Calvin James was able to make out the anomalous shape atop one of the salt piles in almost the dead center of the field.

He quietly summoned McCarter and both observed the woman—and searched for her kidnapper.

Atop the distant salt pile, in a small folding chair, was a woman. From almost half a mile away, James and McCarter couldn't even tell if she was breathing. But she was tied up; she must still be alive.

Adan Neruda clearly had something up his sleeve, which was expected. They had known that he would not attempt something as stupid as a simple transaction, prisoner for money. It didn't happen that way. You have to have insurance, particularly when you're dealing with people obsessed with payback.

But that would be *both* sides in this little exchange. Men of corruption and crime, men who lived their lives leeching off the misery of others, with egos too large to shrug off an insult. Adan Neruda and this man Encina would both be driven to extreme measures to have their revenge on the other. It didn't matter who was wrong and who was right, because neither was right.

James said, "My instinct is to go out and get her."

"That doesn't sound like a good instinct to me," Gary Manning said as he joined them on the roof. "She's gotta be booby-trapped or watched or guarded in some way we can't see."

"We can't leave her sitting there," James pointed out.

"We don't want to inadvertently blow her to bits, either," Manning said.

"And she's not our primary purpose for being here," McCarter pointed out, disliking the words he was saying. "Our top priority is to get one of those aircraft." After a moment he added, "Not that we're going to let her die in the process."

THEY HAD IMPROVISED to come up with light gray clothing covering their typical BDUs. It allowed them to blend in with the off-white coloration of the salt flats. They moved quickly and silently through the near-silent desert dawn, but McCarter knew that they were completely exposed. Anyone from above would see them. If Neruda was staged nearby, camouflaged himself and watching for Encina, he would see them.

A slow breeze whistled over the tops of the little hills of salt, but the air tasted clean. There seemed to be little salt dust in the air. They hiked from hill to hill, taking what little cover the salt offered them.

When they were still a good hundred yards away from the hill with the woman, McCarter called a halt. They examined her again through field glasses.

Now they could see that the setup was not as simple as it had originally looked. There was a tripod placed alongside the prisoner. Atop it was a loudspeaker and what looked like a web cam, covering all four directions. A power supply and some sort of transmitter was tucked under the woman's chair. More alarmingly, the woman was surrounded with several tiny shapes, which seemed to be scattered up and down the sides of the hill. They were cylinders, maybe an inch in diameter, maybe six inches long, each jammed into the rock salt.

"Explosives," Gary Manning reported. "Small, self-contained, black powder charges. For all practical purposes they are firecrackers. Get this—these things are Bluetooth-equipped. You blow them up remotely using your goddamned cell phone. It's supposed to be a safer way to do your fireworks."

McCarter lowered his glasses and looked at Manning. "Are you telling me that this woman is surrounded by a bunch of M-80s?"

Manning shrugged. "I don't know how powerful they

are, but I bet they'll make a lot of pretty colors when they blow."

"What the hell is the point?" Hawkins demanded. "If those are fireworks, they are not exactly going to kill her. They are placed too far apart."

"They blow up a cloud of particulate salt," Encizo said. "You'll notice the air is barely moving here. At seven o'clock in the morning, the winds will move even slower. The sun will begin to seek the surface, and the desert will radiate, and the air will grow warmer, and that will slow the cool breeze coming down from the mountains. If Neruda blows them all, maybe in series, he just might be able to choke her to death. On salt."

"Christ. That's gotta be a miserable way to go," McCarter said.

"We can get up there, and get her out, even if those things are blowing all around us," Hawkins said.

"Heads up," said Rafael Encizo over the headset. To his chagrin, Encizo had been ordered to remain at the work shack, serving as watchman. "Something coming from the south."

McCarter scrambled up the closest salt pile and peered south, finding a spot of haze miles away. After a moment he focused on the shapes of several vehicles crossing the desert floor.

"Son of a bitch. Here they come," he complained. "Everybody's goddamned early today."

THE THREE VEHICLES came to a halt at the far end of the salt field. From there the occupants went on foot—as instructed by Adan Neruda.

But Neruda had not required Encina to come alone. He had not demanded that Encina come unarmed.

So Encina had brought ten men, all of them armed to the teeth. They spread out along the front of the salt field and began to move through the hills of salt, searching for any sign of Adan Neruda.

All they found, at the center of the field, was the hill where the prisoner had been staged.

"Hold up," Encina said as his men coalesced around the hill. He looked up at it, at the woman tied virtually motionless in the folding chair, her drab, full skirt hanging down, possibly hiding something under the chair. And what were all those small black cardboard rolls stuck into the salt rock? The closest that Encina would come was to climb up on the hill facing the woman.

"Can you hear me? Lily?"

The woman raised her head and her eyes rolled back, and even from this distance Encina could see the whites of her eyes. She was heavily sedated. Clear plastic tape covered her mouth, layer after layer of it. But when the hair fell away from her eyes, Encina recognized her features. It was his sister.

He didn't know his sister and frankly had never liked her much. And he didn't especially care about a sister now. What he cared about was addressing the insult that his sister's kidnapping represented.

So here he was, and where the hell was Adan Neruda?

"I'm here." It was Neruda. The voice came from the woman in the chair, but it was clearly the voice of Adan Neruda. There was some sort of the speaker placed beside her chair.

"Where are you?" Encina demanded.

"Nearby."

"I'm taking my sister."

"Don't take one step closer," Neruda said. "I will kill her. I will make sure that she suffers first, but I will kill her."

"You're a fucking coward. Show yourself."

"Where's the money, Encina?"

"I've got it. But we make the exchange on my terms."

"That is absolutely out of the question. We make the exchange under my terms, Encina. You will give me your money. And you will do it in the manner in which I specify. Or your sister will asphyxiate with salt in her lungs. She will die in the most excruciating agony. The best part is, that it will all be on the news in under an hour."

"What?" Encina snapped. He looked around, searching for cameras. He didn't see anything. "You're lying."

"I am not lying. In fact, you are being recorded right now. The video is scheduled to post to a news feed website in thirty minutes from now. If I don't cancel the app, the video of everything that happens here and now goes viral. You will be on CNN and MSNBC before lunchtime. They will be watching you kill your own sister—in Rio and Buenos Aires and in Mexico City and Tokyo. And Beijing and New York City and Moscow. You will be world famous, Encina. You will be the coward who allowed his sister to choke to death on salt. But if you do as you are told and give me my money, and when I'm on my way safely, I'll shut the system down and you will be able to release your sister. The video will never be sent anywhere."

DAVID MCCARTER had to hand it to Adan Neruda. The man knew how to push buttons. A little over-the-top perhaps, but certainly passionate.

Neruda had set this up rather nicely. He was beating Encina at his own game. Encina had ruined his reputation in the social circles of La Paz, but Neruda was going to make Encina into one of the great scumbags worldwide.

But David McCarter also knew the Adan Neruda was a murderous egoist. He had no intention of allowing the innocent woman in the folding chair to escape alive. Neruda had long ago decided that she would die. And he would relish it, watching her on his videotape, knowing how eagerly the news agencies around the world would pick it up, and blur it just enough to show the world over and over again.

McCarter was playing a dangerous game himself, letting this happen. Letting that woman sit in the middle of this conflict. But it wasn't as if he had much choice. He hadn't had time to go in and take her before Encina arrived. And now that Encina was here, going to save the woman would be a suicide run. There were ten men standing around that pile of salt, heavily armed and mad as hell.

By now the man named Encina was practically stuttering with rage, but holding it together just well enough to address the faceless voice of Adan Neruda.

"I get your drift, Neruda. I will follow your instructions. Tell me where to put the damn money, and then turn off the damn video."

"Okay," Neruda said. "Let me see it."

Encina nodded to one of the men behind him, and the man approached, opening a suitcase to reveal banded bricks of U.S. dollars, U.S. bearer bonds and stacks of Argentinean currency.

The contents of the suitcase were displayed to the

drugged woman on the next hill of salt. It made Encina feel even stupider. The voice of Neruda said, "Good. I assume that's five million worth, total?"

"It's there. Count it," Encina said.

"I will," Neruda responded. "Now have your man remove his jacket, shirt, shoes and belt."

"Stop playing games!" Encina snarled.

"This is a game that you started, Encina," Neruda snapped. "You played the first hand. Now it is my turn. And we're playing the game the way I say. Have the man take his clothes off."

"If I don't?"

The answer was a bang. Encina and all of his men were startled; several of them grabbed their weapons and looked for the source.

Nearby, but hidden by hills of salt, McCarter and the others in Phoenix Force were just as startled, but quickly realized what the sound had been.

One of the small explosives wedged in the salt near the feet of Encina's bound sister burst. There was a shower of turquoise-shaded sparks, and then a cloud of salt dust enveloped the woman. She began to struggle and moan, and they could hear the distress in her breathing. She needed to cough to get the salt out of her lungs, but with tape over her mouth she couldn't. The cloud of salt dissipated slowly from around her. It diluted as it drifted away over the desert.

The woman heaved, but she seemed to be able to breathe again.

"That," Adan Neruda said out of the loudspeaker, "is going to make riveting video on the news in London. In fact the video is already on the server. Every second of our conversation and every word that you say is being recorded and stored on a server in Houston, Texas. From there it will be distributed around the world. It will be posted on YouTube. In 1080 P. The programming is already in place to make sure that this happens, Encina. Get this straight—I don't have to do anything to make it happen. It will happen automatically. The only thing I can do now is stop it. You have to convince me that that is what I should do. Do you understand?"

"Yeah, I get it, asshole," Encina said.

"You'd better start acting like it. Or the death of this woman is going to be on your hands. And the people will know that the man responsible for killing this woman is her own brother, Encina Purana, a citizen of Argentina, who happens to run one of the biggest consumer electronics fencing operations in South America. This is all going on the video, right now, Encina."

Encina was trembling with rage and helplessness. He had to restrain himself from screaming at the faceless voice that seemed to reside in the helpless body of his sister. Adan Neruda truly seemed to have him by the balls.

"Okay! All right! We'll do what you say. Let's get this exchange done and over with. Then you can go your way and enjoy the rest of your life with my five million dollars. And I can go my way and we never have to talk to each other again."

"That's all I ever wanted," Neruda said. "To never see you again. Remember, you are the one who started this. This is your fault. You were the coward who attacked a bunch of people at a party in a sky-rise with his toy airplanes."

McCARTER KNEW NERUDA was baiting Encina mercilessly—aching for Encina to lose control.

"All this is happening because you had your feelings hurt twenty years ago, Encina. And you held a grudge like a five-year-old who was kicked on the playground."

"All right," Encina said, loudly but calmly. He was exercising monumental self-control. He turned toward the man with the suitcase, ignoring the ongoing diatribe from a loudspeaker.

He said calmly, "Take off your jacket and your shirt and your shoes and belt. Dispose of any weapons that you have."

The loudspeaker fell quiet. Encina's man disrobed down to his slacks, then lifted the suitcase and gingerly stepped down the pile of rock salt, then stood on the scraped desert floor.

"All right," said Neruda. "Now you will walk forward, for approximately one kilometer to the north edge of the salt field. You will stop there. You will wait. The car will meet you there, driven by an associate of mine. You will give him the suitcase, and then you'll walk back this way."

"What about me?" Encina demanded. "What am I supposed to do?"

"You're supposed to wait where you are. Don't move. None of your men will move. When your man has made the trip and has returned—by that time I should have been able to make a quick assessment of the contents of the case. If it checks out, I will cancel the application that is controlling the video feed."

"My sister?"

"The system will be turned off at the same time I cancel the app. Do you understand?"

"Yeah, I got it."

"I don't know that you do," Neruda stressed. "Keep in mind, anytime I wish, I can end this. I can turn off my broadcast hardware, and I can turn around and leave this place. But if I do, the app continues to function. The explosives blow up. Your sister chokes. Maybe she dies and maybe she lives, but whatever happens to her, it will all be on video, and it all goes global. Understand that it is up to you to turn that process off."

"I understand." Encina's voice shook.

David McCarter, tucked behind a salt hill close by, was getting more concerned. Adan Neruda was pushing his adversary too hard. The man was close to his breaking point.

The shirtless, shoeless man with the suitcase trudged through the rows of salt hills, never noticing the Phoenix Force commandos as they maneuvered to keep themselves out of his line of sight.

It took him several minutes to finally to get to the edge of the salt field.

He stood there and looked at the endless empty desert.

And then he saw the car.

RAFAEL ENCIZO PULLED his Land Rover to a stop in front of the man with the luggage. He stepped out, looked the man up and down and sneered.

"Feet hurt?" he asked in Spanish.

"Fuck you," the shirtless and shoeless man shot back. "Take your suitcase."

"Thanks," Encizo said, grabbing the luggage off the desert floor then shoving it forcefully into the abdomen of Encina's lackey. The impact toppled him onto his back on the desert floor. Before he could get his wits, Encizo knocked his head into the salt crust of the ground with enough force to knock him out. Encizo flipped the man over, hogtied him with plastic handcuffs, then filled the man's mouth with salt and left him facedown on the ground. He shut the suitcase in the rear of the Land Rover.

Encizo saw dust rising in the desert to the north. Another car was coming fast.

"Mr. Neruda's pickup car has arrived," Encizo reported. "Now he's stopping. And now he's turning around and leaving."

"UNDERSTOOD," McCARTER answered in a low voice. "Okay, Phoenix," he said to the others. "Priority one is to get that woman off the hill and safe. Priority two is to raise hell, and put Encina in fear for his life—but we can't wipe them out. Not until he calls in aircraft backup. Understood?"

"T.J.," McCarter said. "Go!"

"YOU FUCK!" NERUDA shouted from the loudspeaker. "What kind of a game is this, Encina?"

T. J. Hawkins was scrabbling, in a gas mask and goggles, over the salt pile directly behind the prisoner, staying hidden as long as possible from Encina and his men. He hurried down, then crept up the far side of the prisoner's hill and managed to get himself to a point within a few feet of the back of the chair. The woman's breathing was labored, as if she couldn't get enough air through her nose. Hawkins had a feeling that another toxic cloud of salt dust would kill this woman. He had to get her out of here now.

Adan Neruda was lambasting Encina from the loud-speaker, but now he made a sudden bark as he finally saw Hawkins sneaking up on the prisoner.

"Oh, no, you don't!" Neruda shouted from the loud-speaker, and several of the nearby rounds burst. A salt cloud billowed out of the ground and sparks and grit tore into Hawkins's exposed skin. He ignored the blasts and lunged to the top of the hill, grabbing at the hard-ware station in its plastic tub underneath the woman's chair. He pulled out a laptop computer and a power pack intended to keep the thing running for hours. Several more explosive rounds cracked open and the salt cloud was so thick the air was actually beginning to darken. The woman in the chair was gagging and wheezing. Her breathing passages were closing up, and the tape meant she could not breathe through her mouth. She was going to suffocate within minutes.

T. J. Hawkins flipped over the laptop, ripped out the power cable to the auxiliary power supply, yanked off the plastic battery panel and took out the battery. The laptop went dead.

The charges stopped bursting.

And he could no longer hear the woman in the chair breathing at all.

He grabbed the chair, yanked it back and dumped the woman to the ground, then looped his arm around her and yanked her down the hill of salt, back the way he'd come.

That was five long seconds after the bullets started flying.

MCCARTER AND CALVIN JAMES were on the move. Mc-Carter stepped into the line of sight of a pair of men ahead, visible through the haze of salt drifting from the hilltop. Both men were firing at the top of the hill and McCarter triggered a burst on the run. He had to get that gunfire to stop, distract those men, while there was any chance they might be hitting the woman or Hawkins.

It was a tough shot—through the haze, over the distance and on the run—but McCarter had been in a running gun battle a time or two and he stitched the first gunner across the crotch, shattering a hip bone. The dramatic effect was that his legs folded sideways under him at an unnatural angle and he screamed. The second gunner was already turning on him when McCarter ran directly at him, triggering the MP-5, and their rounds may have passed each other in flight. But McCarter's shooting was on target, dropping his adversary hard. His adversary's bullets flew over McCarter's head with an angry buzz.

He circled the booby-trapped pile of salt and found another knot of gunners and a pair of bodies bleeding into the dirt. He triggered a long burst from the submachine gun, cutting through the tight collection of Argentinean hardmen, and from somewhere out of sight Calvin James fired at the same moment. The hardmen withered. Three of them collapsed to the ground, one man ducked away behind a salt pile, but another one spun and took rounds in the back. He staggered, lost his weapon and fell against another salt pile. He left a bright pink stain on the pale white rock when he forced himself painfully to his feet again. McCarter cut his feet out from under him.

Then there were no more signs of life. Most of the Encina mob had turned tail.

McCarter retreated quickly to find T. J. Hawkins, apparently uninjured. Another suicide mission had turned out not to be one. The woman was heaving, but her eyes were open, and the frantic rising and falling of her chest was already slowing down. There was no sign of blood, on her, either. Hawkins had the tape off her mouth, and a small plastic mask fed with a thumb-size cylinder of emergency oxygen seemed to be reviving her.

McCarter gave a thumbs-up to Calvin James. The black Phoenix Force commando was jogging down the rows, patrolling between the piles of salt, just in case any of Encina's gunners returned.

"Do you think it worked?" James asked.

It was a rhetorical question. McCarter and James each worked their way slowly and cautiously up to the top of a nearby salt pile. James watched north. McCarter watched south, where he could see, in the long distance, the retreating tiny figures of the surviving Encina men. They'd reached their cars.

And there they stayed. McCarter used his field glasses to examine them more closely. Men were rummaging in their cars, emerging with fresh weapons, but there was no indication that they were going anywhere fast.

If David McCarter was reading their behavior correctly, this was a good sign. He could imagine them, furious and feeling stupid, and Encina, if he was not among the dead, radioing for backup from his new, powerful asymmetric vector. He would bring his nifty new toys out to play. The foot soldiers weren't about to wade into the fray again until the backup arrived.

McCarter spotted the Land Rover, with Encizo at the wheel, at the far western edge of the salt field. He took a sharp turn into the field and drove across the grid, in a row about a hundred yards from the Encina bunch—taunting them.

There were a couple of gunshots, in the distance, paltry and ineffectual.

"They're taking potshots at you, Rafe," McCarter advised.

"Let them," Encizo said. "The worst thing they can do is ding the paint. Did you take out the optional rental insurance?"

"It's not a rental. The car belongs to Uncle Sam," McCarter reminded him. "It's Uncle Sam's paint job. He might be ticked off if you ding it."

The Land Rover had been arranged by Stony Man Farm. It could have come from almost anywhere—a U.S. embassy or some other U.S. government agency working inside Argentina. It was well-enough armored that the small-arms fire from the Encina gang was no danger.

"See anything?" Encizo asked as he reached the eastern edge of the field and slowed to an idle five miles per hour. McCarter was searching the skies over the desert. It was the same hazy blue skies, it seemed to him, as they had seen over southern Mexico. Were the skies of South America always like this—nearly cloudless, blue-gray, slightly hazy? They were perfect for hiding the stealth aircraft.

That notion was reinforced at the moment that one of the aircraft materialized out of the sky, close, and it was like a ghost fading into existence just outside the reach of his fingertips.

McCarter knew those craft were pretty small, but this one loomed unexpectedly large in the sky when it became visible. It was almost on top of them already.

"We have incoming," McCarter announced over the headset. "One bird, from the south, coming in right over our Argentinean friends."

ENCIZO STOMPED ON THE GAS and twisted the wheel, sending the Land Rover into a quick sideways skid that ended with the vehicle facing directly back into the salt field. The quick move also served to raise a cloud of dust from the desert floor to attract the attention of the aircraft, in case it hadn't noticed the SUV already.

Encizo accelerated across the grid of salt hills for several hundred yards before he stomped on the brake again. The crusty desert surface, stripped of its top layer of salt, released another opportune cloud of dust. Encizo grinned to himself. There was no way that aircraft could ignore him.

He pulled a tight turn amid the pile and pointed the Land Rover due north, and he wondered just how close the plane actually was. He couldn't take the time to look for it and he couldn't hear it; it could be on top of him right now and he wouldn't even know it.

He hit the gas again, accelerating rapidly to highway speeds in the narrow corridor between the hills of salt, and his question was answered in the form of a sudden burst of .50-caliber machine-gun fire. It cracked into one of the piles of salt just as he was passing. They were already close enough to have his range.

Encizo touched the brake, slowed by twenty miles per hour, and machine-gun hits on the desert floor in front of him threw up bursts of dust.

The aircraft loomed into view, flying no more than forty feet over the peaks of the salt hills and almost directly over the hood of the Land Rover.

He couldn't hear her engines over the hum of the Land Rover. He was *never* going to get used to that.

"Let's play!" Encizo announced to himself, and pushed on the gas.

DAVID MCCARTER CALLED to T. J. Hawkins.

"Can she be moved?"

"I'm good," the woman said, pushing to her feet.

"This is not over. You stay with T.J. until the danger is passed."

The woman cursed colorfully in Spanish, then demanded in heavy-accented English, "It's my son-of-a bitch brother, isn't it?"

"He might be dead already," Hawkins offered.

"Might be? I will shed no tears if he is killed."

"You may get your wish," Hawkins said.

DAVID MCCARTER HURRIED through several rows, then hoofed it up to the top of a salt pile. He was in time to see the aircraft fire another volley at the speeding Land Rover, and then watched the Land Rover slow down, allowing the aircraft to catch up to it. Then Encizo sped up again, barreling forward, pulling well ahead of the slow-moving aircraft. He was leading it along like a smart fox being chased by a foolish dog.

It was still amazing to McCarter that that thing had been engineered to perform at speeds that slow. Every jet ever made was too damned heavy to get sustained lift at automobile highway speeds—that's just the way it was. They stalled and they dropped.

But this one didn't. It seemed perfectly at home in the air over the top of Encizo's speeding SUV. The plane was stable and responsive, and when the pilot wanted extra speed to catch up with the Land Rover, he got it.

He closed in on Encizo, and a new burst of gunfire came from the machine guns mounted under the nose.

McCarter wondered exactly how well armored the roof of that Land Rover was.

"Gary?" McCarter asked.

"Everything's ready out here," Manning responded. "I see the plane and Rafe coming—but he's too far off the ground."

Encizo urged the SUV to go faster. The Land Rover wasn't designed for speed, but this one had plenty of muscle under the hood. The speedometer topped 100, then 110, but of course the stealth jet had no problem sticking to his tail. Another long torrent of machine-gun fire emerged from under the nose of the stealth aircraft and battered the top of the Land Rover.

McCarter saw dark black paint give way to bright flashes of exposed metal. Craters appeared, a half dozen of them in the roof metal. At that angle, at that entrance point, if they punctured the steel armor....

"Encizo!" McCarter demanded. "Get out of there."

"Nice car!" Encizo said over the noise as another barrage rattled against the roof. "Well made. Think I'll get me one."

Another burst, but now Encizo was slowing slightly, and the puncture marks appeared on the hood. The armor seemed good there, too, at least from McCarter's perspective. The Land Rover kept going. The engine seemed undamaged.

McCarter was running now, trying hard to follow the aircraft and Encizo. He'd noticed something of importance in that last burst of gunfire.

"Rafe! He's having trouble aiming at you. He lowers his nose to fire. He's descending!"

"Keep it up, Encizo," Manning shouted excitedly through his headset. "Keep bringing him down. The lower he is, the better our chances of taking him out."

"Understood," Encizo said, and at that moment he slowed again, just a little. If he slowed too much, the aircraft would simply shoot ahead of him and would need to make another pass. Encizo stayed in the sweet spot: just within the pilot's line of fire, and just enough to motivate the pilot to home in on him.

GARY MANNING HAD LEFT the field of battle long before, jogging to the north end of the salt field and working hard and fast during the few minutes allotted to him. This little plan would only pay off if the plane attacked them from the south, from the same direction that the Encina gang had come. It would only pay off if the aircraft came low enough to the tops of the salt piles. It would only pay off if Encizo could get the jet to the right place and Manning could spring the trap at the right instant.

But then, and even then, they didn't know if they would succeed.

This was the first time he'd used rock salt against a plastic airplane.

In one hand were his field glasses. In the other was the detonator.

Encizo, in his shredded Land Rover, was coming fast, and the little gray jet was right on top of him.

THE SALT FIELDS WERE HUGE. Even at this speed, they kept coming and coming, and Encizo wondered if they would ever run out. He could feel his head pounding and his teeth clenched from the strain of keeping this position. There was the sweet spot, right under the nose of the aircraft, where he could keep himself directly in the line of fire. He could manipulate the pilot, with accelerations and decelerations, enough to motivate the pilot to nudge his aircraft nose down again and again. The jet was coming closer and closer to the tops of the salt piles. How close, Encizo wondered, was close enough?

There was another burst of fire, and more pounding on the roof of his SUV, and it was over again, and something new caught Encizo's eye. At first he couldn't even tell what had distracted him. Then he realized that it was a tiny dot of sunlight on his dashboard. It had not been there before.

It came from above.

No matter how well the vehicle was armored, it would eventually fail under barrage after barrage of rounds.

The trusty old Land Rover had reached its point of failure.

Encizo was finally within sight of the end of the salt fields. Another hundred feet.

There was no way he could give it up now. He hit the gas, pulled himself out in front of the stealth jet, gave himself a little distance and touched the brake a little bit again at the moment he felt was right. He was learning to play with this pilot, using his instincts to judge when the pilot would fire. He was right on this time. The aircraft fired, the rounds traveled over the top of the Land Rover and the pilot compensated by dipping his nose just enough to bring the aircraft down another five feet closer to the tops of the salt piles. That move allowed him to direct his machine-gun fire directly into the roof of the Land Rover. The rounds chewed at the already twisted and battered metal.

Inside the SUV the tone of the impact of the rounds had changed. They were more broken. Less muffled. The armor was giving way. There was a burst of light inside the Land Rover. A major hole appeared above the rear seat. And then another crater opened up above the center seat. And more rounds were slamming into the roof just above Encizo. More light appeared on his dashboard and Gary Manning was shouting into his headset, "Let him go! Let him go!"

The dashboard exploded even as Encizo stood on the brake. Shards of plastic flew around the interior, tearing at his face, and something sliced into his fingers. He ignored the pain in his hands, gripping the wheel hard as the Land Rover skewed wildly, trying to contend with the sudden stop on the uneven ground. Encizo lost the back end and it swung to the right. The wheels slammed into one of the salt piles, slapping the back end in the other direction, and the vehicle lost its balance, its right wheels leaving the earth.

Encizo wrestled for control of the vehicle, finessing the wheel as best he could even as blood trickled between his fingers and he felt the vehicle slam back down onto four wheels. One of the piles of salt swung in front of the SUV, coming fast, and grew huge in the windshield, but the brake finally engaged. The wheels finally got a good grip on the desert surface, and the Land Rover came to a halt with its front end crunched against a wall of rock salt.

GARY MANNING KNEW Encizo was in trouble when he saw the roof blossom open under the final barrage of machine-gun fire. But he couldn't think about that now. The stealth jet dipped low and slowed abruptly as its target vanished underneath it. The thing practically drifted, like a heavy burden, over the last of the salt piles, on the edge of the field. It could not have presented itself better to Gary Manning's booby trap. Manning snapped the switch that detonated the salt piles.

Unlike Adan Neruda, Gary Manning had planted his explosives near the bottom of the salt piles and driven them in as deep as he could, and when they blew, it wasn't powder that flew in the air. A wall of white rock was jettisoned into the air and pelted the slow-moving jet. The salt rock clattered against the belly, bounced off the wings—and was sucked into the pair of engines on the tail.

Abruptly the fanlike noise of the stealth jet engines became a knock, then a rattle and finally the clatter of broken parts. The engines ceased to function, regurgitating broken pieces, and the aircraft slowed even further.

Manning witnessed the aircraft hit its stall speed. The jet went into a flat, quick descent and smacked flat on the desert floor. The body pancaked, leaving the fuselage looking like a flattened tube of toothpaste. The wings cracked off but were still held to the plane by their fiber reinforcement, and then flopped about wildly, disintegrating.

The structural damage was catastrophic at the moment of impact, and Manning hoped for a heartbeat that the thing wouldn't burn. At the same time he witnessed the deluge of clear liquid that exploded from everywhere. It was as if every structural component contained part of the fuel tank. As the engines flopped off their mounts they burst into flame, and the fire engulfed the rest of the wreck even as it was still settling to the desert floor.

Inside something burst apart, and shooting stars were thrown out. There was an explosive few seconds of machine-gun rounds detonating together.

Manning wasted all of three seconds on the airplane. It was a complete loss.

He sprinted back through the piles of salt to where the Land Rover had stopped. He could see huge open wounds in the roof of the vehicle. In the end there would have been nothing left protecting the inside of that vehicle.

He yanked open the driver's door, hoping he would find Encizo still alive and unhurt, and wondering if such a thing was even possible.

The interior of the SUV was even worse. The ceiling was tattered and material dangled in strands like entrails. The dashboard was obliterated. Blood spattered the windows, was smeared on the shifter and glistened on the steering wheel.

Rafael Encizo was holding his bloody left hand high in the air and using his right hand to rummage in the broken glove box.

"GARY!" DAVID MCCARTER shouted urgently. "Did you reach Rafe yet? What's his condition?"

"Uh, he'll live," Manning reported.

"Looking for the goddamned Tylenol," Encizo muttered, maybe unaware that he was transmitting. "I've got a brutal tension headache."

McCarter looked over the tops of the salt piles at the ruin of the Land Rover in the distance.

"You have a *headache,* mate?"

"Like you wouldn't fucking believe."

MANNING GAVE HIS eyewitness account to Stony Man Farm as he helped Encizo limp to the small utility building alongside the salt field.

"The jet burned, Stony. It burned just like the jet in Chilan. We didn't get video this time, but trust me, it was the same scene. Even the pieces that broke off the wreckage went up in flames and melted into the desert."

"And the rest of the Encina group?" Barbara Price asked him.

"They took off after the first plane went to shit," McCarter reported. "They had their plane with them. I could see it—barely. It did a high-altitude flyover of the wreckage of the first plane, and then took off. So did the men in the vehicles. Our vehicle, by the way, is out of commission. We'll need a ride out of here."

The sun was getting higher and the heat more intense, and the hot, dusty little shack retained enough coolness to feel comfortable by comparison. Encizo was directed to sit on the desk, where he could receive first aid on his bloodied hand. The only chair in the little building was occupied by the woman they had rescued. Lily Encina watched Rafael Encizo take his seat.

She didn't look like a woman who had been through a traumatic experience; she looked like a woman ready to kill someone. But her eyes became less fierce when Encizo gave her a pained smile.

And when her expression became less fierce, it became quite appealing.

"Lily Encina," she said by way of introduction.

"Call me Rafe," he said with a smile. Then he winced as Hawkins did something painful to his ring finger.

The woman, younger than Encizo had assumed she would be, glanced at what was happening with his hand, and winced for him.

"It looks bad."

"Not as bad as my head feels."

"Hold still," Hawkins complained.

"I hear you busted your car," Lily Encina said.

"Yeah, you should see it." Encizo sounded positively pleased with himself. "I guess we'll be stuck here for a while, Lily."

McCarter chose that moment to enter from outside. "Jack is on his way. Pick us up within a half hour."

"But I guess we'll be staying in Buenos Aires for a while," Encizo added. "We have unfinished business."

"What is it you do, Rafe, besides ruin automobiles?"

"We're flying back home within the hour," McCarter said. "Back to the United States."

Encizo glared at him.

"Of America," McCarter added.

"Too bad," Lily said. "I would've liked to make you dinner. You sort of saved my life."

"I'd love to," Encizo said.

"Technically," Hawkins interrupted, "I was the one who pulled her off the hill."

Lily Encina looked around the room at the five Phoenix Force commandos with a faint smile. "I would love to make dinner for all of you boys."

"Well, we are in Buenos Aires frequently," Encizo said.

"We are?" Hawkins asked.

"We *can* be," Encizo said. "At least, I can be."

"Well," she said, "consider it an open invitation."

CHAPTER EIGHT

Glades County, Florida

When tourists vacationed in Florida, very few of them came to Glades County. Even when they came to live in Florida, they didn't come here. The county had one of the lowest population densities in the state outside of the Everglades National Park and the various state parks, which filled the map starting about twenty miles south of the county line.

The town of Muse was a throwback. An unincorporated little outpost of civilization in the middle of twenty thousand acres of South Florida swamp. It was 150 miles and a world away from Orlando and the other central Florida tourist destinations.

The old man in the metal chair was also a throwback, the kind of old man who had been sitting in a metal chair in front of a bait shop in South Florida for the past century.

Like the bait shop, he was faded and dusty. But his eyes were alert to the strange car coming up March Road when it was still a half mile away. When it was a quarter of a mile away, he could hear the engine, and it didn't sound like any of the cars he knew. Not that there weren't strange cars passing through the town of Muse from time to time. It was just that he always knew when they were coming.

The vehicle was new and shiny and painted a deep rich green so dark it was almost black. The scorching sun penetrated the layers of paint and threw up an olive-colored rainbow. But the dust was already starting to settle on the hood, dimming that glorious paint. At this time of year, up here you were a good five or six feet above the water table, and the dirt drained and turned to dust. And when some fool drove in his shiny new Jeep Wrangler, coming too fast, driving like he had no sense, then for sure he was going to kick up a cloud of dust.

The old bait-shop owner had learned to accept the dust that came at this time of year. When the car stopped the clouds engulfed his old metal chair and the old man just blinked a little. Didn't cough. Did not try to wave the dust away from his face.

A scrawny-looking young man stepped out of the passenger side, nodded at the old man and just sort of stood there for a minute, looking in all directions.

"Got cold Cokes inside," the old man offered.

"Sounds good." The skinny man removed and wiped at his wire-rimmed glasses.

The man who got out of the backseat was a Hispanic, and he wasn't wearing the forehead of sweat his skinny white friend had been wearing. He smiled at the old man and, like his friend, just sort of stood there for a moment, not in any hurry, as if they weren't on any deadline. Most people who managed to drive their way in such a roundabout route that took them through Muse and who actually stopped their car here, at this old bait shop, were usually in a hurry. To get out. Find out where they took a wrong turn and get back on the road to where they really wanted to be. Almost never was the place they wanted to be the unincorporated South Florida town of Muse.

That made these visitors unusual. Maybe they were on a long slow drive, but nobody made a long slow drive that took them through Muse. Maybe they were visiting somebody here, but the old man who ran the bait shop knew everybody in town. He would probably have known if they were expecting visitors. And he would've specially known if they were expecting these kinds of visitors. People with enough money to buy a shiny new Jeep with the top that could come off and special paint job that seemed to throw up dark green rainbows.

"I like your shop," the Hispanic man said.

The old bait-shop owner thought about that for a moment, thinking about whether he was hearing sarcasm or not.

"Looks like a real place," the Hispanic man added. "Doesn't look like one of those fast-food kind of bait shops."

"No," the old man said. "You are right about that. It really is authentic. This building has been here since the 1920s. Been a general store and a gas station, and now it's just a bait shop. But I sell cold Cokes."

The Hispanic man smiled. "And I bet they taste just as good as a cold Coke coming out of one of those plastic shiny fast-food bait shops."

"I guarantee that it does," the old man said, deciding that he really liked this Hispanic man with the easy smile.

Then he saw the driver. He came around the front of the Jeep, taking off his sunglasses, and for a moment his eyes met the alert eyes of the old bait-shop owner. And the bait-shop owner, on that stifling hot South Florida day, shivered a little. He knew that man. He'd met that man a time or two. He'd met that man in Korea, in a field, and that man had almost shot him in the head. He had met that man again, in prison in the 1960s, where he had been incarcerated for three weeks after a little bit of beer-induced disturbing the peace. That man had been in prison for a lot longer, and that man had decided that he wanted a pack of cigarettes, and he was willing to kill for it.

That breed of man—with the same killer eyes—had been the scariest he'd ever met. The kind of man you encountered on a grisly battlefield and in hopeless incarceration. But not out here, not on the bright afternoon just like the thousands of other bright afternoons that had come before. In front of this bait shop.

The old man shifted in his seat, suddenly agitated.

But the man with the killer eyes slid the sunglasses back onto his head and strolled to the front of the shop. He took the ancient metal chair next to the bait-shop owner.

"Nice place," he said.

He stretched out in the chair, as if he was about to take a nap. The old man expected to hear a threat in his voice, but the man seemed friendly enough. When you weren't looking in his eyes.

"Fishing any good this time of year?"

"Yeah. Some places. Just got to know where."

The scary man nodded, and seemed satisfied with the answer. The skinny one with wire-rimmed glasses came out of the bait shop, allowing the screen door to slap shut, and distributed bottles of pop. He and the Hispanic man leaned against their Jeep, and the man in the chair beside him remained stretched out as if he was about to take a nap.

"I put five bucks on the counter," said the man in the wire-rimmed glasses.

The old man was about to stand, saying, "I'll get you some change."

"Don't bother."

The old man couldn't help but notice that they weren't buying any bait.

So they weren't fishermen. And they weren't visiting anybody in Muse. These guys didn't seem to know what they were doing. They sure were not doing it in a hurry. And then that shiny new Jeep...

In South Florida able-bodied young men in expensive vehicles without visible means of support were easy to label as drug runners. Lots of drugs came to South Florida.

"You boys ain't here to fish," the old man said.

"No, sir," the Hispanic said.

It was the Hispanic man who was throwing off his calculations. You expected Hispanics to be involved in the drug trade. But not this guy. He seemed nice. He seemed friendly.

"If you ain't fishing, and you ain't part of the drug problem, and I think I decided you ain't, then you must be DEA."

The Hispanic laughed good-naturedly. The skinny one smiled and raised his Coke in a toast to the old man. The man in the chair next to him shifted a little, looked at him, and the old man could feel his eyes cutting through the darkened lenses of the sunglasses. But then he closed his eyes again, relaxing.

"You're sharp," the skinny one said. "Ever thought of a career in law enforcement?"

"No, thanks. Spent ten years in Korea one summer. I seen enough of the fighting and dying to last me forever. I like it here. It's quiet, and not much happens, and I don't have to watch people get shot. Hope it stays that way for as long as I'm here. Do you boys think that it will?"

The skinny one and the Hispanic had stopped smiling and now they looked thoughtful. The Hispanic man shrugged at him.

"I wish we had the power to make that dream come true," he said.

"But maybe you are just here to clean up," the old man concluded.

The three young men didn't respond to that, so the old man knew that it was true.

He rubbed his face. He was about due for shave, he decided. He didn't shave much. Grandpa was Seminole. One of the advantages of having Native American blood was you didn't have to shave too often.

And as he was rubbing his face, he saw the second unexpected thing of the day. It wasn't a shiny new Jeep this time, coming down March Road into town. It was farther away, moving faster, and didn't seem to be making a sound. And the fool looked like he was flying no less than a hundred feet above the tops of the cypress trees, and he didn't make a sound.

"Damned fools," he said, waving dismissively at it.

The three strangers hadn't noticed the unusual aircraft, until they noticed him noticing it. Even the man sprawled in the chair next to him read the old man's alertness and followed his gaze, and in an instant they all saw the silent silhouette against the sun-washed pale sky.

And then, so fast it made the old man's head spin, the three men seemed to melt into their new Jeep, and the old bait shop and the old man were left in a cloud of dust.

THAT HAD BEEN SEVERAL hours ago. The old man from Muse had been thinking about those boys a lot. He thought they were good boys. What he based that on, he didn't know. But they hadn't caused any trouble, not so far as he heard.

But then trouble came, literally, knocking on his door. In the middle of the night, too.

It took him quite a while to get out of bed and pull on his old flannel robe and get to the front door. When he opened the door the first thing he recognized was the paint job on the Jeep sitting in front of his house. He blinked a few times before his eyes were working the way they should, and sure enough, those three men were standing on his front doorstep.

"Teach me to answer the door without my shotgun," the old bait-shop keeper said.

"You remember us?" asked the Hispanic man.

"Course I do. And you seemed nice enough. But now I'm wondering what you're doing at my house at nine in the evening. I know you don't need more bait as you didn't buy any the first time."

"You were right about something," the Hispanic man said. "We are here to clean something up."

"And did you?"

"No."

"Not completely, you mean. Still some loose ends that need to be cleaned up. That would be me."

The skinny one laughed. "You got it wrong. We're the good guys. We're not here to snuff you out or anything. We're here to talk about airplanes."

The old man realized he was shaking. He must've been scared, thinking these guys were coming to shoot him. He had decided, at the moment he saw them in the dark on his front doorstep, that they really were drug runners and they had come back to off him.

The Hispanic man took him by the elbow, sat him in his easy chair and got a glass of water.

The old man sipped gratefully. "I don't know anything about airplanes."

"We're looking for more of those airplanes like the one we saw today at your bait shop. You saw it first, remember?"

The old man nodded. "Sure."

"It seemed like you weren't surprised by that airplane. Like you'd seen others like it."

"Yeah. They're fools. Treetop flyers. Gonna kill somebody."

"We went after it," growled the one with the dark eyes. They were the first words that he had said all evening. The way he said it, it was like a bad memory.

"You went after it, but you didn't get it," the old man said.

"Right."

The old man didn't dislike this dark, growling figure so much as he was afraid of him and what he represented. He represented violence. Even if it was violence against violent men, he was the human representation of that violence. The old man who had seen enough of killing in his life had seen enough to know that this was a man who killed exceptionally well.

"And now you want to find it again," the old man said.

"Or one like it," the Hispanic man said. "We think that there have been a few of them jetting around these parts. After we missed that one this afternoon it occurred to us that we needed to get some advice from somebody who spent a lot of time watching the skies over Muse. We thought about you. We thought maybe you'd be able to point us in the right direction to wherever it is you usually see those kinds of planes."

"And if I don't want to help you?"

The dark eyes regarded him silently in the dim living room light. The old man wondered why he was testing this killer. Why he wasn't leaving well enough alone by simply cooperating with them.

"If you don't want to help us," the dark-eyed man said, "then we won't have your help. We'll leave, and you will go back to bed."

"But one thing," said the Hispanic, "that you really ought to know. We can't tell you what we're doing exactly or why we're doing it or who we're working for. But I can tell you this and it's absolutely true—we are the good guys."

The old man believed that. "But I don't want to go out into any swamp. I spent enough time out there my whole life that I don't feel the need to go out there again."

"If you can give us good directions, we'll find it," said the man in the wire-rimmed glasses. "A guy like you knows the swamps so well he should be able to give us directions good enough to get us there. Right?"

"You're right. And I will help you."

"Good to hear," said the dark-eyed one.

The one with the wire-rimmed glasses was quickly unfolding a rattling map, which he laid out noisily on the old man's dinner table. It was an exceptionally detailed map of south-central Florida, with markings that included topography and physiographic features. There was indication of terrain, microregions of vegetation and even a legend indicating typical wildlife. This was on top of detailed roadways and development. It was printed on some sort of plastic paper the old man had never seen before. It was noisy as hell, but it also looked waterproof and didn't seem to wrinkle very much. The old man had never seen anything quite like it.

The one with the wire-rimmed glasses was getting excited now. He poked at the map and said, "We're here."

Then he traced his finger along a sketchy line that had to be the old man's back road. It wasn't even an official road. It had not been since the 1950s, when the county stopped maintaining it. He'd sure never seen it on a map before.

"And this is how we got to your house. And here's the town of Muse."

The old man was trying to make sense of the riot of pale colors, shadings and lines. "Yeah," he said.

"So, where would we go if we wanted to look for one of those planes?"

The old man raised his eyes from the sophisticated topographic map and looked at the wall behind the one with the wire-rimmed glasses. Then the old man got to his feet and shuffled to the junk drawer. He pulled out a composition notebook that he had been keeping there since at least the 1990s. And a pencil. Because if you leave a pencil in a drawer for ten years at a time, it'll still work every time you put the point to paper. And he sat, putting his composition book on top of the sophisticated map, and began to draw circles and rectangles and squiggly shapes. And then he drew a dot. It took him under a minute to do it.

He poked the dot with the pencil lead. "We're here, young man. This is Muse." He trailed the pencil lead to a sloppy square.

"This is the highway that you came into town. This is the intersection. This and this and this, these are all undeveloped roads. You might be able to get through on them, and maybe you can't. I don't know what your shiny new car can do. If you take this one here, you go this way, you go maybe six miles, and then stop and wait at the place where there's a curve in the road like this."

He drew the curve, almost a horseshoe in the road.

"You wait there. If I was trying to find one of those planes, that's where I would hope to see one. You think you can read this map, young man?"

The one with the wire-rimmed glasses grinned. "You better believe I can."

"But the question is," the old man said, "is how long you have to wait. Started seeing those planes a few weeks ago. And I see them maybe every few days. Fair warning. I'd pack a deck of cards if I was you."

"I carry them with me," said the one with the wire-rimmed glasses, still grinning.

CARL LYONS WAS FEELING the frustration. Stony Man Farm had not been able to get its hands on one of these planes. Until that happened, there was no way to find the source. Four times there had been a plane in their clutches. Four times they had come up empty-handed.

Able Team had just spent a long day wandering pointlessly around the back roads of Glades County. Finally they seemed to have a lead on a location. Lyons wasn't sure how much faith they could put in the old man's observation skills—but it was all they had to go on.

While you needed antiaircraft weapons to take down such aircraft, that weaponry wasn't very portable. It was the kind of hardware that works best when stationary, when you can let the plane come to the gun. The second-best option was to mount the thing on some sort of a military vehicle—which was a little too conspicuous, even in the Florida swamps.

Still, Carl Lyons felt like somewhat of an idiot standing knee-deep in swamp water blasting 40 mm grenades at the belly of a swift little jet that was one hundred feet above his head and already starting to blend with the clear Florida sky. Not one of their grenades had scored a hit on the jet.

The plane had been a surprise, despite the fact that they been driving all over the county hoping to spot one. After spotting the aircraft—with some help from the bait-shop owner—they careened around the back roads for the better part of an hour before spotting it again.

It materialized over the trees in front of them, moving whisper-quiet and helicopter-slow just over the tops of the cypress trees. Schwarz had slammed on the brakes, and they had piled out of the SUV and begun to fire everything they had at the underside of the stealth jet.

The pilot of the stealth jet probably never even noticed them. He continued on at his steady, slow speed, making almost no noise, and camouflaged almost perfectly against the clear sky of South Florida. He was gone over the treetops within seconds. Able Team had filed back in the SUV and raced off in pursuit.

But they never saw it again.

"WE'VE GOT TO DO BETTER this time," Carl Lyons said.

The three men of Able Team were sitting in their SUV in a shady spot alongside an unimproved road. As near as they could tell, they were a good five miles from any homes or businesses or people. The night was almost misty with millions of mosquitoes, and without even opening the doors or the windows a few of them had managed to worm their way inside the vehicle.

It was a long night spent waiting and hoping for something to happen. Price stayed in regular contact from Stony Man Farm, and when she failed to report frequently enough they called her, hoping for some indication of activity in their vicinity. But there was nothing. No blips on the radar indicating the identified aircraft. Nothing from air traffic control. Nothing even on the local police bands.

Blancanales had his own eyes on the area. The brightly colored display on his tablet computer showed him the status of several external sensors. He had slipped out of the car in the middle of the night, wearing night-vision goggles. Moving quietly, he had marched up and down several miles of the road, planting sensors. He attended closely to the area they had nicknamed the Runway.

If the old man had been correct in his estimation that the planes were operating in the vicinity of this old stretch of road, then there was just one place where they could be landing. Not that the road didn't have several stretches straight and long enough for the small jets, but they were all overgrown, with trees and shrubs crowding the old road. There was just one stretch of road that was clear enough to allow for a landing.

There the pavement emerged from the heavy undergrowth of the swamp into a wide flat area. The vegetation fell away, and there was open water on either side of the road. It stretched straight for many hundreds of feet. The road had been built on top of landfill when a failed mining operation was originally building its infrastructure here in the 1960s. They had made the road so straight that Blancanales wondered if they had intended for it to be used as a runway.

Blancanales had planted, among other things, audio sensors, far enough away from the Able Team vehicle that the sounds from the car wouldn't interfere with its monitoring of the ambient sound.

The pickup was so extremely sensitive that Blancanales would probably have been able to record their conversation in the car, even from a distance, if he pointed the thing at them more directly. But he aimed it above their heads, into the sky, with a companion sensor pointed in the other direction. They were, in fact, highly directional, which made it more accurate, and could only be utilized because they were assuming that the plane would be coming in from one specific direction or another, lined up with the pavement.

If they were coming in for a landing, they would be coming in low and slow, and using flaps and landing gear, all of which would agitate the airflow over the craft and make it noisier than usual. And it should be noisy enough for Blancanales's devices to pick up well in advance and give them at least some warning.

The app on the tablet was actively analyzing the signals coming in from both of the pickups and isolating them into predetermined frequency ranges, then processing each range for signatures that might indicate an aircraft.

The data was being transmitted back to Stony Man Farm, where it could be reanalyzed later, if need be. If Able Team was lucky, if they got a recording of this aircraft as it came in for a landing, they would be able to use the same system to identify it again later. Perhaps there would be other information that they could glean from the recording.

BLANCANALES DIDN'T KNOW how long he'd been dozing when he heard the soft whisper of a woman in his ear.

"Able, this is Stony," said Price. "Are you reading this?"

"Yeah, I see it," Hermann Schwarz answered. He had the tablet computer now and was watching the app, which showed agitation coming from the sensors. There was something out there causing sound. Hitting one sensor hard, another one just barely.

"It would be a very good thing," Barbara Price reminded them, "to get our hands on one of those aircraft."

"Understood," Carl Lyons said.

Blancanales was blinking away the sleep, dragging on his equipment, getting prepared for whatever might come.

And then the aircraft was just there—settling on the road in front of them.

It was like watching a silent movie. Inside the vehicle, with the windows closed against the bugs, there was only the faintest rush. It didn't make sense that an aircraft, a jet no less, would be able to move as slowly and quietly and touch down on a short stretch of road that quickly.

It came to a rest on the pavement and coasted just a few hundred feet before stopping. It had landed without landing lights, and the aircraft itself was dark.

"Stony," Lyons advised, "it just landed."

"It did?" Price asked. "We didn't see a thing."

Stony Man Farm, Virginia

AARON KURTZMAN was shuffling through the display options offered by the drone aircraft that Stony Man Farm commanded at this moment over Glades County, Florida. He was looking down on the scene, right where Able Team was waiting. He could see the beacon from the Able Team SUV, pinpointing their presence, and he could see the road in front of them. The road was still radiating some of the heat it had absorbed from the sun during the day. The waters around it were comparably cool. He glared at the display, bringing his face close, and finally saw the shape of a small aircraft now sitting on the road. The heat signature was barely discernible from the road itself.

He heard Lyons communicate with Barbara Price. "Please tell me we don't need to wait and see who shows up to meet this aircraft."

"No way," Price said. "Let's secure that aircraft now."

"Too late," Kurtzman interrupted. "I see another vehicle approaching now." The thermal display showed him the unmistakable image of a pickup, warmed by its engine.

"From which direction?" Lyons asked

"From east of your position," Kurtzman responded. "Looks like they are pulling up on the other side of the aircraft."

"They will unload, then taxi back in this direction to take off," Lyons said.

"It would be far better," Price said, "if you could take control of that aircraft before it moves again."

"We're way ahead of you, Stony," Lyons said.

BLANCANALES LEFT THE SUV first, slinking across the road in the blackness, keeping his eye on the dim and distant shadow where the aircraft now sat. He stepped into the marshy weeds on the far side of the unmaintained road and approached the personal watercraft that they had staged there hours ago.

The watercraft had been arranged for Able Team. If their first day of searching the county by road yielded no results, the plan had been for them to spend the second day hunting the swamps. There were stretches of dry ground that were not accessible by road but still had the potential to serve as landing strips.

The wide-open water in this location gave them a use for the watercraft, which was secured to the bank using lines staked into the ground—and was covered in a camouflage tarp. Blancanales uncovered it and stepped aboard, then shoved himself away from the shore. He drifted into the open water alongside the road, his night-vision goggles giving him enough detail to see where he was going. He used a small boat paddle to propel himself, dipping it gingerly into the water and gently sweeping himself forward. He was not in a big hurry yet. Quiet was more important than speed right now.

He saw the headlights approaching from behind the aircraft. They swung out of the trees close behind the parked aircraft, creating a silhouette momentarily. Blancanales was struck again by the size of the thing—the plane looked like a toy. How could such a thing be causing so much trouble in the world? Then the pickup went black, as well.

Blancanales eased himself along the waterway, staying parallel to the road, and he could already hear the conversations from around the aircraft. The pilot and the driver of the pickup were greeting each other as if they were old friends. They were speaking English. No South American accents here. They were talking about a shipment, and Blancanales heard mention of twenty bales.

"Okay, let's unload," one of the voices said.

Okay, good. That would take them several minutes, which would give Able Team enough time to get into position. Schwarz would be making his approach on the other side of the road, in his own watercraft.

The challenge was to get this aircraft under control, without burning it up. These aircraft were becoming notorious for their flammability. There were theories that these aircraft were built with fuel housed in their bodies and wings, providing more interior space, but also making the aircraft easy to ignite. Able Team had to stop this aircraft—gently.

The small alert came in from Lyons over the headset. Fifteen seconds. Blancanales counted them down in his head, fingered the starter, and when the countdown reached zero he thumbed the switch. The watercraft roared to life. The lights blazed on, illuminating the scene in front of him. Schwarz's watercraft came to life at the same moment on the other side of the road.

Blancanales twisted the throttle and accelerated alongside the road, closing in on the aircraft and the pickup and the surprised-looking pair of men standing in the road. They both were carrying shrink-wrapped bales, which they had been busily moving from the cargo bay in the aircraft to the storage bins in the bed of the pickup.

Blancanales laid down cover fire, triggering the M-16, cutting into the road at the feet of the two men. Both of them shouted, dropped their bales and dived for cover behind the front end of the pickup. Blancanales's rounds bounced over the pavement, wiggled underneath the pickup, and scored one of the tires. A front corner of the pickup abruptly sank to the pavement.

The smugglers opened fire with their weapons, but Blancanales was faster and more decisive, and his rounds found the top half of the man exposed over the hood of the pickup, about to trigger a shotgun. The man flopped back onto the road with his weapon unfired. It clattered on the pavement, then into the grass on the far side of the road. The second gunner adopted a firm, two-handed pistol stance, triggering a 9 mm handgun into the water at Schwarz. Blancanales stitched him across his shoulders and the man collapsed.

Then Blancanales saw unexpected movement. The aircraft was moving silently, its engines too quiet to hear over the splutter of his own watercraft. There was a pilot still inside and he was eager to make an escape. Blancanales was just as eager to make sure that it didn't happen. He cut a tight circle on the surface of the water, and again paralleled the road, and unloaded his M-16 at the tires of the aircraft. There was no effect. There seemed to be some sort of a shielding over the wheels. Flimsy plastic shells, it looked like, but maybe it was enough to keep out rounds from his automatic weapon. The aircraft was accelerating rapidly, and the hatch cover wobbled and slammed down into place.

Blancanales cursed—he was going to have to target the body. He aimed at the wing tips. The aircraft accelerated, pulling away from him.

At least one of Blancanales's rounds penetrated the wing, and Blancanales glimpsed a pockmarked blossom in the plastic, but then the aircraft was pulling away from him, and he was out of speed. He noticed the angle of the wings—almost impossible to see in the wild swaying of the only light source—his headlight. The aircraft seemed to be limping.

Blancanales had taken out a tire after all. He throttled up again, trying to stay hot on the tail of the accelerating aircraft. Now it seemed as if the rear tire was shredded, and the rear end of the aircraft might even be fishtailing slightly. Yes, the aircraft was compromised. No matter how short its taxi distance was, it was going to have a hard time making a safe takeoff with its rear tire blown.

"Christ, Ironman, get the hell out of there," Blancanales said into his mike. "This guy may be cracking up any second."

Lyons had anticipated this. He started the SUV and dragged it into gear and slammed his foot on the pedal, steering the thing out of the bushes and onto the road. For a fraction of a second he envisioned himself turning to face the aircraft and driving directly into it. Maybe he could head-butt it into the water. The more likely result would be to immerse himself in the aircraft's conflagration. He spun away and fled the coming crash.

The aircraft was struggling for speed. The blown tire was slowing it down. At the end of the open water the long straight stretch of swamp road curved gently to the right. That was the end of the line in terms of taxi distance for the aircraft. Blancanales managed to stay close enough to see the thing fishtail again, and then the pilot must have given it an extra jolt of fuel, desperate to get the thing off the ground, as the curve came under his wheels. The aircraft, unbelievably, left the ground and seemed to grab at the air. The trees came up underneath it, and Blancanales thought the thing was getting away from them.

Then, unbelievably, he watched the side of the aircraft open up—it was the unsecured hatch cover flopping open. Bales of plastic-wrapped narcotics tumbled out and the turbulence ripped off the hatch. The wind buffeted into the hatch and the aircraft's aerodynamics became wildly unstable. The aircraft twisted on its side and descended to the ground, unbelievably adjusting its flight to match the curve of the road. It touched a wing tip on the pavement and the wing was wrenched off. Instead of cartwheeling, the aircraft settled on its side on the pavement and slid, maintaining its integrity for a hundred feet, shredding parts and sending up sparks, until a buckle in the pavement sent the aircraft bouncing a full yard into the air. It landed on its nose and disintegrated in earnest.

And there was the Able Team SUV, right in its path. Carl Lyons must have felt he was far out of the danger zone, unprepared for the chance that the aircraft would crash into the road again, and now the thing was chasing him down. Lyons slammed the SUV into Reverse and backed away fast from tumbling wreckage.

He only needed to move another forty feet. What was left of the aircraft abruptly lost forward momentum.

Blancanales pulled his watercraft to a smoldering nose cone piece, with the remains of the pilot still strapped to his seat inside it. It was resting, nose-down in the water, lodged in the mud.

It was the largest of many fragments of the aircraft that were now scattered everywhere that he could see. Fires burned in the grass and oil burned on the surface of the water, but the violent destruction had dispersed the parts—and presumably the fuel load.

Lyons approached on foot. Already most of the flames were flickering out, with the exception of the large fuel spill spread across the road and the water at the place where the plane had cracked into the earth.

"Stony," Lyons said, then he was momentarily at a loss.

"We saw the crash on thermal from the drone, Able," Aaron Kurtzman said. "Did it burn?"

"No. Most of it escaped the fire."

"Thank goodness," Barbara Price said. "Good work!"

"But," Blancanales said, "you're going to need a big cardboard box to carry it home."

CHAPTER NINE

A high-security go team from the U.S. Air Force Aerospace Accident Investigation Board had been dispatched to the scene. Barbara Price charged the AIB team with the responsibility to locate, tag and remove every piece of the crashed aircraft.

They were to remove evidence of the crash occurring, including sandblasting scorch marks from the pavements and clearing fuel-burned vegetation. This was to befuddle any behind-the-scenes investigations that might come later. It was standard practice for a supersecret agency like Stony Man Farm to cover its tracks.

A National Transportation Safety Board investigation might allocate weeks to investigating the crash site before moving the wreckage. Price gave the AIB go team twelve hours to get in, do their job and get out.

The remoteness of the spot helped. The road was unused. The AIB's tagalong commandos spent the time tucked into the vegetation, but no one ever showed up— no innocent civilian on a fishing trip or criminal suspect coming to investigate why a drug shipment had never returned home.

The AIB team did what it was commanded to do, leaving the scene eleven hours and forty-five minutes after it arrived, and making haste to a private hangar adjoining LaBelle Municipal Airport.

JACK GRIMALDI STOOD in the long-unused hangar, put his hands on his hips and frowned at the pile of rubble at his feet.

The go-team leader approached. He was an Air Force lieutenant colonel, but with special security clearance— and at a higher pay grade than many full colonels.

"Colonel Ricks," Grimaldi said, shaking the man's hand.

"You are my liaison?" the colonel asked, frowning. "You're Jack?"

"That's me," Grimaldi said. "Expecting somebody military, I imagine?"

The colonel shrugged. "What I was expecting doesn't really matter. Let me walk you through what we've got so far."

"Sure. Just so you know, I'm a pilot, but not an expert on air crash investigation. I'm looking for all the input you can give me. My main goal is to figure out the nature of this beast."

The colonel nodded. "I think we can give you a good idea what this thing was like. But I have to tell you, this is the strangest piece of work I've ever seen."

Jack looked hard at the colonel. "You have been briefed, Colonel? You do understand that this is one of the stealth aircraft that's been getting all the play on the news?"

"Like the one that attacked the hotel in Bolivia," the colonel added. "I understand. I can also tell you, Jack, that this is one of the most dangerous aircraft I've ever seen. It was clearly made with very little consideration for the safety of the crew. It was made to be stealthy, to be quiet and to be lightweight. All kinds of safety compromises were made to achieve that."

Jack looked from the man to the mess of parts that littered the hangar, and back to the man.

"You and your people figured all that out in just the last few hours?"

The colonel laughed. "Jack, we figured that out just from picking up the pieces."

The colonel snatched up a section of the plastic fuselage that had been placed on the floor of the hangar. They had not tried to position all the body pieces in the correct place. They were just shoved together. This section was the size of a magazine, and it was curved to indicate the shape of the original aircraft. It smelled of fuel. The colonel grasped the piece in both hands and bent it in two.

"Christ," Grimaldi said. "Not big on structural integrity, are they?"

"You'd be surprised. Let me tell you all about it."

AN HOUR LATER, THE TEAM was gone from the hangar. They would return to their work later. First it was time for Jack Grimaldi to conduct a solo briefing with Stony Man Farm.

Able Team members Schwarz, Lyons and Blancanales were back at the Farm and sitting at the War Room conference table, eager to find out about the aircraft they had helped acquire.

Jack Grimaldi had set up cameras at various points inside the hangar. He spoke into the central camera, his face appearing on the main plasma screen.

His first order of business was to relay the initial comments of the colonel from the Accident Investigation Board.

"The colonel was absolutely correct. These planes

are unbelievably dangerous—by design. They are essentially privately designed and manufactured Very Light Jets, or VLJs. They're also death traps."

"You and I have discussed the pros and cons of VLJs in the past and I thought you were okay with them," Schwarz said. "At least on a philosophical level."

"Commercial VLJs, sure," Grimaldi said. "They're cute for my taste but they're well engineered and safe."

"Why don't you give us the well-informed civilian briefing on *this* VLJ," Price suggested. "From the top."

"By the top, I assume you mean the brain." Grimaldi strolled to the pile of junk near the front, where the remains of the seat could be seen. It was the nose that Blancanales had found stuck in the mud. The body of the pilot had been removed, although a lot of his blood still stained the interior of the nose cone.

"Here's the cockpit. Two seats. This specific aircraft had no other seats. First thing you notice about the cockpit—there are no redundant controls. If somebody needed to take over the controls of the aircraft, the pilot has to move or be moved. But once you get behind the controls, piloting this plane would be relatively easy. It's got a pretty incredible degree of computerized automation. We've got the most fully electronically controlled power plant I've ever seen on a jet, with a full-authority digital engine computer, or FADEC. There's data coming in from a large bank of sensors.

"The engines are made with their own sets of sensors and limiters, which feed into the FADEC's electronic engine controller, or EEC. The thing is built with all kinds of standardized parts. You see the same component profile again and again. Here's the thing—half the parts are off-the-shelf, hardware-store grade. Not aircraft grade."

"But have you figured out how it's so stealthy?" Aaron Kurtzman asked.

"Yes, I think so," Grimaldi said. "Look at this." He held up the piece of the body panel that Colonel Ricks had showed him when he arrived.

"Looks corrugated," Schwarz said. "They making stealth jets out of cardboard?"

"What they're using is a little better," Grimaldi said. "This is what my friends have figured out—through some quick material analysis. This is ceramic matrix composite or CMC. It's a crystalline structure used to make a carbon fiber–reinforced carbon material.

"It's not unique as a class of materials. They use them to make high-performance braking systems, space shuttle parts, other very high temperature applications needing thermal stability and fracture resistance. But this material, specifically, is something special. We haven't identified its specific properties yet."

Aaron Kurtzman broke in. "We've got samples in-house and others going to labs all over the country. All we know thus far is that it is not a cataloged material grade. I'm confident we'll find it is the source of the stealth properties."

"But there's more to it than that," Grimaldi said. "What's so unusual is that whoever produces these aircraft actually used this rigidized CMC compound material as the structural foundation of the entire aircraft." Grimaldi picked at the part and came away with a few tufts of beige fabric. "They start with a molded plastic shell of the aircraft—fuselage, wings and all—and adhere this on the outside of it. The exterior is then a foamed thermoplastic shell, probably molded on top of the material. It's a semitranslucent light-absorbing plastic that gives it the ability to actually reflect the colors of the environment. The interior is a thin layer of an engineered material, molded around a capillary liquid storage system. And that's the gas tank. This aircraft has miles of it—strong plastic tubing built into the body of the aircraft."

"We know just how innovative that is," Carl Lyons said.

"It would be innovative if it weren't extremely dangerous," Grimaldi reported. "On the one hand it allows for maximized interior space with a massive dispersed fuel storage tank. I bet they could double the fuel tank and the range of this jet using this technique. Because the fuel is dispersed throughout the body of the vehicle, the capillary feed could easily be designed to keep the weight constantly balanced, front to back. That helps with stability. All that's outweighed by the danger, if you ask me. Put a hole in the wall and all of a sudden you have avionics fuel leaking into your plane."

"So that's the purpose?" Barbara Price asked. "For range?"

"Weight is another factor. All that plastic makes it very lightweight. Too lightweight to control safely, I'd wager," Grimaldi said. "Very low mass means reduced inertia on the runway. You get takeoffs and landings in world-record short distances."

"All this sounds too good to be true," Schwarz said. "Except for the extreme danger."

"Maybe, but you know what? I think that the reason was cost," Grimaldi said. "Once they figured out the stealth capability I think the entire design was driven by the need to make it dirt cheap to manufacture. I've seen Happy Meal toys with more structural integrity that this aircraft would have. This thing is molded out of cheap plastic, assembled with cheap parts. The fuselage, including the wings, are manufactured as one huge molded plastic part so they don't have to use expensive alloy connection components. The light weight also allows the use of these small, quiet turbofans. They're made just as cheaply as the aircraft itself. Sure, they're quiet, and they are powerful enough to make this aircraft maneuverable, but I give them a useful lifetime of maybe ten thousand hours. After that you can't even fix them. You have to buy a new one."

"That seems to sum up the entire aircraft," Barbara Price said. "It's quiet and stealthy and invisible to radar, but it's essentially disposable. And it would only be used by people with disposable lives, quite frankly. A flying death trap."

"But it's a bargain," Schwarz said.

Kurtzman said, "So the aircraft body itself can be made inexpensively, as can the engines. What about the controls?"

"More off-the-shelf components in the controls," Grimaldi said. "They're not designed for use in aeronautics. They are not tested to that kind of reliability. The programming—we can't know about the programming. Judging by cockpit, this thing is programmed and engineered to fly with video-game skills. Almost anybody should be able to do it. There must have been some custom software that got all these components to work together as a system. Frankly, if the electronic control firmware was put together with the same level of expertise as the hardware, then I'm surprised these things aren't diving out of the sky when someone pushes the wrong button in the cockpit."

"Who in the world would buy aircraft like these?" Blancanales asked.

"Any drug runner in the world would salivate to get their hands on them," Lyons said. "These are not the kinds of people who put a lot of value on their coworkers' lives, if you know what I mean. If they can get their hands on a jet that is virtually guaranteed to get past border security, fly into the United States unnoticed by the DEA, with the ability to strike at a rival gang with impunity, and all for a bargain price? Why not?"

"There are three selling points, if you ask me," Grimaldi said. "Stealth, price and usability. We know they're stealthy. The remains suggest they're cheap to make and sell. The simplistic cockpit suggests they're made to be easy to fly. Somewhere there's a factory that is cranking these things out, fast and furious, all exactly the same, all dangerous as hell."

CHAPTER TEN

Ali Zordun had lived with the stench of burned plastic for so long he didn't even smell it anymore. His assistant, however, wore a mask to work and constantly complained of headaches and nausea. She said the fumes were too great.

His sister—she complained constantly. Someday soon he would transfer her to the factory floor.

He made no comment as he walked down the hall from his office to his media room to watch his precious video feeds.

The video feeds were one of the design upgrades that had been made from the original prototype. One of his electronics designers had mentioned that, as long as Zordun was equipping each aircraft with video pickups it would be extremely easy to install a cellular transmitter—very low power, but one that would operate almost constantly. Whenever there was video saved in the nonvolatile memory of the aircraft computer, it would be streamed back to Zordun automatically.

What was more, it was a simple trick to program the aircraft operating system to run the video pickups constantly—whenever the aircraft was powered up, or even when the motion sensors indicated it was occupied. When the electronics designer had suggested this feature Zordun assumed it would be too expensive. His electronics designer had made a simple case for it. A few extra motion-detection sensors would add almost nothing to the overall cost of the aircraft. A few tweaks to the programming and the power supply took care of the video pickups. A few adjustments to the aircraft operating system meant that the aircraft operator would never know the camera was in operation when its app claimed it was dark.

He would have a constant stream of video intelligence coming in on the people who bought from him. He thought of it as a way of getting to better know his customers.

He still wondered if it had been a good idea to have this functionality added to the aircraft. It had, frankly, turned out to be a major distraction for him. He spent too much of his own time tapped into the activities of his customers.

But he was a hardworking man and he hadn't taken much time off for himself in years. He looked at it not as work, but as entertainment.

He was especially entertained by the video of in-air trysts, which were an almost universal trend among his buyers. Once they purchased one of his aircraft, and once they convinced themselves that they could actually fly the thing with the help of its highly automated software and a few flying lessons, the first thing they invariably did was have sexual relations on board while the plane flew in autopilot.

But much of the real intelligence garnered from the video feeds had long-term, marketable value. What could be more potentially valuable than operational evidence from people in highly illegal businesses?

He had a big market among heroin movers in the Central Asian states and in Southeast Asia. They must have thirty or forty of his planes by now. At least that many again were on order.

Even some Afghans had found the wherewithal to come up with the three-quarters of a million dollars for one of his planes. Several of them had portrayed themselves as drug smugglers, but had turned out to be in far different businesses.

There were several cowboy Australians whose careers consisted of flying cocaine and marijuana into and out of Sydney, mostly from the outback or from routes through Indonesia. These cowboys liked the fact that their aircraft came equipped with video cameras, and they loved the idea of recording their own dramatic flights, and burning them to DVD to impress the women.

Of course, they did not realize that those video streams were also transmitted back to Zordun.

Someday he would use them. For now, they were simply his private entertainment.

CHAPTER ELEVEN

It happened again. David McCarter came out of a nap in the uncomfortable seat of the transport jet with the odd feeling that they'd just changed direction. Jack Grimaldi had left them, returning to the United States to help Stony Man make sense of the jet remains acquired by Able Team. The Phoenix Force flight was being piloted by two United States Air Force pilots on loan to the Farm.

The monitor and workspace at the front of the jet had come to life with an alert. There was an incoming call from Stony Man Farm.

Barbara Price appeared on the screen as the others gathered around the worktable.

"Where are we headed?" McCarter asked.

"Southeast Asia," Barbara Price said.

"I thought maybe we forgot something in Buenos Aires," Encizo muttered.

Price didn't hear him. "We've got a lead on the source of these aircraft."

"And it is not in South America?" Calvin James asked.

"The attacks have been escalating worldwide, not just in South America," Price said. "The number of attacks blamed on stealth aircraft now exceeds two hundred, in fact. But the stakes have just become much higher."

On the right-hand side of the screen, a small window opened up of its own accord, showed a small fighter jet, almost invisible against a cloudy sky.

"This was taken fifty miles from a Chinese air force testing ground by an undercover U.S. operative. This operative is looking into Chinese industrial espionage that has nothing to do with aircraft. But she happened to catch this photo and transmitted it to a contact in the CIA. This happened approximately four hours ago. She reported that the aircraft descended to within two hundred feet of her position outside a small village near her manufacturing district. She said that there was no noise coming from the aircraft, and that it was virtually invisible to the naked eye."

"It doesn't match the profile of the jets we've seen," Gary Manning said, staring closely at the image from China. "It's configured like a fighter jet."

"With stealth capability," David McCarter added.

"Yes. We think so. That started a flurry of activity," Barbara Price said. "This woman was within one hundred miles of the known Chinese air force testing facility, and where the United States happens to have drone activity—offshore, so we're not violating Chinese airspace. But we do have radar monitoring of the skies in that area. We put eyes on the ground in the vicinity, and simultaneously monitored the radar. In the past several hours we've had sixteen sightings of virtually silent aircraft, all of them slow-and-low jets, and at least three of them marked as Chinese air force. None of them appeared on our radar."

"The Chinese bought the technology," McCarter said. "They're creating their own stealth air force."

"With a significant tactical advantage over the United States, or any other adversary," Price added.

"The United States wouldn't fly such an aircraft," Manning said. "If the only way to keep this aircraft stealthy is to keep it extremely lightweight and inherently dangerous, the U.S. wouldn't do it."

"China would," Price said. "Ethical or not, it gives them a military edge."

Youngstown, Ohio

THERE WAS NOTHING WORSE than being in the middle of the mission with nothing to do. Sitting around Stony Man Farm, watching all the activity but with no opportunity to be a part of it, was maddening to Hermann Schwarz. He was glad when Barbara Price dispatched Able Team to the western edge of Ohio.

Half a day later he wasn't so thrilled.

They had been sitting on what was essentially a low-grade stakeout, in front of the rented townhome of a man named Noah Brezius. The man may or may not have been instrumental in the development of the material that was being used on the stealth aircraft. He was a special sort of crystalline-ceramic-engineering genius.

"Being a crystalline-ceramic-engineering genius must not pay too well," Schwarz commented as they sat in their blacked-out Toyota Highlander, watching a pair of working girls stroll down the street, unsteady on their high heels. It looked like a rough night for the girls, in a seedy neighborhood. And Noah Brezius lived in a run-down townhome, with a view of a pawn shop and a liquor store. It was a neighborhood that had an air of desperation about it.

Brezius wasn't at home and had not been all day. Schwarz had let himself in through the back door and taken a look around the townhome. The man was still living there, as evidenced by recent food purchases in the fridge and recently dirtied dishes in the sink.

It was after 10:00 p.m. when Able Team saw a figure pausing in the darkness of a sidewalk-wide alley alongside the townhome. The figure poked his head out just long enough to check up and down the street before he hurried to the front door, unlocked it with nervous energy and slipped inside. A minute later one dim light appeared on the second floor behind the heavy curtains.

"I don't know if he's interested in having company this evening," Schwarz said.

Lyons grunted. "I think he'll see us."

"Wait," Blancanales said. "What the hell?"

He pointed out the windshield, at the same dark passage from which Noah Brezius had emerged. Two more figures were now crouched there, in a state of high alert. They were in black, and they were armed. Seriously armed, judging from the glimpses of the weapon profiles that Able Team could see from their vehicle.

"And up there," Schwarz said, indicating the balcony of a townhome on the other side of Brezius's house. Another man in black, also with what appeared to be an automatic weapon in hand, was crouched on the balcony. He was watching the street and seemed to be satisfied that there was no one observing the movements of his hardmen. He gave a hand signal, which was quickly acknowledged by the pair down below. They waved to the rear, to someone else out of sight, then disappeared into the passage.

"The Youngstown street gangs," Schwarz said, "are getting pretty sophisticated in their techniques."

"Those look like Special Forces," Lyons said as he triggered his headset. "Stony, I don't think we're the only black ops with a line on Mr. Brezius. There appears to be an insertion team here right now. Can you check that out?"

Barbara Price sounded doubtful. "Even if Brezius is the target of multiple investigations, what are the chances of two blacksuit teams coming for him on the same evening? Hold on, Able."

She came back a minute later. "Able, from what I can tell, there is no FBI activity in your area—but there's no clearinghouse of such operations, either. Even the local law enforcement wouldn't post plainclothes operations to some central database."

"Understood, Stony. But I'm not going to go in at the same time these guys are on-site and risk taking or delivering friendly fire."

"Understood," Price said.

Seconds later Lyons advised, "Change of plans, Stony. We are on the move."

AT THAT MOMENT, the figure that they assumed was Brezius had opened his front second-story window and climbed out onto the roof covering his front door. He held on tightly, and inched backward toward the edge. At that moment the man in black crouched on the nearby balcony shot at him.

Brezius had the good luck of scooting off the roof at the moment the man fired, but the round struck where he had just been, and where his hands were still gripping roof shingles. The shingles were shredded and

Brezius fell with a cry. He landed on his back on the concrete stoop, then rolled quickly onto his stomach and pushed himself to his feet, leaving bloody prints on the concrete. The handprints were decimated by a quick burst of automatic rifle fire. Once again, moving fast had saved his life.

By then Carl Lyons had stepped out of the SUV and lain across the hood, targeting the man on the balcony with his own weapon.

"Hands up," he commanded.

The figure on the balcony turned his weapon on Carl Lyons, unleashing a burst into the hood of the Highlander. Lyons dropped out of the burst and peered around the front of the vehicle. It was entirely unethical for any SWAT or Special Ops team to try to shoot a man in cold blood—and that's exactly what these men were doing to Noah Brezius. Lyons nevertheless gave it one more try.

"We're law enforcement. We're on your side."

In answer, the hardman on the balcony squeezed on the trigger of his weapon and held it there, emptying the magazine into the Highlander. The rounds bounced off the armor and cracked against the bullet-resistant windows.

Schwarz was on the ground alongside Lyons.

"Ironman, I just don't think he's on our side."

"Yeah." Lyons lifted himself over the hood of the Highlander and targeted the black-suited shooter on the balcony. He triggered a brief, far more efficient burst than his adversary. It cut through the wooden railing on the balcony and into the legs of the crouched hardman. He sagged, moaning.

BLANCANALES BOLTED AWAY in pursuit of Brezius, closing the distance rapidly. Brezius was wavering on his feet, weeping blood from his hands, and could well be suffering other damage from his fall—and he wasn't a fit man. Blancanales closed in on him fast.

"Noah, I'm a Fed," he called. "I can get you to safety."

Brezius looked over his shoulder with terrified eyes, and veered between buildings. Blancanales pursued him and found himself in a dark, junk-filled alley. He tried to find Brezius in all the clutter, but there were a handful of places the man could have hidden himself. Harsh white light mounted high above on the side of the building created a number of deep shadows.

Behind him came the sound of gunfire.

THE FRONT DOOR OF BREZIUS'S townhome was yanked open and a pair of gunners emerged in a big hurry. They looked right, left, and one of them shouted at the man on the balcony. He only got a groan in response, and then, from directly in front of them, came trouble. The two hardmen faced two new, unfamiliar blacksuits emerging from behind a parked Toyota SUV.

One of them was nothing but a pair of baleful, murderous eyes in the blackness. The second one, by comparison, looked almost harmless—thin, with wire-rimmed glasses.

"Don't move," said the one in the glasses.

They responded like well-trained, no-surrender-at-any-cost commandos, turning their weapons immediately on Hermann Schwarz and Carl Lyons. Schwarz and Lyons triggered their weapons before the pair had their targets. Rounds slammed into both hardmen, sending them toppling to the ground. One of them met the concrete step with his temple. Something went crack, and the body went limp.

The second man rolled, managed to get to his feet and attempted to bring his weapon to bear. Schwarz was already on top of him. He snatched the gun, knocked it solidly against the man's forehead and tossed it away. The man sank to the ground, his eyes going glassy. The hardmen were bound in plastic cuffs in seconds, and Lyons searched the unconscious man for some sort of identification. There was none. He did find body armor, which explained why the two weren't dead from the gunshots. He also removed a Beretta 9 mm handgun and a combat knife.

Schwarz got up close to the face of his own prisoner. "Who are you? FBI?"

The man with the glassy eyes managed to focus on Schwarz, and laughed at him bitterly.

"Forget them," Lyons snapped. "Let's go."

They didn't go. Instead, Schwarz grabbed Lyons by the belt and yanked him aside as another gunner emerged from the dark alley and triggered an Uzi. The rounds flew wide of the Able Team warriors but the unconscious hardman took the hits and grunted.

The man with the Uzi wasn't concerned about wounding his own men. He pulled back into the passage and ducked out a moment later to deliver another long burst. At the moment his top half emerged from cover, Schwarz and Lyons fired simultaneously, aiming for the unarmored neckline, and nearly decapitated the man with twin bursts. The body slumped, half in darkness and half out.

"What the hell?" Schwarz demanded.

"I wish I knew," Lyons said. They heard gunfire

ahead, in the darkness up the street, where Blancanales pursued Brezius.

"Christ, Pol." Lyons bolted to his feet. "Come on."

BLANCANALES HEARD the gunfire at the townhome become intense. Able Team had met more resistance than it had bargained for in the act of taking Noah Brezius into custody. Not that they couldn't handle it.

Blancanales couldn't worry about his teammates or the nature of the unidentified gunmen. His one priority was to get Brezius to safety.

"Noah, are you still here?" he called into the alley.

There was no response, but he heard something creak, like old metal. Maybe a trash can that Noah was hiding behind.

You couldn't blame the guy for wanting to keep quiet. Somebody was after him, and they wanted him in the worst way.

"Noah," Blancanales called, "you have to believe me. I'm here to protect you and to get you somewhere safe. I don't know who is after you, but I'm going to try to get you away from them. Trust me."

Blancanales thought he heard a faint, derisive snort from far deeper in the alley.

A shadow shifted at the opening at the far end of the alley. One hundred feet away, where only the faintest gleam of the overhead light could reach, it was a human, all in black.

At that moment, Lyons spoke into his headset. "Pol?"

"Stay out of the alley until I give the word," Blancanales responded under his breath, hoping Lyons could hear him.

"Understood," responded Lyons.

With his eyes shaded by his hand from the overhead light, Blancanales began to get a better feeling for the layout of the alley. After many seconds a dark shadow separated itself from the blackness at the end of the alley and began to move carefully, slowly, against the wall. It picked its way around some rubble and its foot nudged a piece of trash lightly, enough to make a clink, and the figure froze in place. By then Blancanales had spotted the profile of a second figure, standing guard at the far end of the alley.

The shadow announced, loudly, "Your friends are all dead now, Noah. We killed them. You come with us, and everything will be okay."

The hardman was answered with silence.

"You come out," the man insisted. "You come out, or I might just start shooting my way around this alley until I flush you out. It's that simple a choice."

Now Blancanales could hear the faintest movement very close to him. A slight scraping sound. The rubbing of fabric against the greasy pavement. From a shadowy place against a trash bin something emerged on all fours. It was a bleeding, tattered-looking man trying to make a surreptitious escape.

But he wasn't good at it. His foot nudged a discarded beer bottle, which rolled a foot and a half and tapped against the brick wall of the building, and in the blackness it sounded as if it was amplified over loudspeakers.

The hardman trudged forward, clearly blind to Blancanales's presence.

"You little shit," he said, and bent to grab Brezius by the collar. Instead he took a snap kick from Blancanales to the kidneys. It sent him tumbling against the wall himself. Another kick rocketed his skull against the wall and sent him into blackness.

Brezius yelped and tried to push himself to his feet, even as the new shadow at the far end of the alley detached itself and strode forward. Blancanales tackled Noah to the ground and shouted into his mike.

"One gun, far end of the alley. I need cover!"

There was a burst of gunfire from the far end of the alley and Blancanales fought to keep Brezius from getting up; the man was trying to leap directly into the gunner's limited line of sight. Blancanales twisted awkwardly, aimed through the clutter at the distant gunman and triggered his M-16. The figure dropped away, but there was another hardman there in a flash, blasting blindly into the alley with a combat shotgun.

Lyons and Schwarz stepped around the corner and fired over Blancanales and Noah Brezius and cut down the gunner before he could pump his shotgun.

BLANCANALES HUSTLED Noah Brezius into the backseat of the Highlander, then stayed there with him as Lyons and Schwarz lugged one of the men from the alley and one of the men from the front yard of the townhome. The others were corpses. The two gunmen were manhandled into the rear of the Highlander. There was no time to go for the man on the balcony, who may or may not still be among the living, or to collect the bodies of the other gunners. The sirens were already wailing and the first squad car skidded around the corner, lights blazing, even as Schwarz drove the Able Team Highlander away from the scene at an unhurried pace.

Lyons contacted Stony Man Farm. "Barb, we're leaving behind a hell of a mess in Youngstown."

"We have to let the locals deal with it," Price said. "Any idea who these people are?"

"Not a clue," Lyons said. "No ID."

"The one who was talking in the alley was an American," Blancanales said.

"But these were definitely not friendlies?" Price emphasized.

"No," Lyons said. "U.S. friendlies don't shoot each other." He explained to her how one of the dead men resulted from friendly fire from another black-suited hardman.

"And how is Brezius?" Price asked.

Lyons turned to the man in the seat behind him. "How are you, Noah?"

The man glared at him. "Scared shitless. Who are you? I didn't do anything!"

"Don't worry," Blancanales said. "We really are harmless."

Brezius nodded, but his eyes were drawn to the battered, unconscious men piled in the rear of the Highlander.

CHAPTER TWELVE

Ali Zordun sold his aircraft as a package deal. This package included the aircraft and an intensive week-long training program. He guaranteed that anyone who drove a car could learn to fly his aircraft in just a week of lessons.

He used the lessons to emphasize the dangers inherent in flying—and the special limitations of his own aircraft. Because the aircraft was so inexpensive there were necessarily some compromises required in the aircraft's function.

For one, the cockpit did not pressurize well. For that reason, his aircraft were not meant for long-distance transport so much as they were meant for special-purpose missions.

The fact was that the substrates used in the fuselage of the aircraft, while providing the stealth capability, also give the aircraft a number of inherent shortcomings. Aside from the inability to pressurize, there was less overall structural integrity of the craft. It could simply not stand some of the higher forces another jet would typically endure. Because the engines of the jet were designed for short missions, and didn't have the thrust of some other small jet engines, Zordun's jets wouldn't achieve the speeds that would produce those forces. Particularly on the wings. Still the training sessions taught users what maneuvers were inadvisable.

And users were instructed to trust the aircraft's operating system at all times. It monitored stresses and wing flex and interior-exterior pressures, and its automatic flying routines specifically altered performance to keep all the measures in the safe zone.

The jets were also inherently vulnerable to impact with other airborne objects. Because they were quiet, because they blended in visually, because they were equipped with emergency-only exterior lighting, it was quite possible for another aircraft to simply fly into them without ever knowing they were there.

These were the kinds of things that Zordun instructed his buyers to be aware of.

Another was collision. The aircraft were designed to be extremely small, but with proportionally large interior space. This was meant for users who routinely shipped special cargo.

His users knew what he meant.

To achieve this, virtually none of the interior space was used for mechanics or for fuel storage. Fuel was stored in the wings, but also in a capillary piping system within the body of the fuselage. This, Zordun emphasized, made the aircraft especially well balanced in flight. Fuel drained not from a single source, which would have changed in-flight weight distribution, but from throughout the aircraft, keeping the aircraft balanced throughout the flight.

It was his way of selling this feature as a safety benefit, when in fact it was perhaps the most dangerous aspect of the craft.

Zordun knew that designing the aircraft that way would make it more prone to fire, but even he was surprised at how easily and quickly his aircraft, with even a small puncture, could ignite, burn and melt into little more than a puddle of waste plastic.

After the first few fatal accidents, Zordun began offering his buyers an extended, month-long training program. No one had taken him up on that offer. The one-week program was sufficient. He made them sign affidavits—entirely non-legal and nonbinding, of course—affirming that they had been advised of the specific operational idiosyncrasies of the Zordun stealth aircraft.

In fact, if there was anything more entertaining than watching his clients' in-flight sexual activities via his secretly streamed video feeds, it was watching them crash.

He had become enthralled with these videos, from the first one he had ever seen.

There had been a buyer from Zordun's home province in China. Liang was a longtime acquaintance of Zordun, who despised the man. It didn't bother him that Liang brought heroin into their hometown; Zordun simply thought that the man was crude and petty.

But Liang made a good living, and Zordun convinced him, without too much effort, that his business would boom if he used one of Zordun's new stealth aircraft to move product into and out of China. He had demonstrated the aircraft to this man, using Zordun's own personal aircraft. It was essentially like the models that he had just started to sell, although with some safety upgrades.

Zordun and Liang buzzed the local municipal airport, and Liang was furious, convinced they would be arrested the moment they landed. Only later did it become apparent that the airport had never seen the aircraft on radar. They had only become aware of it when it had buzzed the traffic control tower—and of course there were no markings to identify it. Once it left visual range, it was untraceable.

Liang purchased an aircraft. He learned to fly it, and was soon enjoying remarkable success. He could move large shipments in and out of China with no danger of detection or arrest. This enabled him to cut transport costs and still sell at a discount. Business and profits boomed.

As Zordun's first buyer, his video streams were also the first videos in Zordun's media archive. He had video of Liang christening the aircraft with his mistress, and another video of him christening the aircraft with his wife and an Urumchi whore simultaneously. The exterior cameras had recorded video of Liang landing at an isolated field in Tajikistan and loading up a shipment of narcotics.

But the true masterpiece was captured by both the interior and exterior video cameras. They showed Liang climbing into the aircraft, unsteady and intoxicated, with a bottle of vodka in one hand, and giddily flying the aircraft through rock formations several miles outside the city. The video of him skimming those cliff faces was exhilarating. The moment when he flew the aircraft into the cliff face was so startling it almost gave Zordun a heart attack the first time he viewed it.

He had been so excited he had watched that video again and again.

Finally his curiosity had overwhelmed him. He'd gotten in his car and driven out to the rock formations, where he'd found the remains of the aircraft—still there, four days after the crash. He'd also found the remains of Liang. No one had reported him missing, apparently—

or if they had, no one had bothered to follow up on it. And how would they have known to come and look for him in the rocks miles from town?

The wreckage had also demonstrated to Zordun just how catastrophically his aircraft could fail. There had been no remaining piece bigger than a shopping bag....

Since then, there had been a number of dramatic wrecks, preserved forever on video in his personal library.

But until recently the video feature had been little more than a novelty. There had been nothing, strictly speaking, useful to the business that had come out of these videos.

Even the video from South America, of the aircraft being destroyed in the Mayan ruins, had been only an entertainment at first. There really was little to see on the video, which faced front, and showed him just distant images of the shootings and mayhem.

But one time he did get a close-up view of one of the faces of the attackers. A man had passed close by on the right-side nose-cone video pickup, and for a moment he was rendered in crisp detail.

He was some sort of a soldier, well outfitted, with a serious-looking weapon and a competent demeanor. Whoever this man was, he was very good at what he did, and he knew it.

When the man spoke he revealed himself to be, of all things, British.

Zordun could not imagine circumstances that would have brought British Special Forces to the jungles of southern Mexico.

The most interesting and exciting moment of that particular video was the four-camera shot—front, left, right and interior—of the moment the aircraft was hit with an explosive round and it burst into flame. The cameras continued to function for several seconds as the aircraft burned in vivid detail.

One of the most amusing videos came from a buyer in southern India. The man was smug and considered himself superior to everyone he had ever met. He had only grudgingly attended the pilot-training sessions, and even then had paid little attention. And his superior attitude had been his undoing.

He flew his aircraft on a pleasure jaunt out of Chennai, out over the ocean, but he'd failed to heed warnings about the inconsistency of the fuel gauges. If he had paid closer attention during the training sessions, he would have understood that the nature of the fuel tanks, which were actually capillary tubes threaded throughout the fuselage of the aircraft, made the gauges notoriously inaccurate. There was simply no reliable way to measure the amount of fuel left. The fuel drained from the tanks in inconsistent increments. One could not get an accurate measure of the remaining flight time based on the fuel gauge alone. One had to make use of a special fuel-use app included in the aircraft operating system.

This buyer from southern India had never gained a good understanding of reading the operating system and its warnings. Thus he had been a good five miles from the Indian shoreline when his fuel supply was used up. He began to shout angrily at the gods and at the aircraft and even at Zordun himself for selling him a faulty product. And then he had wept and kicked his feet on the floor like a stupid little boy. Zordun laughed to see this self-important, self-righteous man brought so low in the final seconds of his life. When the aircraft hit the surface of the Bay of Bengal it had essentially dismantled itself, and for a moment one could glimpse the back end of the aircraft separating from the front end and floating away. And for a moment, one could see the hands of the self-righteous man flapping at the surface of the water as he was dragged down with the cockpit, his seat belt still latched.

Of course, Zordun was not held accountable for the accidents that happened in his aircraft. These accidents were not reported to any authorities. The accidents often happened in out-of-the-way places. Missing aircraft and their pilots were usually written off.

Zordun had considered offering the aircraft with GPS homing beacons that would allow a search party to find the aircraft, should there be an accident. In fact, he'd offered it to some of his potential buyers. Of course, none of them had been interested in any sort of technology that would make the aircraft easy to find by any sort of authority.

Zordun had been alarmed at another similar video shot in southern Florida by one of his aircraft just before it, too, was destroyed. It happened in the night. It was a drug shipment gone bad. Soldiers emerged out of the darkness to attack the smugglers, and in the light, briefly, the video showed images of the soldiers. There had been something familiar about them. But when Zordun analyzed the video, he realized that they were not the same soldiers as in the video from southern Mexico. Different faces. Even different equipment. But they seemed to carry themselves with the same self-assurance.

Still, Zordun returned to the video from the Mayan

ruins again and again and froze the image of that face.
The British soldier. Something about the man disturbed
him. He was an unknown entity. Zordun could not shake
the lack of rationale for a British soldier being active
in the Mayan ruins.

But it was ridiculous to think that the British soldier
could be dangerous to him.

Zordun did face real danger—from his customers. It
was inevitable that he would be blamed for deaths that
occurred in his aircraft. That was why he went to such
pains to convince people to study the idiosyncrasies of
the aircraft. That was why he stressed that these aircraft
needed to be handled in special ways.

All the disclaimers and all the training and all the
warnings would be of no value if and when one of his
customers became convinced that his aircraft had failed
to operate as promised.

And the people who were his customers were not
the type to take him to court to prove civil damages.
They were the type to come to him with a truckload of
hardmen to express their disappointment.

He had also had disagreements with the government
of China. He provided them with only enough material to allow them to construct eight prototype aircraft.
They had demanded much more material. They had also
demanded that Zordun build them a facility to produce
the material for themselves. Instead, Zordun fled China.

He could never work for a single customer. Where
was the profit in it?

But Zordun began growing his personal security
staff as a contingency against China or other disgruntled customers.

He also needed to do a better job of hiding himself.

He created a remotely located distribution center in the middle of nowhere. The aircraft were shipped out of Taiwan in a dozen different ways, taking a dozen circuitous routes, before finally ending up at the distribution center in the middle of the jungle in Malaysia.

Zordun was no longer even involved in the sales of the aircraft. He had independent reps to do that for him. He had people around the world with special contacts, who earned a special commission on every aircraft sold.

Meanwhile, he had further diffused his operation by separating production of his most important component, the CMC material, from the molding operation of the aircraft itself. He placed his operations in the middle of one of the biggest industrial districts on the planet, where he was in close proximity to dozens of electronic suppliers and dozens of glass suppliers and dozens of specialty rubber suppliers and all the components he needed to construct his aircraft.

He bought out a specialty ceramics-engineering firm, and was using it to create his own CMC material. He purchased a defunct plastic-molding operation, upgraded the equipment, and was now using it to construct the complex one-piece molding of the aircraft.

He had to admit that molding the jet of multiple substrates in a single pass was quite the engineering challenge, and it did lend itself to the occasional structural weakness in the end product, but the manufacturing efficiency could not be beat. His facility could now mold one jet in 5.5 hours. Soon he would have the process down to under five hours. He would be capable of molding two jets in a shift.

He was beginning to think of himself as some sort of a manufacturing genius.

CHAPTER THIRTEEN

Akira Tokaido loved a challenge—particularly a hack. The Stony Man Farm cybernetics expert was one of the most skilled hackers on the planet.

Once upon a time, it was easy to figure out what being a hacker meant—a digital burglar who broke into secure electronic systems. These days, anybody who managed to learn his best friend's Facebook password and post embarrassing pictures on his wall called himself a hacker.

Tokaido had little in common with such hackers. He was a man who could probe the most secret computer networks on the planet. There were few electronic systems that he could not break.

The electronic systems on the GPS homing devices planted on the hardmen from Youngstown were tough—but not really. They sent a cellular signal back to a specific monitoring site. It took him under an hour to extract all the information that could be had from the devices.

"Not too good," he said dismissively of the devices that sat on the table in the War Room, where he was briefing Aaron Kurtzman and Barbara Price, with Hal Brognola on the big screen.

"Chinese," Tokaido added. "They're still not up to speed with the rest of the world."

Tokaido handed over a tablet computer, which

showed the location of the monitor of these GPS devices. Price took it, and read the name and address.

"Joe Zhang. Chinese?"

"It is," Kurtzman said. "He's a known PRC spy, operating in the United States for the past three months. The CIA identified him almost immediately after he set up shop here in the U.S. and has been keeping an eye on him, just to see what he was up to. So far that appears to be nothing."

"The CIA was mistaken, obviously," Hal Brognola growled. "It looks like he's been up to something after all, and the CIA never saw it. What about these Special Forces? Did Zhang recruit them?"

"Unlikely, not in such a short time in the country," Price said. "The FBI took Zhang into custody half an hour ago and he's being questioned. I predict he won't have anything to tell us."

"It's a bad day when China is able to hire our own military people to work against us—and on United States soil no less."

Price stood, with her arms folded on her chest, gazing up at the plasma screen and Brognola's image.

"Hal, there cannot be many individuals with Special Forces training that would turn traitor as these men did. You and I both know that it would take a tremendous effort to coordinate a team of American commandos to operate against the United States's interest, especially from within the United States."

"I'd like to believe that's true," Brognola said, sounding disillusioned.

"If we take that as stipulated," Price insisted, "we can also assume that this group must have been an extremely valuable tool to the Chinese espionage operation in this country."

Brognola looked at her from his office in D.C. He was wondering where she was going with this. "Yes?"

"I think this makes it clear that Brezius must be an important cog in this machine," Price concluded.

"It also means," Brognola added, "that the Chinese are into this more than we thought. Up to their elbows. One minute this whole affair is about cheap drug-running planes in South America. Another, and it's about the balance of military power between the United States and China. What about Brezius?"

"Noah is in a safehouse in Philadelphia," Kurtzman said. "Our friend Rosario has been babysitting all night, and I think he's convinced Brezius we really, truly, aren't going to murder him. He's apparently been on the run for some time."

"So what's the nature of his involvement?" Brognola asked. "It doesn't sound like Brezius is the man running the operation."

"Clearly he is not," Price said. "There is every indication that he's been living in the United States—while trying to stay off the radar, so to speak—for months. He's been a specialty-materials-development expert for several years, and there are records of him working for different global engineering plastics and ceramic specialty firms. Most of his developments have been less than innovative, until the point he started working on new developments in CMC materials approximately two years ago. He may have developed the stealth material after leaving his last legitimate employer. There's no record of employment for a long period, although there were frequent trips out of the country."

"To?" Brognola asked.

"Sydney. Honolulu. Singapore. And a three-month stay in Kuala Lumpur. Malaysia was the final Asian trip for him. As soon as he returned he packed his stuff and moved out of his apartment in San Francisco. He's spent four months since then moving from place to place, all over the country."

Brognola nodded. "I get the picture. He was involved, got scared, knew his partners would execute him if he tried to bow out. So he went on the run."

"We'll know more when he talks," Kurtzman said. "But I'd agree that's the likely scenario."

"So he developed the materials, but he is not the one currently exploiting the material. He's not the one making these aircraft. So the question is, who's making the aircraft? That should be the first thing you ask him."

"It will be," Price said. "In fact, Rosario's been picking his brain already this morning. We'll let you know when they come up with anything worthwhile."

AKIRA TOKAIDO ALSO LOVED a new type of target. For example, he had never had a good reason to hack into a network television meteorological center before.

It came about as a result of a morning intelligence report from Rosario Blancanales. Noah Brezius had provided them with a theoretical way to see CMC on radar. Blancanales had put Brezius on the phone with Tokaido to discuss what was needed to make the theory a reality.

As soon as he ended the call, Tokaido started hacking.

"Nice," he announced.

Aaron Kurtzman pushed himself away from another table and rolled across the room, coming to an abrupt halt at Tokaido's side, peering at a huge, crowded display.

"Worldwide Weather News," Tokaido said, waving at the screen. "They've got new satellites, five big daddies, with fifteen little satellite children, all in geostationary orbits. The children satellite feed signals into the main satellites, which gives them a leg up on tracking storms around the world. Cost them, like, three hundred million dollars, but it just might give them the ability to identify hurricanes before anybody else. Even government hurricane centers."

Kurtzman made a face. "Not really?"

"No, probably not really," Tokaido said, "but even if it doesn't work, they can tout their new system of satellites and make it *seem* like they've got better information than anybody else. Perception is everything. Anyway, what they do have is a dynamically fluctuating ground-based Doppler radar system that nobody else does have. So what they do is feed the signals from the Doppler radar from other analysis systems, along with their proprietary satellite climactic imaging, and they crunch it and come up with some pretty accurate current weather pictures. Maybe the most accurate simulated, real-time weather imaging on the planet."

"I see," Kurtzman said.

"But here's the cool part," Tokaido said. "They can take pictures of the shapes of meteorological activity at resolutions that nobody else has ever been able to achieve. They can image storms in real time using their fifteen satellites. They don't even have to have clear access to all of them because the children feed their signals to the big daddies, and the encrypted data comes back down through the feed from the daddies. But they can have multiple satellites looking at a single storm system and get incredibly detailed pictures. Makes for really excellent weather-channel video."

Kurtzman rubbed his forehead and tried to process this information. "What, exactly, is fluctuating dynamically in the ground-based Doppler radar system?" he asked.

"The frequency," Tokaido said. "The network meteorological gurus claim to have an algorithm of Doppler fluctuation that is supposed to give them better on-the-fly pictures of the current weather conditions. Like high resolution of wind speeds and precipitation and even cloud density."

Kurtzman considered that. "I can see the usefulness when it comes to making pretty weather simulations. How's it help us?"

"So," Tokaido continued, grinning broadly, "what you do is, you fluctuate the radar and you analyze the signals on the fly. And that way, you find anomalies. And when you find them, you tune in the frequency in that vicinity. The frequency is always going to be different, depending on things like air pressure, humidity, wind speed, and that's why it's impossible to find using regular radar. The thing is, you program it to do this automatically. Like I've just done. And then you turn it on, and it will automatically find the thing that can't be found with run-of-the-mill radar. And the fifteen satellites make an image of the weather where that is."

Kurtzman finally felt like he was catching up to what Tokaido was explaining to him.

"Or," he suggested, "it can let you digitally visualize a CMC stealth airplane?"

"It will." Tokaido was still grinning.

"You sure?"

Tokaido nodded. "I'm *sure*." He touched his keyboard and pulled up a colored radar view of two hundred miles of the U.S. border with Mexico, centered at El Paso. On the screen, highlighted by red circles, were the faint images of two aircraft.

"Those are both stealth aircraft?"

Tokaido nodded. "Probably. The system cross-references with known aircraft. Again, it's gotta have a feed from air traffic control, military, whatever systems are out there tracking aircraft. Then you have to cross-reference those with the weather satellite reading in order to cull the known aircraft. Other factors can narrow them down, too. Speed. This plane is moving too fast for a prop plane."

Tokaido tapped one of the aircraft on his screen.

"It's not on any digital flight plan. It's not military. On every other method of looking at air traffic, *it does not exist*."

Kurtzman was grinning himself now. "These weather network satellites provide full coverage?"

Tokaido nodded. "Worldwide Weather News isn't just a name. Their new satellites cover the globe. The question is, will the weather news network be ticked off about us stealing bandwidth and data right off their proprietary system?"

"They'll get over it," Kurtzman said.

CHAPTER FOURTEEN

East Malaysia, Borneo Peninsula

The locals claimed there had once been a rich man living here. They said the facility was a huge private vacation home owned by a Hong Kong underworld millionaire. It was certainly a beautiful location, in the midst of a valley five miles long and three miles wide and surrounded by hills blanketed with rain forest. It was remote, seventy miles by air or rail from the nearest metropolitan center.

Once the local indigenous people had prospered from the generosity of the Hong Kong millionaire who'd chosen the spot for his outlandish home. He'd bought the locals' loyalty with outlays of money and gifts. He'd given them houses, televisions and cars.

Then the millionaire's business ended badly, and the vacation home burned dramatically to the ground. It moldered for more than a decade before someone new arrived to make use of the land. The locals got gifts again—new cars, new cell phones—and some of them even got jobs. Today the land housed a warehouse—a distribution hub with its own power-generation facility, a landing strip and a water supply.

There was one unique skill that locals offered, and it was invaluable to the new operation. The locals knew the river. The Sungei Paitan began in the hills far south of the valley, and quickly became deep, but also twisting and tortured. It was navigable only by a skilled pilot who was familiar with its tricks and hidden dangers and narrow, treacherous passages. The locals had been riding the river all their lives, bringing in a meager income by selling locally produced lumber.

It took lumber-herding boats to bring those logs down to the ocean docks. The new distribution operation also used similar shipping vessels to bring their cargo to the docks on the coast of the peninsula.

Business was apparently good. In the three months that the operation had been in place there had been almost a hundred shipments going downriver.

The locals were told that the only way the company could keep this operation here, in this town, with all the benefits that it offered the villagers, was if no one knew about it. Indeed, the shipments came into the distribution facility by rail in strange wooden crates on open railcars. There might be twenty such crates on a single train, and they were quickly moved inside the new warehouse.

The distribution facility apparently did nothing other than store them temporarily, and then move them out again.

It was a curious operation. There were, at most, twenty employees at the place who spent most of their time sitting around doing nothing, or so the locals reported. Few of the locals had actually been inside the place.

There were aircraft flights that came and went from the warehouse. To be more accurate, the locals said, the aircraft went, occasionally, but it never seemed to come.

The locals witnessed that quiet little aircraft leave the place several times, but never saw it arrive.

The locals could not understand why anyone would want to choose their valley for a warehouse. It was far too remote from the big outside world to be practical. But the locals were enjoying their new cell phones, and the frequent payoffs that came from the owners of the distribution plant, and they weren't about to mess with a good thing.

A large transport prop plane could be heard over the valley an hour after dark. A young man from the village looked up from the game on his smartphone and watched the aircraft. It flew over and was gone a few minutes later.

The young man went back to his Angry Birds.

It was too dark for the young man to see the five parachutes that were descending into the jungle not a mile from where he was sitting.

THE INSERTION WAS UNEVENTFUL. The five Phoenix Force commandos put down in a clearing, quickly wadded up and hid their parachutes and set out through the Borneo jungle.

The jungle ended at the bottom of a long incline, where the groundscape changed oddly. The big valley had obviously been heavily landscaped. There were gravel walkways, brick courtyards, raised stone planters and wooden gazebos and atria. When it was active, a small army of gardeners must have been required to maintain it.

Years later, everything made of wood had disintegrated, the jungle had invaded the walking trails and the plants had surged out of their planters.

There were a few trees growing in the valley now, but it was mostly clear, giving them good visibility. In the clear night, under a bright moon, the area appeared empty and silent. The warehouse at the far end of the valley showed some light, but there was no sign of activity.

Gary Manning and Calvin James had volunteered to make a soft probe of the building. They had little trouble approaching across the valley. The access road was cobblestones, installed by the Hong Kong millionaire and utterly impractical in the hot tropical climate of the Borneo peninsula. When the millionaire had left and grounds maintenance ceased, the weeds had taken over and the cobblestones had almost disappeared. The new occupants of the valley had brought in heavy equipment to build their warehouse, ripping up the weeds and the cobblestones. The road was a wreck.

But there was no security here. No electronics on the road. No camera. Soon Calvin James found himself standing with his shoulder against the warehouse building, undetected.

He began to doubt they were on the right track.

The warehouse had been their first and only Asian target identified so far, and it had come as a result of intelligence obtained from Noah Brezius.

"The man has latched on to Pol," Price had reported to Phoenix Force hours before. "He wouldn't speak to anyone else, but he's talking to Rosario. He identified the warehouse in Malaysia as the only permanent site he ever set foot on. All his other technical meetings with the buyers were at temporary locations. At some point they brought thermoforming equipment into the industrial building at Sungei Paitan and test-molded parts using the CMC material that Brezius provided them. He was at the site for several weeks, helping them test-mold large components. The other tests had been in rented industrial spaces, but Sungei Paitan was to be used for the stealth jets. Brezius thought they might be manufacturing them there, although in the end he learned that the molding equipment would be shipped away from the site, and Sungei Paitan would be strictly for distribution."

The remoteness of the location appeared to be a success, as well.

"The Chinese have been looking for the source of the aircraft itself—so much so that they were willing to offer Brezius millions for his assistance. And when he refused, they were willing to sacrifice a highly secret in-country Special Forces cell to kidnap or kill Brezius."

"But he doesn't know the source of the stealth planes," McCarter said.

"That's what we need to learn from the distribution point in Malaysia," Price said.

When the conference with Stony Man Farm was done, McCarter glared at his commandos. "Able Team got the bloke with the intelligence and Able Team got an unbelted stealth plane."

"Think we can be as great as Able Team when we grow up?" said T. J. Hawkins.

"All I know is we better bring something useful to this damned party, mates, or that dick Lyons is gonna be acting awfully smug," McCarter said. "There is nothing gets my goat worse than smug Carl Lyons."

THERE WERE OTHER GOOD reasons to track down the source of the stealth aircraft other than denying Able

Team bragging rights. Keeping the balance of global military power was one.

Several cars arrived at the warehouse, forcing Calvin James and Gary Manning to halt their reconnoiter and seek the sparse cover of low scraggly shrubs. Fourteen cars arrived in total, with nineteen men. It was the night shift. There was no sense of urgency in their behavior. Just a bunch of guys coming to work.

James and Manning made their way along the building to a gap in the plywood exterior, where they had a view of the inside of the building.

The interior was stacked with huge wooden crates or small, freestanding wooden structures. James estimated they were better than thirty-five feet square and more than ten feet in height. Each was big enough to hold one of the small stealth jets. To James the big plywood packages reinforced the impression that these things were not real aircraft at all, but toys.

Sure enough, the night shift was busily opening one of the crates. Power screwdrivers backed out the wood screws holding wooden cover panels in place. They were apparently going through what passed for a safety inspection on the product.

After removing the lid, one man jumped into the crate to activate an aircraft, trailing, of all things, jumper cables. The cables snaked back to a charging box and were clamped on the inside of the cockpit. The aircraft was allowed to charge for several minutes, then the systems were powered up. The men went through a series of checks. Electrical readings were taken. Fluid levels were checked.

The jet was deemed shippable in a matter of a half hour. The lid was put back on the crate and screwed into place, and an overhead crane was employed to lift and carry the bulky crate across the warehouse to an interior dock. There, a dilapidated shipping boat was waiting. Cargo doors were opened and the aircraft was slipped inside, to be followed by several dozen more crates of goods. Paper products, canned vegetables, boxes of textiles marked Made in Malaysia. They were all piled on top of the crated jet.

Calvin James relayed his observations to David McCarter.

"I count ten crates in the warehouse," James said.

"What about locals?" McCarter asked. "Any of them in evidence?"

"No," James said, "these are all well-dressed Chinese-speaking employees."

"All right," McCarter said, "let's shut them down and drive them out."

James and Manning circled back along the exterior of the warehouse to the generator shack they had identified upon their approach. Manning spun the wing nuts on an access panel, finding a bank of circuit breakers. He flipped them and returned the panel to its place.

"All dark," Manning reported.

"Hold, Phoenix," McCarter said. "We've got activity on the perimeter of the valley."

"What kind of activity?" Manning asked.

"Uncertain," McCarter responded. "I think when you turned off the power, you may have alerted a guard force we didn't even realize was there."

"Report, Phoenix," Price said via the headset.

"Six or eight figures, all becoming active at the perimeter of the valley," McCarter said.

Manning switched his night-vision goggles to Thermal and found the human-shaped hot spots becoming active at the base of the jungle. "I see them. There's more than eight."

"There sure the hell is," McCarter said "We now count twelve. Fifteen. They're on the south perimeter, as well. We're seeing weaponry and equipment. These are not locals."

David McCarter was quickly reassessing their situation and their strategy as the figures materialized via his thermal lenses. A lot of heat signatures, with enough detail to show battle gear, automatic weapons and electronics. This was *not* a bunch of local villagers patrolling the jungle with hunting rifles and fifty-dollar shotguns.

McCarter's mind went back to the briefing he had received from Stony Man Farm on Able Team's recent activity in Ohio. In hunting down Brezius, the man who'd given him the lead on this facility, they had found themselves unexpectedly engaged with American mercenaries—hired by China.

The Chinese were consistently the playground bullies on the global weapons front. They wanted what you had, and then they wanted you to not have it anymore.

"It's the Chinese," McCarter declared.

Encizo and Hawkins gave him a curious look.

"Do you have intelligence I don't have?" Encizo asked. "Or is it just that your night-vision glasses are so much better than mine?"

"It's all guesswork," McCarter said. "But I know I'm right. Who else would it be? Who else would be trying to shut this operation down?"

"I'd say anybody," Hawkins said.

McCarter ordered urgently, "Cal, Manning, pull out now, via the west jungle."

"No, abort that," Hawkins snapped. "Check it out. They're coming in from the back end, too." He pointed to the far west side of the valley, where the jungle reached out close to the warehouse.

"Shit," McCarter said as he looked to the far end of the open plain. Another force of unfriendlies was emerging from the jungle, a swarming green monster in his night-vision goggles. McCarter had a sinking feeling in his chest: a quiet, clandestine probe may have turned out to be a suicide mission. These new arrivals were closing the pincers, using a coordinated approach, and James and Manning were caught inside of the trap.

"Stony," McCarter said quickly, "we've got trouble. Approximately twenty-four heavily armed troops have joined the party. They were stationed in the jungle. They must've been biding their time to take the facility themselves. I think they reacted when we shut off the power."

"Are they moving in to engage the crew in the warehouse?" Price asked.

"It would appear so," McCarter said. "But Manning and James are on-site, and they're not getting out without being apprehended by the new arrivals."

"Chinese?" Price asked.

"That is my assumption," McCarter responded.

McCarter was thinking fast. Their only advantage in this situation was that, as far as he could tell, the new arrivals were not aware of the presence of Phoenix Force. They were totally ignoring himself, Hawkins and Encizo, ensconced in a small copse of decorative trees gone wild some two hundred yards east of the warehouse.

As the Chinese closed in on the warehouse it became more clear that they were not targeting McCarter's hiding place. It was time to make their presence known, McCarter thought.

He snapped out his orders to Hawkins. The young Texan crawled out of the copse of trees and quickly crab-walked through the undergrowth across the dark field.

"Cal, Manning—stay put," McCarter ordered. "You're outnumbered on every side. We're going to try to draw off some of those troops."

HAWKINS KEPT A CLOSE EYE on the marching line of Chinese hardmen as he circled the south side of the valley and found cover among some old decorative shrubs now overgrown and ungainly. He unsnapped a pack of rounds for the M-203 mounted on his M-16.

The night was eerily quiet, considering the number of men with violent intentions who were on the move in this still and peaceful field.

Time to get their attention, Hawkins thought.

Time to raise some hell.

He started off with the illumination round, triggered it, and before it had completed its arc he fired a second one. The rounds deployed via parachute and turned brilliant, bathing the valley in illumination. The encroaching Chinese were alarmed by the sound of the rounds being fired, but that was nothing compared to what happened when the lights came on. They had been moving in darkness and in silence for all this time, and suddenly found themselves under the stage lights, completely exposed and easily targeted. The Chinese found themselves with just one logical response—they dropped down, to minimize themselves as targets, and peered into the night for their enemy.

Easy targets, indeed. Hawkins thumbed in an M-406 high-explosive round and triggered it. The HE sailed into the lighted zone and detonated amid a trio of crouched Chinese attackers, killing two instantly and sending a third flopping to the ground, where he moaned, attempted to rise and fell limp. The nearby attackers were scrambling away on hands and knees when the second HE hit the ground in their midst. Several attackers were in the kill zone. One of them shouted a warning as the round hit and he leaped away as the round detonated. The blast hit him in the back and tore him open. Nearby companions suffered shattered bones and massive head damage while their exposed flesh was ripped apart. They went to the ground without hope of ever rising again. Another man dived for the ground, hoping that the blast would roll over him, but he was too close; the concussive force crushed his rolling body.

From his position on the south side of the valley, Hawkins had just enough range in the M-203 to reach the attackers on the north side of the warehouse. He stuck in another parachute round and sent it sailing over the heads of the attackers, and they, too, found themselves in the spotlight of the brilliant white flare. Seconds later, the high-explosive rounds began to land in their midst. By then the entire north wave was in retreat, and when a third round hit the ground the shrapnel chased after them and further mutilated the already fallen bodies.

GARY MANNING AND Calvin James crept alongside the warehouse, making their way to the front and out into the open. On either side of them, fifty feet away, the flares had landed and were sputtering out in the tall grass, giving them enough darkness to allow for an escape.

Manning went to ground and pulled James with him as a pair of gunners emerged from the front of the warehouse and faced in both directions. A third man emerged between them and fired directly in front of the building. If they'd been any closer, James and Manning would've caught some of the buckshot. The man was firing blind, hoping to scare off the attackers, and managed to miss the pair of Phoenix Force warriors.

Now the other two men started firing into the dark night. One was pumping a shotgun, blasting up the grass, the other cocking a hunting rifle and firing off rounds over the tops of the shadowy undergrowth.

The man in front, the one with the combat shotgun, was holding his fire and peering out into the darkness, looking for a target. Maybe he saw the crouched shapes of Manning and James, and maybe he was still firing blind, but when he directed his shotgun in their direction it was time to fight back.

Manning triggered his M-16, cutting the man down. James turned his weapon on the one with the hunting rifle, now rapidly pivoting in their direction, and cut into him. And the one with the pump shotgun was taken down virtually simultaneously by Manning and James before he could duck back inside the warehouse.

A torrent of machine-gun fire came through the half-open door to the warehouse. It ripped into the plywood and showered the fallen bodies with wood splinters. The rounds whacked at the weeds around James and Manning. James instinctively aimed at the invisible source of that machine-gun fire and triggered his own weapon. The machine gun turned off, as if with a switch.

For a moment they seemed to be in the clear. James and Manning leaped to their feet and raced eastward, on a path to rendezvous with the rest of Phoenix Force.

They dropped hard when volley after volley of automatic rifle fire came from the north. Flora turned into confetti, and Calvin James found himself hugging the earth to stay under the bullets.

DAVID MCCARTER WAS BLIND now to James and Manning's predicament, his night-vision goggles useless. All he knew was what he'd seen in the last bit of sputtering flarelight—Manning and Hawkins were hurrying across the valley one moment, pinned down by multiple gunners the next.

"Phoenix," Barbara Price said.

"Not now, Stony," McCarter snapped.

"Listen, David!" Price insisted. "We have a stealth aircraft on its way to your position. From what we can tell, it is one of the Very Light Jets."

"Great," McCarter said through gnashing teeth. "Bloody great."

The Chinese configurations—from what little they knew of them—didn't include VLJs. "In all likelihood, it's coming to protect the warehouse," Price said.

"ETA?"

"Five minutes."

"Stony," McCarter said. "What are the chances of us getting cooperation from the Chinese?"

"Cooperation?" Price responded.

"I know it sounds mad, but we got a real mess here," McCarter said. "Cal and Gary are pinned down or just down. The Chinese are firing at us, the warehouse is firing at us, but we and the Chinese are both sitting ducks when that stealth aircraft gets here. We want the same damned thing. We want to destroy that warehouse. If you have any sort of line into the Chinese special operations, now is the time for some instant detente. We could stop killing each other, get the job done and get the hell out of here."

"I'd say it would take months to negotiate," Price said.

"'But can you do it in the next few minutes?" McCarter demanded.

"It can't hurt to try," Price said.

Stony Man Farm, Virginia

BARBARA PRICE DID IN FACT have contacts in the Chinese military, but they weren't people she liked, or who liked her or were likely to respond to any request. In fact, there was zero chance she could find anyone in the Chinese military who would admit to knowing anything about this operation—let alone jump to acquiesce to a request for instant international cooperation.

She spun her chair and practically shouted across the War Room, "Akira!"

The Japanese hacker rose up from behind a distant display cluster, and for a moment Price had the amusing image of a groundhog emerging from a golf course with a wide-eyed, questioning look on his face.

"I need to get a message into China's Ministry of State Security at their office in Shanghai. I have this number, but I know for a fact that it's inactive. I also know that there are other active numbers at this location." She was speaking carefully, quickly and clearly. If this was going to be done, and if it was going to work, it had to be done right the first time. The seconds were ticking away.

"I need you to hack in and ring one or more numbers at the same location. If you can get me in and get someone who can speak fluent English, I will talk to them. But I need it *now*."

She read off the old phone number. This contact was now dead, and when he was alive he had never been cooperative or even civil. But he had been a high-level intelligence officer, and if she could reach someone of similar rank...

Akira Tokaido took the number and sank down below his displays without a word, like the gopher going underground, and Barbara Price bit her lip. This could be a waste of time, and right now, with Phoenix Force in the middle of a firefight, there might be other ways she could assist. How long would this take? Could it possibly be done quickly enough to beat the stealth plane that was en route to the warehouse in Malaysia?

A hack like this could take *hours*—

"Got it," Tokaido barked from across the room.

Price snatched up her phone. "Hello?"

"Who is this? Why are you calling here?"

"I'm calling from the United States government."

"Why would you call here?"

"I know for a fact that I'm calling an office of the Ministry of State Security Operations, Special Forces."

"This is an office building for product export services," the man said belligerently.

"Listen to me," Price said, "and you and I may be able to help each other out. There is a situation ongoing at this moment in Malaysia. There are more than two dozen Chinese Special Forces on the ground, engaged in a firefight. There is a good chance that they are moments from being wiped out by a stealth aircraft attack. We have men on the ground engaged in the same battle. It is a stalemate. We can break the stalemate by working together. Do you understand what I'm saying?"

"This is absurd!" The man was obviously Chinese, but also obviously fluent in English. He had the accent of one of the high-profile British universities.

"Of course it's absurd!" Price snapped back at him. "But it might save lives on my side and on your side. And it might achieve what we both need to achieve. The destruction of a warehouse in Malaysia filled with stealth aircraft. You know what I'm talking about. You want that warehouse destroyed, and so do we. If we all get wiped out in an aerial attack, then neither of us gets what we want. Now, we have two minutes and counting before your men start taking machine-gun fire from above. I'm giving you this intelligence for free. But someone there has got to have the balls to make a decision—right now."

"Wait," the man said.

Price fumed. She was furious with herself. This was a useless gesture and a waste of time. The Chinese would never cooperate with some unknown United States intelligence agency, particularly one that they were known to be engaged with at that very moment. Totalitarian government officials did not act impulsively.

She could hear the man speaking on another line, in rapid-fire Chinese.

He came back on the line. "I am acting as liaison and translator."

"Yes?" she asked, almost desperately.

"What is it you want?"

"Cease the attack on my men in that valley in Malaysia. If your men pull back, mine will pull back, and we can all take cover before we are wiped out from the air. Altogether. It is for mutual benefit. And then we can see about destroying that warehouse and everything inside. That is what we both want."

She was practically shouting at the man. And then she heard him translating rapidly into another phone.

And then her line went dead.

Sungei Paitan, East Malaysia

"JAMES, MANNING, do you hear me?" McCarter said.

Manning offered some sort of a response, but at the same moment another wave of automatic rifle fire came from the north side of the valley and the transmission halted. More of the Chinese troops were moving into the valley, filling it with gunfire, and for the first time began using grenades themselves.

A STAND-ALONE GRENADE launcher was erected on the north side of the valley and triggered in the general direction of the warehouse. The round hit the ground and detonated brightly, and by then the man had fired a second round. The next round detonated a hundred yards closer to where they had seen James and Manning go to ground. The next grenade would land right on top of them.

Encizo jammed the sniper rifle on the tripod, flopped

behind it and sighted the man behind the grenade launcher, cursing at the flashes of chaotic light. He pulled the trigger.

Luck, and maybe desperation, guided his hand. The soldier at the Chinese grenade launcher was firing the grenade that would land on James and Manning's position, but then he keeled over onto the launcher as it triggered. The high-explosive round detonated against his body and obliterated it.

And yet he was replaced almost instantly by another wave of gunners who emerged from the trees and rose up from the ground. They put down more suppressing fire, cutting a broad swath across the valley, determined to hold this ground. McCarter's estimate of the Chinese forces was now at least double his original guess of twenty-four.

"Hawkins!" McCarter shouted into his headset mike.

HAWKINS GRUNTED IN RESPONSE as he was falling to the ground. He twisted and fired a burst behind him, where yet another wave of Chinese commandos emerged. They recoiled from the unexpected fire and sank to the ground, and Hawkins thumbed in another HE and placed it dead center of the group. The man in the middle of the pack disintegrated. His partners were merely hacked apart by the explosive force of the round. Most of the wave was dead in a heartbeat—and more were behind them in the jungle, scrambling for position.

"I got an unknown number of unfriendlies coming up behind me."

"You need to get your ass back here and we're all going to have to give cover to Manning and James if we want to pull them out of there."

"On my way."

ENCIZO FLATTENED HIMSELF as more rounds buzzed at the trees that gave him and McCarter scant cover. He judged that he was out of range of any sort of a precise hit, so he rose up behind the tripod-mounted rifle again, looked for the muzzle flashes and pecked at them with high-velocity sniper rounds. It was impossible to see in the darkness if he was scoring any hits; the confusion of lights and flashes was too much.

Then a pair of Chinese soldiers jogged into the field and faced down Encizo's sniper rifle. In front of them they held shields, like police riot shields, and when the pair stopped, the shields formed a solid wall in front of their crouched bodies. Encizo reloaded the sniper rifle and aimed for the shields, finding them to be easier targets but also finding them impenetrable to his rounds. He could see when he actually scored a hit because it jerked the shield in the soldier's hand.

The soldiers were pros, and they waited until he had used up his rounds before they picked up and rushed forward again, trying to get themselves close enough to target Encizo with their own weapons. David McCarter spotted another knot of Chinese soldiers waiting at the tree line, watching the encounter, waiting for this pair of shielded soldiers to remove the resistance the Phoenix Force pair represented. Then they would be free to move in and take the warehouse, and likely take down Manning and James in the process.

The pair of commandos paused again, crouched behind their shields and held their ground. For a moment there was a kind of eerie quiet over the battlefield. Encizo was holding his fire, knowing there was no value in chipping away at their riot shields. Then he witnessed another shield raised up between the pair, and this one was slotted to allow a shoulder-fired rocket launcher to get through. Encizo triggered his weapon in rapid succession, but he wasn't going to stop them from sending a round directly at himself and McCarter.

But someone else was going to stop them.

CALVIN JAMES ROSE painfully into a crouch in the darkness of the valley, unseen and unlooked for by the Chinese commandos, and he had an unshielded side shot. He triggered the M-16 and cut into the soldiers, and kept firing as the first man fell and the rounds chopped into the second commando, and then the third. They collapsed together, and their shields fell atop them.

Then the Chinese group in waiting rushed forward, finding a new target within their range, and unleashed a barrage of automatic fire at Calvin James as the Phoenix Force commando fell back to ground.

McCarter could only hope that he had wormed his way far enough through the undergrowth to avoid the onslaught. And he saw, to his dismay, still more Chinese soldiers gathering at the tree line.

Sometimes, regardless of your skill in battle, you could be overwhelmed by numbers.

But there had to be away to extricate that pair without getting any Phoenix Force warrior killed in the process. He was beginning to think it would take some sort of a miracle.

And that was when the firing stopped.

THE MEN AT THE TREE LINE seemed to step back into the shadows. They were still there—McCarter could still feel their eyes and he could still see the occasional glint of metal or an LED—but the Chinese were holding back. All around the Chinese could be seen slinking away, out of the exposed valley and into the cover of the jungle.

The valley was filled with a potent and almost poisonous silence.

"Stony," McCarter said into his mike, "the Chinese are pulling back. Did you do it? Did you actually get the Chinese to play along?"

"Stony here," Price said. "I don't know. They just hung up on me."

"Cal? Gary?"

"Stay put. We're making our way out." Gary Manning was speaking in a tense, carefully modulated voice. It was as if no one dared to speak out loud.

"Are either of you hurt?" McCarter demanded, his eyes roving the dark undergrowth that filled the valley, unable to see his two missing commandos.

"Almost there," Manning said.

And still the cease-fire held. From the south, the bushes rattled slightly, but it was Hawkins who emerged, eyes scanning back the way he had just come, his M-16 in one hand and a handgun in the other.

He came to a halt in a low tense crouch alongside McCarter.

"What the fuck is going on?"

McCarter didn't even hear him.

"Manning!" he barked.

Manning seemed to materialize out of a low bush ten feet away from McCarter, crawling slowly and dragging something heavy.

Dragging Calvin James.

"Shit," Hawkins said, and crab-walked over to Manning and Hawkins quickly. He felt around the body armor covering James's abdomen—body armor that looked as if it had been exploded from the inside.

James seem to spasm when it was touched.

"Hurts, motherfucker."

"You broken?" Hawkins demanded.

"Check Manning," James said.

Hawkins looked at Manning. "Gary? You all right?"

"Busted my headset," Manning said as he pulled off the shattered plastic and a dangling wire to show Hawkins. His eyes weren't focused and his voice seemed distant, and Hawkins could see well enough that Manning's head had taken some damage, as well.

"Shit," McCarter said. "Phoenix, we are out of here."

McCarter himself shouldered Gary Manning to his feet, and began walking him out of the valley, away from the battle. Encizo and Hawkins gathered up James, who placed his feet on the ground without bearing weight.

James was struggling in their grip, trying to watch their backs, but the valley was silent, until they heard a rush of air, like a vigorous fan, over their heads.

Now, David McCarter knew, the shit was really going to hit.

He turned back in time to see a silent flood of commandos emerge from the forest and coalesce on the warehouse, and he was amazed at the number of them. Even in the dim light of the jungle night he guessed there were more than fifty.

The Chinese really wanted those aircraft—and wanted to make sure that nobody else had them.

The warehouse door swung open as the assault was renewed and several gunners emerged with their hands in the air. There was a rattle of machine-gun fire, and the men were gunned down where they stood. Then came an answering burst of gunfire from above their heads as the tiny stealth jet swooped down low and peppered them with gunfire.

Even as the Chinese troops took fire and several of them fell, others began lobbing grenades into the open warehouse while others directed gunfire at the sky. There were bursts of fire inside the warehouse.

The small stealth jet was already making a quick U-turn over the top of the jungle, and it came diving down again, firing tracers, and then targeting the men who were now fleeing through the valley. Behind the plane, the warehouse was quickly becoming a ball of flame. The aircraft inside, along with their crates, and the plywood walls of the building itself—all of it flammable—was going up fast. The Chinese were in quick retreat now, their mission accomplished—almost. They had destroyed all the aircraft in the warehouse. But there was one aircraft left at the Malaysian site.

From out of the jungle perimeter came a blast of heavy rocket fire. It was an antiaircraft gun.

The Chinese had indeed come in well prepared.

And the slow-moving, low-flying stealth jet was no match for a ground-based antiaircraft rocket, once it got a bead on the vehicle. The launcher unleashed rocket after rocket, which slammed into the body of the jet and sent it plummeting into the middle of the valley, already a mass of broken parts and melting plastic.

CHAPTER FIFTEEN

Stony Man Farm, Virginia

"Ali Zordun. An ethnic Uyghur who's made a career in materials production at a factory he owned in the East Turkistan region of China," Barbara Price stated.

Zordun's face appeared on the screen.

Hal Brognola was there, in the War Room, sitting at the conference table with Price and Kurtzman. There were others at work in the room. The older black gentleman, dapper in a jacket and tie, was Huntington Wethers; the attractive redhead was Carmen Delahunt. Both were part of Kurtzman's cybernetics team and they were huddled around a terminal with Akira Tokaido.

"Zordun has run highly engineered materials production operations—plastics, ceramics, fibers—at the same manufacturing campus in China. He's a troublemaker and a capitalist, from the PRC point of view, but he's always brought good business into China so he was given a long leash," Price said. "He was considered one of the bright technical minds in China. Unfortunately his expertise is in process, not development. He's been accused time and again of industrial espionage—stealing proprietary materials research and making the stuff in his own factories, undercutting the patent holders."

She related what they had learned from Noah Brezius about Zordun. Zordun had actively courted Brezius for his developments in ceramic matrix composites. He did license some of Brezius's early CMC technology legitimately, but when Brezius came up with the material that enabled the stealth aircraft, Zordun really became excited. But this time, the processing of the CMC was too sophisticated for Zordun to replicate on his own. He needed Brezius to assist in getting the production variables right.

Zordun found a high-paying customer for the stealth aircraft substrate in the Chinese government. He also realized that he was getting in too deep with the PRC. They would never allow him to market his material.

Zordun got out of China early. He left his home and his factory and never returned. Brezius believed that the PRC put its own people into the plant to continue production of the CMC, but they would have been stymied as soon as they had to calibrate for a fresh batch of raw materials.

"Brezius claims only he had the knowledge needed to crunch the numbers on the raw material specifications in such a way as to get the right end-product characteristics," Price said.

"Is that his ego talking?" Brognola asked.

"We think he's being honest," Price said.

"So the Chinese have a very limited supply of the material. But surely they could reverse engineer it, eventually."

"Maybe. Maybe they already have. But in the meantime, they pursued Zordun. He was a man on the run for months—trying to stay ahead of the Chinese, who wanted to shut him down, at the same time he was trying to start a new production plant outside China. Brezius was getting paid big-time consulting fees by

Zordun, but he was also seeing the increased danger from China and it made him nervous. Brezius even admitted to helping with the design of molding machinery for the stealth aircraft, but by then he was in fear for his life. When he returned from the test-molding runs in Malaysia he was a nervous wreck. He called Zordun and bowed out of helping any further. Then Brezius went into hiding."

Brognola nodded. "So where is the Zordun factory?"

"Nobody knows. Brezius never knew where it was going to be. He was certain Zordun was cutting him out of the operation anyway, as soon as his technical usefulness was exhausted. Zordun wouldn't have wanted Brezius to be walking around with that knowledge. Zordun would have known he'd be a target as soon as the aircraft went on the market.

"But," Price added, "we and the Chinese may both be on the verge of locating Zordun."

Brognola raised his eyebrows.

"There was at least one other stealth plane in Malaysia that did not join in the ground strike against the Chinese forces," Price said. "It left the scene quickly about the time the Chinese rolled out their antiaircraft artillery. We're tracking it, and it has now left Malaysia and is heading out over the South China Sea. It's very likely headed back to some sort of safe haven. It's unlikely that it knows it can be tracked. It may very well be headed back to the Zordun base of operations."

"But we *can* track it?" Brognola insisted. "Throughout that part of the world?"

"Thanks to the Worldwide Weather News new satellite deployment, we can," Kurtzman said. "The system we've pieced together utilizing their hardware appears to be holding together as long as we keep finding and feeding localized air traffic radar for auto-comparative purposes." He nodded back at the three members of his cybernetics team. "It's keeping them hopping. But I think we can do it."

"How does Worldwide Weather News feel about us appropriating their satellite?" Brognola asked.

"We're not sure. They must know they're being hacked, but as long as they maintain partial functionality of their system they're not going to shut the whole thing down. They can't see what we're doing with the satellite. I assume they're scrambling to find a way to block the hacker."

"They won't block Tokaido?" Brognola said.

"Unlikely."

Brognola nodded. "Fine. But, Barb, you said the Chinese may soon know the location of the Zordun facility."

"That's the real issue," she said. "It seems the Chinese are tracking the same stealth plane we are."

"How is that?"

"Not using our methods. Something more crude," she said. "We tracked at least four Chinese air force aircraft in the vicinity of that battle very soon after the warehouse went up in flames. They did some sort of a high-altitude chemical dump—a liquid solution containing heavy metals. It blanketed the vicinity for several square miles, and the solution adhered to the second stealth aircraft. Whatever was in that solution, it appears to be effectively reflecting radar on a specific frequency. It is giving the Chinese the ability to keep track of the thing from a very short range. One of the Chinese aircraft from Malaysia has followed the stealth plane out over the South China Sea, and has been sticking to its tail, keeping a very tight window. It's also staying well above the stealth jet, presumably so the stealth jet won't know it's being followed."

Barbara Price pulled a map of Southeast Asia up on the big screen. The map showed East Malaysia and the path of the fleeing stealth jet.

"The Philippines," Brognola said. "That would be an ideal spot for such a manufacturing facility, right?"

"We don't think so," Price said. "We have identified every known specialty ceramic materials plant in the Philippines. There are no plants in-country that can process the CMC material Brezius developed. Incentrifuge simultaneous firing, knitting and foaming. There's nothing we know of in the Philippines that can do it."

"Where then?"

"Following the current route, could be anywhere. Japan has all kinds of high-tech CMC molding capability. South Korea does, as well."

Brognola's eyebrows shot up. "What about North Korea?"

Price and Kurtzman exchanged a look. "That occurred to us, as well. They can't possibly have the technology in-country unless they brought it in very recently. Of course they would be eager to get their hands on state-of-the-art military technology."

Brognola massaged his brow. "That would be a problem. A worst-case scenario."

"We just don't know where that plane is going right now, Hal," Price said. "We have Phoenix Force in the air regardless, and they'll be able to insert themselves wherever this aircraft happens to land."

Brognola nodded. "How is Phoenix?"

"Black-and-blue," Price said. "James was hit by a round in the back. He seems to be okay. Full range of movement despite extensive bruising. He claims he's fine but we've got a full battery of testing scheduled for him upon return home. Manning has a mild concussion and took a few stitches to the head. Nothing debilitating."

"We can't afford for anybody to be debilitated right now," Brognola said. "Tell me again, Barb, why you made contact with the Chinese secret-service military branch."

"I was hoping to save James and Manning, that's why. They were pinned down," Price snapped. "The forces that the Chinese had on-site were significant—far more than I ever would have estimated. There was no way we were going to fight our way out of that situation. I took a gamble."

"And do you think," Brognola asked, "that they actually responded?"

"It's hard to say. Phoenix Force reported that they did halt hostilities long enough for Phoenix to pull out."

Brognola nodded. "They were not cooperating," he said. "They were giving us an out so they could get in and destroy the jets in the warehouse."

"Or they simply used our intelligence to pull their own forces out of harm's way during the stealth jet airstrike, and that just happened to give Phoenix an escape," Price added. "But it achieved my goal. James and Manning were, in fact, given a window of opportunity to extricate themselves."

Brognola turned to watch the big-screen display, where the stealth aircraft seemed to be stationary over the South China Sea. But, indeed, it seemed to be on course to skirt the Philippines.

Zordun couldn't have a factory in China.

Japan and South Korea were quite a distance from the distribution hub in Malaysia.

"Oh," Brognola said.

He fished an antacid out of his pocket and chomped it—and then another one.

"It's in Taiwan," he announced.

"Possibly," Price said.

"Zordun is in Taiwan. It makes sense logistically. They've got the high-tech manufacturing infrastructure. They've even been vocal about supporting the World Uyghur Congress and Uyghur rights inside the PRC. Check for the facilities. Check for any sign of Zordun in Taiwan."

Kurtzman shook his head. "Hal, I really hope you're wrong."

"I'm not. But I was mistaken about saying North Korea being the worst-case scenario. Taiwan is. And the worst-case scenario is what we're getting."

CHAPTER SIXTEEN

Price had no idea what instincts were telling Brognola with such certainty that they would track the Zordun operation to Taiwan, but the big Fed was an intelligence genius. She trusted his instincts.

Kurtzman began making a thorough sweep of Taiwanese industry. Meanwhile, he pulled Carmen Delahunt off air-traffic-control programming and dedicated her efforts to looking for other signs of Zordun in Taiwan. He had almost certainly changed his identity, or else the Chinese and Stony Man Farm would have identified his location long ago. But even under a new identity, there would be other signs pointing to him. Particularly if he had started his own factory in-country. That would require significant paperwork, exchanges of money, and perhaps even biometrics were now on record. Any of these records could include traces of the old Zordun identity.

Kurtzman followed his own gut instincts to guide their search.

"We are going to concentrate our search in the southwest region of the country. The Port of Kaohsiung is one of the biggest container ports in the world, and Pingtung County is one of the biggest industrial centers in Asia outside of China mainland. If I were going to try to hide a specialty materials factory anywhere in Taiwan, I would hide it in plain sight—in Pingtung."

"I'll start there," Delahunt said.

And that was where Kurtzman started, as well. His efforts paid off almost too well. There were a hundred specialty materials firms, large and small, in Pingtung County. A full third of the shops had specialty ceramics capabilities. But when it came time to drill down further, to find out if they had the special combined firing, fiber knitting and centrifuge capabilities, such information was simply not easily available.

He resorted to scanning each company's website, and Kurtzman found himself pounding the keys in frustration. This was going far too slowly. On the big screen at the end of the War Room, the stealth plane inched ever closer to Taiwan.

Every mile closer that the plane advanced, the sooner international tensions would begin to boil.

He flipped open his phone. "Gadgets? It's Aaron."

Hermann Schwarz showed up in the War Room in minutes, still removing ear protection. He had been testfiring new weapons configurations with the Stony Man Farm armorer, "Cowboy" Kissinger. It was something to do to kill time while he waited for the possibility of a new assignment related to the current crisis.

Surfing industrial websites was not exactly part of his job description, but it was *something*.

"Anything to help," he said. Kurtzman quickly explained to him what they were looking for. Schwarz began going down the list of thirty-odd specialty materials facilities in the Pingtung County of Taiwan, in the southwest corner of the country, looking for the capability to make the Brezius CMC material.

Schwarz had not been in the meeting with Brognola, but he got a drift of the situation from Kurtzman, and he could read the tension in the War Room. And he could see all eyes turn again and again to the plasma screen, where the stealth plane out of Malaysia crept along over the South China Sea and homed in decisively on Taiwan.

As Schwarz scanned one website after another, he processed the information. China wanted this technology for itself. China wanted this technology very badly. China would be particularly eager to keep this technology from being manufactured and distributed to anybody, anywhere, with a million in cash.

It would be particularly galling to the People's Republic for the distribution to be coming out of Taiwan, the island nation that it coveted and claimed and had threatened again and again to conquer.

Such a conflict could be very bad news for Taiwan and for Asia—and for the United States, which would be forced to intervene in some way.

As Schwarz scanned one website after another, he found that he, too, was glancing again and again at the big plasma screen, where the small icon of the stealth jet moved inexorably toward the circle that signified Taiwan.

"BEAR," SCHWARZ CALLED.

Kurtzman wheeled over quickly when he heard his nickname, and Barbara Price joined him.

"Shin Zed," Schwarz said. "If you want a ready-made source for the CMC materials in the southwest corner of Taiwan, this is it. Nobody has the capabilities in larger quantities."

Price nodded. "We can send in Phoenix."

"This could be a long shot, Barb," Kurtzman said.

"Zordun could be getting his materials from a source elsewhere in Taiwan. He could have purchased the equipment to make the materials in-house. Zordun operations might not even be where I think they are in the first place—they could be elsewhere in Taiwan."

"I understand, Aaron," Price said. "But it does make sense that Zordun would choose the industrial center in the southwest for his operations. He's got the port, and any other port on the island would slow his delivery time to Malaysia. He's got the critical mass of industrial infrastructure to hide in. And I seriously doubt that he would have had the time to put together his own in-house CMC specialty production on top of starting up the molding operation and assembly for the planes. It makes sense that he is using an outside supplier for the CMC."

"Maybe," Kurtzman said.

Schwarz said nothing. He was staring at the screen. Shin Zed Specialty Fiber Materials used a tiny animated roll of material, with bug eyes and a big smile, as its logo. It danced in place, hopped up and down, and danced in place again. Schwarz was trying to reconcile the cute animated GIF with the production of materials making unbelievably dangerous weapons.

He'd been convinced this was the right place a minute ago. Now, like Kurtzman, he had his doubts.

Something didn't fit.

He looked again at the notepad beside his keyboard. He had checked thirty-three websites. He had scratched off four of them. Out of business.

"Wait," he said.

He began a new search, quick and brief, this time

looking not at live websites but at the archives of dead sites.

He hit pay dirt.

"Here it is," Schwarz said. "I realized just now that Zordun would not risk having his material made at a contract manufacturing plant. He would want a proprietary facility. And he would have the money to pay for it. I'm betting that he went out and bought one of these companies, and shut it down, or maybe even found one that was already shut down—just so long as it had the equipment he needed. And here it is. QS Materials. The last website archive was taken four months ago, and the capabilities page includes one of the world's largest fiber stitching and firing centrifuges. More capacity than any of the other plants. Now the website is down. The industrial register lists QS Materials as OOB."

Price nodded. "Out of business." Already fully up to speed, she conceded, "I know this is pure guesswork, but we can't ignore it. I am getting Phoenix on the ground in Taiwan and I am sending them to that location."

"We do have other avenues of investigation under way here," Kurtzman said.

"And if you come up with a more likely target, we will change our focus," Price said.

"Personally," Schwarz said, "*my* gut is telling me we're on the right track."

Over the South China Sea

THE STEALTH AIRCRAFT never made it to Taiwan.

Minutes before it entered Taiwanese airspace, the long-range surveillance aircraft that had been shadowing it all the way from Malaysia was suddenly joined by a Chinese air force fighter.

The fighter pulled up to within a hundred meters of the stealth jet and the pilot fired manually. The stealth jet became just burning scrap, and most of it burned to ash before it hit the ground.

Then the two Chinese aircraft veered off, returning to Chinese soil.

But on their way, passing underneath them, was the amassing Chinese naval fleet, heading due west, to Taiwan.

Hsiaogang Airport

"HI," SAID THE GIRL in the trench coat. "You Mr. M.?"

McCarter found himself looking down at a very attractive and young-looking Chinese girl.

"I'm your ride, Mr. M."

"You even old enough to have a driver's license?"

"Sure, I am. Driver's license, hunting license, even one of these." She thrust her Langley ID in his face.

"Fine. Let's go," McCarter said unhappily.

The Chinese girl led them through the terminal and turned to regard her followers. Five extremely fit and somewhat battered men.

"Can't remember the last time I had an entourage like this," she announced.

They quickly exited the secure airport gate and stepped into a big Mercedes G-Class SUV. She took the wheel. As soon as the doors closed McCarter turned on her. "We're not your entourage."

"But I know Taiwan, Mr. M.," she shot back. "Xiaoliao Jiahua," she announced to all of them. "Call me

Cello. CIA, although I'm officially off the clock on this one. I'm here to help you guys get the job done. I've been in Pingtung for a few years and I can get you around town in a big hurry."

"Fine," McCarter said.

"Old friend of Barb and Bear, by the way."

The interior of the Mercedes was silent.

"Okay, so I talked to them on the phone a time or two. But I did fieldwork with another guy you know. Belasko."

She floored the SUV into Reverse and tore out of the lot.

"Did you know that?" she prodded.

"We knew," McCarter said. They had received a very brief report on this CIA operative before landing. Cello had indeed done fieldwork with Mack Bolan when he was going under the alias Mike Belasko. She had impressed Barbara Price. Her CIA activities in China had been successful, much to the chagrin of the People's Republic of China—and she was no longer welcome in mainland China.

"I guess Barb's been keeping an eye on me since then. Thinks I'm doing an okay job and that you could use somebody to make your visit to Taiwan very efficient. Can you tell me something?"

"No," McCarter said.

"Belasko. Is he, you know, still alive?"

McCarter regarded the young woman behind the wheel. She looked like a kid despite being in her thirties. And she glanced across at him with concern in her eyes. She had liked Bolan and all she wanted was some reassurance.

"He's still alive," McCarter said.

She smiled broadly. "Wow. That's good to hear. Because *that* son of a bitch lives on the *edge*."

ZORDUN GLIMPSED THE NEWS from his bed. There was a buildup of Chinese naval forces in the South China Sea. This happened every few years. He wasn't worried about it. In a few days the Chinese would dissolve their attack formations and pass the buildup off as simply "maneuvers."

China was too financially vested in Taiwan to go to war with Taiwan.

What truly unsettled Zordun was the rising tide that seem to be turning against him outside of Taiwan—and that was exacerbated by the events in Malaysia.

He had never dreamed the Chinese would be so determined to get access to his technology. The resources they had put into their Malaysian attack were huge.

But this came on the heels of other worrisome events. He rolled out of bed. It was early evening. The manufacturing shift started soon and he was too worried to sleep.

He wanted to watch his most recent collections of videos. He felt as if they had something to tell him—something he had yet to discern.

It was the video from Argentina that began to give Zordun serious cause for concern. It was the recording of a stream from an airstrike in a desert, with piles of rock neatly arranged on the desert floor. Zordun was mystified until some research revealed that it was in fact salt in those orderly rows, scraped up and piled for quick loading and transport to market.

Why one of his customers was attacking a rival at this specific locale was unknown to Zordun.

This was the same customer who had used the aircraft to attack a high-rise hotel in a mountain city in Bolivia. That had been dramatic and exciting video. It had been all the more exciting when he read about the attack in the web news. The news was full of unanswered questions, but Zordun had the answers. He alone knew the full story of the technology. He had a ringside seat to this great news show that was staging itself all over the world. He should have been delighted by it all.

This buyer had used his aircraft next at the salt desert. The video was exhilarating for several moments, as the aircraft chased down a fleeing vehicle and hammered it with machine-gun fire. Then the end of the salt field had come up, and the fleeing vehicle finally seemed to have been stopped, and there was a man climbing on one of the nearby salt piles, activating something. At that moment the salt piles in front of the aircraft had risen into the air, pelting the aircraft. The video pickup on the interior of the aircraft showed the pilot in a panic—until the aircraft hit the desert floor and all video ceased to function.

All very exciting, but Zordun could not enjoy it. He thought he recognized the image of the man on the salt pile. He did what he could to enhance the video, but the camera was too far away and the image was too blurred. The hair color didn't match the man he had seen in the Mayan ruins. But the more he looked at the video, the more the man on the salt pile seemed to be of the same *type*. His clothing was different, but his self-confident manner was like that of the British soldier from Mexico.

And now Zordun wondered if he was detecting a pattern. Over three days, three videos had shown soldiers tracking down and destroying three of his aircraft.

But this was to be expected, he told himself. Soldiers and police and drug enforcement agencies were perpetually on the trail of the kinds of people who bought Zordun's stealth jet. Invisible on radar or not, his buyers were mostly stupid gangsters making stupid mistakes that would get them apprehended.

Stealth aircraft could make their jobs easier, but it would not cure their stupidity.

And so they would still find themselves being tracked down and arrested, and of course the law enforcement agencies would be eager to track down a stealth aircraft and destroy it on sight.

And it was out of the question to believe that it was the same group of British soldiers in all these cases. In Mexico and Argentina and in Florida.

And yet, Zordun could not stop thinking about it.

CHAPTER SEVENTEEN

The global crisis deepened.

She shouldn't have been surprised, but it was some-how bewildering to Barbara Price that this had come so far so quickly. How could an imbalance of power lead to a near declaration of war in a matter of hours? And indeed, that was happening now. It was the promise of war. It was the stoking of flames. It was the inevitability of conflagration.

Price's glance was drawn to the rear of the War Room. A man was there and then he was gone.

"I'm taking five, Aaron," she said.

When she entered her private room there was a man waiting for her, silent and dark. He was unshaved, and there was a bruise on his jaw and there was a wound on his hairline. He had the eyes of a killer. And when she saw him, standing in the shadows in her room, she felt a deep well of relief. She crossed the room and took him in her arms.

He said nothing, held on to her, giving her a rare mo-ment of protection. Usually she was the one protecting the world; right now, he was her shield against every-thing that was bad.

Finally she released him and went to the sink to wash her face. She pulled a fresh blouse out of the closet and changed into it. He looked at her, waiting for her to speak.

"It's getting bad," she said. "Have you seen what's going on?"

"Yeah. Nobody seems to know what got the Chinese going," Mack Bolan said. "It's like all of a sudden they decided it was time to go to war."

"They will go to war," Price said. "They've wanted to for years. Now their pride and ambition may force them to finally do it."

Briefly she explained the events leading up to this point.

Mack Bolan, the man that some called the Executioner, listened without interrupting her.

"They go to war to save face," Bolan said finally.

Price shook her head. "No, they go because they want that technology, and want it exclusively. For all their power and money, China simply has not found a way to foster innovation domestically. They can't stimulate their own technological breakthroughs, so they have to get it from the outside world. It's shameful to them, and yet it's the only way they can maintain their status as a superpower. They need this technology to keep them at the forefront of military state of the art."

"But it's more important to them that they save face. For the very reasons that you said, Barb," Bolan said. He was sitting on the bed now, looking tired, but somehow still powerful.

She considered his words.

"For decades, China has struggled with this humiliation of being unable to create leading technology. With all their people and all their money and all their industry, they still can't innovate themselves to the forefront. And now, to have Taiwan, the bastard child whose very existence is an embarrassment to them, create a leading military technology—it's unacceptable."

"But Taiwan didn't develop it. In fact, it came from an American researcher."

"It doesn't matter," Bolan said. "It comes from Taiwan now. That's bad enough. But China would stand down if the source of the embarrassment was removed."

Price looked at him, crinkled her brow and considered his words.

And then she was leaving her room, and leaving Bolan, and buttoning her fresh shirt as she ran back to the War Room.

"Aaron," she said, "I think I know how we can defuse the situation.

Kurtzman rolled over to the conference table, curious. "Tell me."

"China wants this technology. Taiwan has this technology. If the technology becomes worthless, there's no reason to go to war."

"How can you render this technology worthless?" Kurtzman asked.

"By telling the world. Right now, Stony Man Farm is the only entity on the planet that knows how to track those stealth aircraft."

"Which is exactly why the U.S. military wants it. And you know that no one is going to want us to give it to them. We have Brezius, which means we know how to create this technology. As of right now, the Chinese do not. Even in Taiwan, they know how to formulate the CMC, but only Zordun's learned the process. If he's gone, there's a very good chance they won't be able to re-create his processes. At least not in the near term.

That will give the United States a huge head start on the exploitation of this technology."

"All well and good," Price said. "But far better to defuse a war between China and Taiwan. If it starts, what will happen when Russia becomes involved? When the United States does, how will we respond? Which side will we engage and which side will we ally ourselves with?"

"You know I can't answer that question," Kurtzman said.

"Most importantly," Price said, "what will the toll be? Will the people of Taiwan merely be decimated? Or will they be defeated, and then face punishment for their years of rebellion against Chinese rule? There is no good outcome here. If we can stop this war before it starts, it's a far better thing than handing over some new technology to the U.S. military."

"The U.S. military might not see it that way," Kurtzman said.

"Yes, they will," Price said. "When they see how easily this technology can be turned against itself."

CHAPTER EIGHTEEN

Cello Jiahua was all business as she steered the SUV through one of Taiwan's sprawling industrial districts.

"I did a drive-by on QS Materials before you guys landed," she reported. "There's a lot of activity for a place that has supposedly closed up shop. Coming up on the right."

She slowed only slightly as they drove by QS. There were lights on, and several trucks and cars were parked in the lots. A truck was backed into the loading bay.

"The trucks are all labeled as engineering and construction firms," she said. "They're not. I've checked them out." She indicated a truck with bright blue characters painted on the body panels. "That says Dea Contract Structural Engineering. The firm exists but it's not at that address, and the vehicle is not registered to the company. It was purchased used by an individual three months ago. That individual used fake identification. So the owner is unknown. The truck at the loading bay—same story, different fake ID."

"What about the building itself?"

"Ask Barb. She was looking into that."

McCarter contacted Price. "Ms. Jiahua's got our clearance to participate in this exchange," Price said. "She's already gathered time-saving intelligence."

Jiahua grinned smugly at McCarter.

"The building and all the equipment was purchased

by a shell company two months ago. We're still try-ing to backtrack the names of the individuals behind the shell. They overpaid by as much as two hundred percent. Looks like they had to convince the former owner to sell and finally offered him so much cash he couldn't say no."

"So we can't find a single real name tied to this op-eration?" Manning said from the middle seat.

"The good news," Price responded, "is that it's look-ing more and more like Zordun's CMC plant—and not a wild-goose chase."

"So what are we waiting for?" McCarter said.

McCARTER, ENCIZO AND Manning left the Mercedes and approached on foot, moving through the darkness to a cold truck parked near the loading bay. James and Hawkins were using the other entrance.

"We are in position," Calvin James relayed.

"Make your entrance in fifteen," McCarter replied.

"Understood."

With a hand signal, McCarter indicated the ap-proach. The three of them emerged from behind the cold truck and spread out, with Encizo and Manning mov-ing quickly to stacks of pallets as McCarter marched boldly up an empty loading ramp and into the open loading bay.

Two Chinese men were moving large, long wooden crates, but the forklift came to an abrupt halt. Without hesitation, the driver was out of the forklift, and he and his companion stalked toward McCarter. They were shouting at him, and he shook his head, indicating he didn't understand. This only increased their agitation, and one of them got in his face.

McCarter cold cocked him. The shouting stopped, and the man flopped onto his back, while McCarter snatched the second man by the collar.

The man reacted with a quick sweep of his arms designed to dislodge McCarter's grip. McCarter allowed his grip to be moved, but in the same instant snatched the collar with his other hand and used the first to bash the man across the face. The man made a pained sound in his throat, went momentarily limp and then lashed out viciously. The Phoenix Force warrior ducked the high blow and put his fist low under the man's rib cage, making good use of the man's forceful leg jab. The figure bent double, coughing viciously, and McCarter walked him headfirst into the closest wooden crate.

McCarter twisted the collar viciously, cutting off the man's already labored breath.

"Zordun?" he asked.

The hacking stopped. The figure rolled his eyes at McCarter. Then he pushed himself away and wrenched his shirt free with a mighty effort, staggered and grabbed a wrench from the floor of the forklift. He swung wildly at McCarter, broadcasting his move well in advance, and McCarter sidestepped it and swept the man's feet out from under him. He landed flat on the floor, but swung again at McCarter's feet. McCarter had had enough. He lifted the wrench from the man's hand and brought it down hard on the base of his skull.

A man stepped from behind the forklift, covering McCarter with an old Chinese-made version of the AK-47. McCarter froze, hands in the air, and glared at the gunner.

"I'm looking for Zordun."

The Chinese man sneered. "Why do you think you would find him here?"

"It's his factory."

The Chinese man did not deny it. "Get on the ground," he told McCarter. "Hands behind your back."

"No, thanks," McCarter said, and lifted the AK-47 away from the guard.

"Only amateurs get close enough to let their adversaries take their guns," McCarter snarled—and put the barrel of the AK-47 against the man's forehead. The man rolled his eyes up to the barrel, then with what he likely thought a smart idea, made a grab for the barrel. McCarter lifted it away from his grasping hands.

"Just keep your hands in the air," McCarter commanded. "Now where is Zordun?"

"How would I know?"

"Because if you do not know then you are dead."

With that, McCarter nodded, and the prisoner looked over his shoulder. Gary Manning and Rafael Encizo were close by with M-16s leveled at his middle.

The guard panicked and snatched an old 9 mm handgun out of his belt. What he planned to do with it would never be known. McCarter's AK-47 cracked into his skull and his world went black.

"They know Zordun," McCarter said. "At least we're in the right place. Now let's find somebody who can give us directions to the man himself."

Encizo examined the wooden crates, but shook his head. "No shipping labels. Not that I expected any."

"They don't need them if it's all going to the same place and nobody else is supposed to know where that place is," Manning said.

"So what we need is a delivery driver," Encizo said.

McCarter passed into a hallway and into a small lunchroom with three tables, a refrigerator and a hotplate. No one was there.

Across the hall, Manning yanked open the door to the restroom, found it empty.

McCarter nodded up the hallway, where there appeared to be an office and lights were on. McCarter signaled for a quiet approach.

At that moment, gunfire erupted from deep within the building.

There was a curse from within the office, a chair was pushed back and a man stalked into the hallway, slapping a magazine into a 9 mm handgun. He took several steps down the hall, then stopped and spun, falling into a crouch and triggering his weapon directly into the Phoenix Force warriors. He never made target acquisition, with Rafael Encizo cutting him down with a burst from his M-16.

McCarter jogged to the corner of the hallway and looked around.

There were two entrances into the bowels of the plant from the loading bay—the hall and through the factory itself.

"I got this route," McCarter said. "You two move through the factory. Let's make it a controlled approach. Nobody gets out to the bay. Let's control the movement of the population. Remember, we need just one man who knows where the Zordun factory is located."

ENCIZO AND MANNING jogged back to the loading bay and made their way through the industrial warehouse section of the plant, which seemed to be filled to the ceiling with empty wooden crates. None bore labels.

Another forklift sat there, cold. Two men with AK-47s ran headlong into the storage area, took one look at the Phoenix Force warriors and raised their weapons. They never fired them before Encizo and Manning cut them down with quick bursts.

Another figure ran into the storage area just in time to see his coworkers dance and die. He halted his forward momentum by grabbing the doorjamb, and fell back the way he had come. He picked himself up and unloaded half his magazine through the door, putting holes in wooden crates. Encizo slipped to the door and stepped around just long enough to deliver another brief burst that cut the man down.

The hallway was empty but McCarter heard several men approaching together, talking on top of each other, nervous and agitated. He risked glancing around the corner and found the men entering one of the rooms off the hallway. He heard the opening of chests and the distinctive and familiar sounds of weapons being readied. That room was an armory, and a large number of reinforcements was about to be added to the guard at the factory.

But not if McCarter could help it. He snatched a flash-bang from his belt, primed it, then stepped into the hall and rolled it into the armory. It clanked across the concrete floor noisily.

McCarter sprinted back the way he had come and ducked around the corner, where the cinder-block wall was some protection. He fell into a crouch, squeezing his eyes shut and putting his fingers in his ears.

He still saw the flash, and he still heard the raucous screech of the grenade. As soon as the noise and the light show were done he ran back to the armory, where the would-be reinforcements were staggering out, holding their heads. The grenade would have temporarily blinded and deafened them.

But one of the men must have inadvertently avoided the flash, because his eyes were open and his gaze was locked on McCarter.

McCarter had his submachine gun pointed directly at the man. He shook his head. The gesture said, "You can't win."

The man raised his own weapon, regardless, and McCarter cut him down. The other men went into a panic, a pair of them stumbling down the hallway, feeling along the wall. A man staggered out, shoulder falling against the doorjamb, his red eyes forced open, trying desperately to find the attacker. He swept his AK-47 across the hall, cutting down one of the fleeing men before McCarter put a burst of submachine-gun fire into his rib cage.

McCarter stepped to the door of the armory and found another man waiting in the corner for him. The man was completely blinded still by the flash-bang, but that didn't stop him from triggering his own weapon at the door when he heard McCarter's footsteps. His aim wasn't good. McCarter's was. The man flopped to the ground.

With one eye watching the hallway, McCarter took a quick inventory of the armory. There was nothing noteworthy about the lineup of old Chinese-made weapons. McCarter dropped an explosive grenade into the weapons cabinet and left in a hurry. He strode down the hall and grabbed the last conscious figure, who seemed to finally be regaining some of his sight. He recoiled from

McCarter's approach, and when the HE round detonated inside the armory, he yelped and pleaded for his life.

As his eyes finally focused again, the man looked up to see a commando in black, wreathed in smoke, the bodies of his comrades strewed around him. McCarter terrified him.

"Where is Zordun?"

The man answered in Chinese.

McCarter shook his head. "Speak English." It was not a question.

"I do not know Zordun."

"If you do not know where Zordun is then you are no good to me alive."

The man spoke rapidly in Chinese, shaking his head vigorously, and he was saying the name Zordun again and again. For not knowing the man, he certainly seemed to be familiar with the name.

It was as if he was more afraid of Zordun than he was of the commando standing in front of him.

Gunshots came from the far end of the hall, and a pair of starbursts showed two gunners shooting from around distant corners. McCarter dragged the Chinese man by the biceps, but the man shouted in fear, pulled away and ran into the AK fire. The gunners at the end of the hall targeted the man and he withered to the floor.

THE GLASS FRONT DOORS to the materials plant were locked. It would've taken Calvin James seconds to punch through the glass, reach in and unlock the door from the inside. It took only a few more seconds for T. J. Hawkins to slip the lock. And it was quieter. The entrance room inside was dusty, and looked as if it had not been used in some time, but behind that was a series of lockers and showers, including a decontamination shower. They passed through and found themselves in a laboratory. There was a curious collection of equipment, some of it obviously sophisticated and expensive, but shoved into the back of the room and grimy with dust. Only a few pieces appeared to be in use. There were test bins containing strips of fibrous material. There was also a bin containing fragments of solid material. Hawkins absently grabbed a few pieces and pocketed them before they left the lab and ducked into the CMC processing room.

The room was dominated by some sort of a mixing bin on one side and a gleaming stainless-steel oven on the other.

A pair of men, busy scooping material out of the mixing barrel, dived for cover the moment they saw the Phoenix Force warriors. They had weapons conveniently staged near the barrel, but by the time they grabbed them James had cut both down, while Hawkins covered two surprised-looking men working the huge oven.

Hawkins gestured with his M-16, and the two men put their hands in the air. Hawkins backed to the wall, then mounted a few steps to the raised platform they were standing on. He could see through the access window, into the interior of the oven. There was a circular machine operating under the fiery glow of heating elements.

The access door had not even been closed all the way, and heat seeped out, burning his skin. The heat was so intense that it must be about to ignite the clothes on the two workers' backs.

"Shut the door."

The worker nodded, backed slowly to the door and nudged it closed with his foot. It latched in place and instantly the room cooled.

Hawkins touched his headset, and adjusted the lipstick cam mounted at his temple.

"Stony, are you seeing this?"

"Yes," Price said. "Hold on. Can you give me a better look at the nameplate?"

Hawkins detached the camera from his headset and held it close to the nameplate on the equipment. He touched a button that lit an LED on the lens mounting.

"Got it," Price said. "That is exactly what we were looking for. I do not believe that there are any further doubts that this is the source of the material."

"Understood," said Hawkins, whose own doubts were satisfied long ago. "We're shutting it down."

He waved the men off the platform and marched them across the room, but they were intercepted by more gunmen. Hawkins and James fell back and triggered around their captives, but the enemy fired first, and fired without discretion. The prisoners were cut down.

James and Hawkins blasted them as their own men dropped. One of the gunners fell dead. The second grabbed his side, letting his AK rattle on the concrete floor.

Calvin James would never understand the mind-set of murderers who could kill the very men they worked with, who had no respect for the lives of their own comrades.

He grabbed the wounded man, marched him to the hatchway of the oven and quickly bound his hands to the handrail with plastic cuffs.

The man looked through the fiery red window into the oven's interior, then at Calvin James's dark, sweaty, grim expression.

"I'll let you go when you tell me where to find Zordun."

"I won't do that."

James shrugged and walked away, then turned abruptly and fired his weapon. It missed the prisoner, but smashed into the red window. Raw burning heat poured out, and the prisoner wrenched as his clothing burst into flames.

"Cal? T.J.?"

"We're here," James replied. "We've identified the equipment. We've got material samples. We can use them to positively ID this as the Zordun material source, if needed."

"What we need," relayed McCarter, "is an address for Zordun."

"Nobody here was very helpful," James said bitterly.

"Phoenix," Barbara Price radioed, "your driver says you have got a truck coming to the dock."

"All right, Stony," McCarter said. "Let's go have a talk with the driver."

Gary Manning, the demolitions expert, met up with Hawkins and James and wasted no time planting a packful of explosives throughout the material processing room. He avoided the heat blasting from the centrifuge oven window, and the grotesque burned corpse, and calmly planted his plastique on the base of the oven.

The three of them left the plant quickly, emerging at the loading bay. A second truck was now parked there, and the driver sat calmly on an empty wooden crate, under the watchful gaze of Encizo. Manning distributed more plastique charges throughout the finished-goods warehouse, and McCarter called for their ride.

As Cello pulled up the Mercedes SUV, Encizo shrugged his shoulders.

"Our friend is not exactly cooperative."

"He speak English?" McCarter asked.

"He claims not to," Encizo said. "But he does."

"I'll talk to him," Cello said, emerging from the SUV and almost skipping up the ramp. She was in well-worn formfitting jeans, and she slipped a strand of dark hair behind one ear as she sat on the crate next to the prisoner and chatted easily with him in Chinese.

She looked up, like a young girl who just found herself inside a grand cathedral, but the man shook his head. She nodded and responded almost brightly, as if she was saying *that's okay* in Chinese.

Manning returned from the finished-goods warehouse, holding a complicated remote detonator control. Cello popped up and spoke urgently with Manning in private, and then she returned to the truck driver.

She asked another question. He responded again, tersely, shaking his head.

She smiled brightly and nodded her head at Manning. He touched a button on the remote. The processing room on the far side of the facility was obliterated and the impact of the explosions seemed to rock the foundation of the warehouse.

She turned to the man, got close to his face, and spoke in a very quiet voice. His smile was somehow tainted.

He shook his head slightly, but before the words were out of his mouth Cello turned to Manning again.

He activated the second batch of explosives. The long hallways and the laboratory were ripped apart by plastique charges. They heard a rain of debris flying into the finished-goods warehouse just behind them, and even before it settled, she turned on the prisoner, grabbed him by the lapels and pulled his face close to hers and demanded an answer. She was vicious and snarling. It was an amazing transformation.

James rolled his eyes at the others and mouthed the word *freaky*.

"Think I'm in love," Manning muttered to Hawkins.

Hawkins shook his head. "I saw her first."

The driver was still obstinate, but he visibly flinched when she grabbed him by the wrist. She walked him quickly into the finished-goods warehouse, accompanied by Manning. She yanked out a pair of plastic cuffs, which she looped through the cuffs already on his wrists. She attached the old man to the forklift.

One of the plastique charges was three steps from where he was standing.

"Ready?" she said.

"Sure," Manning said.

"Let's go."

As soon as they were out the door the man began screaming and pleading.

Cello tapped her foot.

"Is he ready to spill?" McCarter asked.

"He just did. But he ticked me off. I am letting him stew a little."

"He's stewed enough. Where?"

Cello translated the name of the place where they would find Ali Zordun.

The prisoner was retrieved, marched to the rear of the Mercedes and piled into the back. Just before they closed the hatch, Manning flipped the switch that detonated the final set of charges in finished-goods warehouse. Flame belched out of the loading bay.

The man's eyes went wide.

"Good decision," Manning said, and closed the hatch in his face.

CHAPTER NINETEEN

His computer beeped to signal an alarm. An important video stream had ceased. It was the video stream from his second Malaysian stealth jet.

Ali Zordun played back the GPS signal, time-synced to the end of the stream. The stealth jet had ceased to send its video signal while still over water, probably within sight of Taiwan. The GPS had ceased simultaneously.

Zordun played back the last few minutes of the video. From the three exterior cameras, he saw nothing of interest. Water. Land coming closer. And then suddenly darkness. The video stopped functioning.

He played the video from the interior of the aircraft. He saw the pilot, almost nodding off after so many hours in the cockpit, then perking up slightly as land came into view. Then the pilot became excited. He saw something. He was leaning forward, trying to peer up through the cockpit window. There was something above him.

There was another aircraft tracking him.

Then the pilot made a gasp and the video ended.

Zordun thought carefully. He must not jump to conclusions, but all evidence indicated that this aircraft was shot down. The pilot had seen something directly above him. This was not an impact. It was something that deliberately destroyed his aircraft.

How could that be?

He replayed the video, and replayed again. He learned nothing new.

He went back to the video from the previous night. His first Malaysian attack plane had flown over the valley and wiped out Chinese soldiers by the handful. Then those Chinese bastards had unleashed an antiaircraft gun on him. The video revealed the weapon just as he fired.

That craft, its video feed, had ceased to exist the moment the first antiaircraft round slammed into it.

He switched immediately to the time sync of the second stealth aircraft. It had been flying over the jungle in large circles, and the camera on its nose caught a glimpse of the dramatic destruction of the first stealth jet.

The pilot had then been ordered by Zordun to flee the battle. No amount of stealth could give his plane the advantage over antiaircraft artillery with line-of-sight targeting.

As the stealth aircraft winged away over the jungles of Malaysia, there had been a brief, glimmering rain shower.

And that was unusual.

Zordun replayed the rain shower. It was indeed just moments of strangely fine mist. It seemed unnatural for such a mist to be in the skies over the jungle in the late evening.

So could it have been man-made?

The rain did indeed have a curious scintillating quality to it. It released a rainbow of color in the dim illumination of moonlight. The mist appeared almost oily.

Curious, Zordun switched back to the interior camera. He watched the video at the time sync of the mist. He saw the pilot frown and peer through the windshield. He was having difficulty seeing, as if the rain was not being blown by the wind immediately off the windshield.

As if it was adhering.

Zordun nodded. Now things were falling into place.

The Chinese had devised a method of tracking his stealth aircraft, even if they couldn't see it on radar. They had showered it with some sort of oil, perhaps containing infrared reflective particles. The oil would allow them to track the path of the stealth jet, and they had followed it to Taiwan and blown it up minutes before it would have landed.

And now they would assume Zordun was in Taiwan.

Could this explain the reason for the sudden Chinese buildup off the coast of Taiwan? Did they want this stealth technology that badly?

Could the soldiers in South America have been Chinese-hired agents? There were always mercenaries for hire, from every country in the world. Would the Chinese hire a British merc to track down Zordun's aircraft in South America?

It didn't make sense. What purpose would it serve the Chinese to destroy aircraft in South America?

Another beep and his eyes were drawn to a red and blinking icon on his screen. He switched to it. It was a security alert from the CMC plant.

Had the Chinese already landed agents in Taiwan to track him down?

He hurriedly pulled up the most recent video streams from the cameras at the CMC plant. He saw fire. He saw bodies. He saw the wreckage of equipment.

He backed the video up several minutes and watched in growing horror as a group of soldiers infiltrated his materials plant. He stopped cold on one of the faces. For some reason, this man, standing in his materials facility not ten miles away, reminded him very much of the blurry image of the man standing on the salt pile and detonating the explosives in Argentina two days ago.

It seemed impossible that it could be the same man.

And the image from Argentina had been too blurry to make any sort of identification.

But he kept watching. And there was another face. He switched from one camera to another and witnessed this man roll a grenade into his armory and shoot his guards dead. The invader appeared in almost perfect profile in the camera for one brief instant—

Zordun felt sick with dread. This man he *recognized*, without a doubt.

It was the British soldier from the ruins in Mexico. Somehow this soldier had tracked him down. From Mexico to Argentina—which he believed now must be connected—and all the way to Taiwan.

He looked at the time code, his common sense suddenly and finally kicking into gear.

The time code showed the departure of the soldiers from the CMC plant eight minutes ago.

Zordun had no doubt where they were headed. They were headed here. To his plant. To his home. And they would arrive any minute.

CHAPTER TWENTY

Darrell Carpenter—Carp to his friends—got a call on his personal cell while he was in the middle of a round-table meeting.

The topic of the meeting was system security. The company had sunk almost half a billion dollars into a satellite network that was supposed to make the World-wide Weather News network the star in its field.

But two days ago the system had been hacked and some asshole had been using it with apparent impunity ever since.

Darrell Carpenter, who right now wasn't Carp to anybody, wanted to know why they couldn't stop it. And he wanted to know why he couldn't stop the god-damned phones from ringing when he was in the middle of this meeting.

He thumbed off the phone midbuzz and dropped it into his pocket. The conference room phone began to ring. The second conference room phone began to ring. His secretary, Alice, poked her head in at that moment and said, "Mr. Carpenter, there are some people trying to reach you by telephone."

His cell began to buzz again in his pocket.

Both phones in the conference room stopped, then both started ringing again.

What in the hell?

"They seem to think is very important that they speak to you immediately, Mr. Carpenter."

"Which line?" he demanded.

Alice looked nervous. "All of them."

His personal cell phone buzzed insistently. His subordinates around the conference table weren't sure what was going on, either.

"Give me a minute," he said. He poked at the screen of his smartphone. "Who is this?"

"Hello, Mr. Carpenter. This is Aaron."

"Aaron who?"

"Just Aaron. I'm calling about your satellite security problems."

Oh, great. The media had finally got wind to the breakdown of the WWN system.

Time to deny, deny, deny.

"What satellite security problems?"

"I know you have satellite security problems, Mr. Carpenter." Aaron said. "I'm friends with a guy who hacked you."

Darrell Carpenter's mouth became very dry. "What?"

"I know this is going to be hard for you to believe, but your satellite system has been seconded by a certain intelligence agency to assist in a certain highly volatile geopolitical crisis. Believe it or not, your new satellite system has been an extremely useful tool."

"What the hell do you want with us?" Carpenter stormed.

"As I said, it's going to be very difficult for you to believe what I'm about to tell you. Please open your mind and listen to what I have to say. We have something to offer you. We discovered a new capability that you did not even realize your system possessed. It's going to enable a new and truly unique type of programming. Not the kind of programming your network has ever done in the past, but I guarantee you it will be of great interest to viewers around the world."

Darrell Carpenter simply did not know how to respond to the crazy person on his line. And he was deathly afraid that the crazy man truly was the hacker. And if he insulted the man, the man would retaliate by crippling the WWN satellite system permanently.

"Mr. Carpenter, you still with me?"

"I'm still here."

"I'm going to explain to you now what your system has been used for."

"Okay, buddy. You go ahead and explain it."

And then the man who called himself Aaron explained to the CEO of Worldwide Weather News Corp. exactly how the WWN satellite system had been appropriated for intelligence use. The explanation left Darrell Carpenter flabbergasted.

"You are with...who? Taiwanese intelligence?"

Aaron said, "I would never try to deny such a thing, Mr. Carpenter. But I don't know how you could possibly believe a word I've said without me actually proving it to you."

"How could you prove it?"

"Here's what I will do," Aaron said. "I would like to have my technical man talk to one of your top system specialists. Somebody who understands the satellite operating system. My tech guy is going to send your expert the same software we have plugged into your system. You can run it in a digital vault if you're worried that it might contaminate your system. But when you do, you're going to see that what I say is true."

"We're going to see unidentified flying planes," Carpenter said incredulously.

"You're going to see stealth aircraft that belong to the Chinese military, as well as drug smugglers from around the world. A very specific kind of stealth technology will be made visible on your systems. And when I give this to you as my gift, the only thing that I ask of you in return is that you broadcast it."

Stony Man Farm, Virginia

THE AMASSING CHINESE FLEET was the focus of the news on every channel. U.S. senators were calling the move by China simple, bald-faced aggression. Unprovoked and unmotivated.

Others were saying that China had been planning this move for decades and simply now decided that the time was right.

Even Taipei had been mystified by the abrupt change in tenor in its relationship with China. The ongoing stalemate had changed so rapidly into preparation for war that it had caught the government in Taipei off guard.

Publicly China was making no demands. Behind the scenes, the story was different.

The message had been delivered to the government in Taipei.

Taipei was stalling for time. It had no idea what exactly it had in-country in terms of the stealth technology. It had not even heard of this technology until the message was delivered by China.

Taiwan's leaders reasoned that if China was willing to take the geopolitical gamble of making war, or even the gamble of preparing for war on Taiwan, then the technology they were after must be immensely valuable.

There were some who suggested that Taiwan should confiscate this technology and exploit it for its own good.

Put Taiwan in the seat of power for a change.

Cooler heads seemed to prevail. Whatever the technology, and however it could be exploited, it could not possibly be located and exploited in the few hours remaining before China's aggressive military buildup turned to military action.

And there were those who worried both privately and in the government houses in Taipei and in Washington, D.C., that nothing would stop China this time. That China would send its force into Taiwan, if for no other reason than to confiscate the technology that it claimed ownership of, and as long as it was finally taking an aggressive act against Taiwan, it would go for broke. Exert control. Conquer Taiwan.

The problem for China had always been one of global perception. It had Taiwan outgunned easily. Militarily there was nothing stopping it. The problem with a military takeover of Taiwan would be the large-scale damage done to China's interests the world over. Its economy would suffer devastating losses when nations chose to no longer do business with China.

This reality had been mystifying to China in decades past, but as the leaders became more exposed to the Western world and understood the depth of the world's disdain for aggression, if not the sentiment behind it, China knew it was stymied in this regard. Military expansionism was simply no longer tolerable in a world filled with billions of bleeding hearts.

China had long ago determined that there was more to gain in appeasing those bleeding hearts and supplying them with consumer goods than there was in alienating them and hamstringing China's own industries.

It was a matter of simple market economics versus military ambition.

And yet there were times when military ambition became the top priority. Because the military was required to protect the business interests. And thus China had put a focus on making its military the superior global force.

And for once, they found the technology within their own borders that gave them military predominance. A technology that they did not have to steal or reverse engineer. It was theirs. It belonged to them.

The fact that the technology had actually been developed and perfected in the United States was conveniently ignored.

When the demand was passed along to the government in Taipei, there was no mention of the fact that this technology originated anywhere but China. It was characterized as technology that belonged completely to China. The message to the government in Taipei reminded them how highly China valued intellectual property and how it brokered no casual or premeditated violation of intellectual property rights.

The message delivered to the government in Taipei was quite clear: China felt justified in invading Taiwan, if for no other reason than to retrieve that which Taiwan had stolen from it.

THE GOVERNMENTS OF THE WORLD, and the pundits populating the global news-media industry, speculated endlessly on the motivation behind China's actions. When the timeline became publicly known, the speculation escalated.

There had been no activity from the Chinese military as recently as twenty-four hours ago specific to its military buildup. Such a rapid buildup on this scale was unprecedented.

This had also not played out like simple military exercises or scheduled maneuvers. In the past, when China decided to flex its muscle, it let the world know. It moved ships and positioned military resources for weeks at a time. It deployed troops. It sometimes made veiled threats.

This time, nothing until just a few hours before. Peace had transformed into the largest single-location buildup of military power in years, or decades. There was evidence of inefficiencies and sloppy work, clearly indicating that this had been an unplanned venture.

The more the world watched, the more the pundits became convinced that something had happened behind the scenes. Some diplomatic disaster or international insult must have triggered the activity.

And now, even as it was still moving ships to the South China Sea, China had delivered some sort of a deadline to Taiwan. It was not a deadline of days, but of hours. Someone had leaked the information or had overheard it in the conversations among high-level Taiwanese leaders. It was a deadline of twelve hours.

"TAIWAN IS RESISTING," Price said.

"How can you blame them?" Kurtzman said. "Why should they suffer these fools?"

"Because they can't win. Not if it comes to war."

"That's always been the case. Taiwan has always

faced that inexorability. If China ever found itself truly willing to attack Taiwan, they could throw a million soldiers at the island. They would sacrifice whatever materiel and lives were required to not lose. It was always about saving face for China."

Barbara Price had heard too much about saving face. Intellectually she understood it; as a human being it revolted her. "Sacrificing one million soldiers to save face? Even if they did it, they'd look like fools. It would reinforce the world's view that they care about their power base far more than about their people."

"The old boys and the militarists are still there, still breeding and still in positions of power," Kurtzman said.

Price turned away from the news screen and looked at Kurtzman. "Aaron, do you think they would really do it? They'd really turn this crisis into some sort of impulsive expansionist aggressive act?"

Kurtzman nodded. "Maybe. The keyword is *impulsive*. Taiwan has been an itch under their collar for as long as they can remember. Every time they threaten Taiwan, you better believe there is always that urge to actually follow through. Despite the cool heads in Beijing, there are hotheads, too, and the hotheads might someday have the political leverage to make the attack actually happen. Is it today?" Kurtzman spread his hands helplessly. "I don't know."

"To save face," Price said bitterly.

"Not if we can help it," Kurtzman reminded her.

CHAPTER TWENTY-ONE

Darrell Carpenter gazed at the flat panel, not daring to believe what he was seeing.

His tech was trying to explain it to him.

"This is an aircraft being picked up by our satellite system. This is the air traffic control radar signature."

He flipped back and forth. The aircraft was there, and then it was gone, and it was there, and it was gone.

"And that's Chinese?"

"Not officially. But yeah. We're looking at the South China Sea. That is a Chinese stealth aircraft."

"And this software in our system, it can see only a specific kind of stealth aircraft?"

"With the programming that's in place, yeah."

"Listen, kid," Darrell Carpenter said, "if we go public with this thing there has to be no doubt that we're not compromising U.S. military technology. We do that, we're traitors. We're out of business."

"On the other hand," the IT guy said, "if it's only the bad guys, then we're heroes."

"How are we supposed to be sure?"

The IT guy shrugged. "I just barely have an understanding of what's going on here, let alone how the programming makes it happen. The stuff is beyond me. All I can tell you is this thing can see stealth aircraft in all parts of the world. When we tested it an hour ago with Aaron we saw eight or ten of these things flying around in South America. We saw some in Europe. They're concentrated outside of the United States, although I was told that there are also drug smugglers who do use them to come in and out of the United States. From what I have seen, and from what I've been told by these people, and for whatever that is worth, Carp, these are all bad guys."

Carpenter nodded. "So do we risk it?"

"This is one of those days," the IT kid said, "when I'm really glad I'm not the boss."

IT WAS ALMOST MIDNIGHT in Taiwan, and getting on to noon in Washington, D.C.

Tokaido leaped up from his seat and pointed at the plasma screen. "Worldwide Weather News has just gone live with Stealth Cam Global!" he exclaimed. "Check it out!"

The image was on the screen. It was Tokaido's software, prettied up with better graphics.

The announcer was explaining, and the words were scrolling at the bottom of the screen, but Barbara Price only caught some of it. "Some connection to the crisis in the South China Sea…stealth technology claimed by China…dozens of aircraft around the world using the technology…China assumed to be selling stealth technology to drug smugglers, crime organizations and possibly even terrorists. Proprietary software provided by an unknown source with direct connections to the crisis in China."

The network was making it very clear that none of this had come from the United States.

Price turned to another screen and found that CNN had already picked up the feed, crediting Worldwide

Weather as the source. MSNBC had it, as well. Even the local news stations were showing it now.

"Well," Tokaido said happily, "China did want to claim it was their technology. I'd say Worldwide Weather News is giving them full credit for it."

CHAPTER TWENTY-TWO

The plant sat between a wide, slow-moving waterway on one side and a near-empty parking lot on the other. A long access road at the rear led to the shipping bay. Chains stretched across the front entrance doors.

David McCarter saw no time available to look for another entrance. This probe was not to be finessed. He ordered the team to cover and lobbed an HE grenade at the front doors, removing the chain and the doors they were attached to.

Phoenix Force entered the factory and were welcomed with gunfire. Heavy-duty metal tables had been set on their sides and provided excellent cover to an unknown number of gunmen in a parts logistics room. The blast had already dumped shelving units, and tens of thousands of tiny plastic and electronic parts were scattered on the floor. They crunched underfoot.

Hawkins was ready with a flash-bang, which he lobbed underhand across the sorting room, then put his fingers in his ears and squeezed his eyes.

The team entered the room and gunned down the three stumbling, temporarily blinded and deaf men struggling to find the exit.

There was no time for mercy.

Encizo stepped behind the tables and found another gunman on the ground. The man made a last stand. His

AK-47 lifted toward Encizo, but the Cuban fired into his chest. The man fell limp.

They moved along to an assembly line, where racks of parts were organized in carts around manual workstations. The cowling segments and fan parts indicated that this was where the jet engines were being slapped together.

David McCarter didn't care about the equipment. He saw movement on the other side of the parts racks. He targeted through the grates and triggered his MP-5, and submachine-gun fire took down a fleeing man.

Manning clambered over the assembly line, pulled himself up a wall-mounted access ladder and kicked at the top of the rack. It was ten feet tall, heavily weighted on the bottom, but with enough leverage it toppled. It carried the next two racks with it. There was a rattle of rifle fire, as if someone was trying to fight off the collapsing racks. The racks clattered heavily together—tons of shelving and components.

There was a burst of gunfire from under the wreckage. One of the trapped men, unbelievably, was trying to cut them down. Gary Manning found a gap in the wreckage, inserted the barrel of his weapon and triggered it.

After which there was silence from under the wreckage.

David McCarter was already leading the others down the assembly line, searching for the way deeper into the factory. The wall ended and the ceiling extended up another fifty feet, opening into a huge room intended for manufacturing large-scale parts.

Two men leaped from what might have been a janitorial closet, paces away from the four warriors—without realizing there was a fifth. Manning chose that moment to catch up and he gunned the pair down before they realized he was there.

They entered the expansive manufacturing facility, filled with machinery, molding equipment and crates of materials. Hanging from an overhead crane was the molded fuselage of a stealth jet. Just the one piece of wings, body and tail. Glass, motors and controls were all still to be added. It seemed to be curing under specialty infrared lamps, which would harden and strengthen the engineered thermoplastic exterior.

The molded fuselage had been pulled from a massive molding machine that dominated one end of the manufacturing chamber. The machine's two-sided mold was closed, and the control panel indicated an operation in progress. There was another fuselage being compressed into shape even at that moment.

"So this is where they come from," Gary Manning said.

"Not anymore," McCarter responded.

"Yeah," Manning said. He stepped up, quickly adhered a pair of plastique bricks, activated their igniters and waved his teammates back the way they had come.

A burst of gunfire from deeper inside the manufacturing chamber chased after them. Manning scrambled behind the wall and opened his igniter control—but held off. He and the other members of Phoenix Force were listening to the approaching footsteps. At the proper moment McCarter said, "Now."

Manning grinned and flipped the igniter switch. The plastique bricks detonated and a cloud of debris gushed into the engine assembly sector from the manufacturing chamber.

They allowed the flying debris to settle and returned to the manufacturing chamber to find several gunmen strewed on the ground. Another foursome marched into view, peppering Phoenix Force from far across the chamber.

McCarter triggered a long burst from the MP-5, cutting down two of them. The other two attempted to run, but Hawkins took a careful shot, shouldering his M-16 like a sniper rifle, and delivered a burst at shoulder level at them both. They fell.

Manning jogged to the molding machine to inspect his own work. The controls were obliterated. The screws that held the mold were twisted, and at least one piece of the massive mold tool was cracked and broken. A mess of molten plastic and wadded fiber was oozing from the bottom of the broken metal slab.

"She's a goner," Manning said.

"You sure?" McCarter said.

"They're not going to be making any more aircraft anytime soon on this thing. Give them a month, and maybe they could repair this mold and get this thing functional again."

"If we give them a month," Hawkins added.

"Not up to us," McCarter said. "Let's finish this cleanup job and get the hell out."

They circled the molding facility and found themselves at the base of wide concrete stairs that led up to an oversize upper-level supervisor's office overlooking the factory floor.

Large steel barrels had been rolled into place and a trio of men waited at the bottom of the stairs. They blasted away at Phoenix Force.

Encizo found good cover and returned fire, targeting

the metal barrels. The results were satisfying; the metal barrels amplified each bullet strike into a raucous clang. Encizo laid on the trigger and turned the steel drums into a loudspeaker. The gunners found the cacophony unbearable and retreated up the stairs in a run. Fully exposed, the four other Phoenix Force warriors took them out with quick, efficient bursts.

A burst of automatic gunfire came back at them from the top of the stairs, followed by the click of a grenade landing on the floor nearby. Phoenix retreated and ducked back behind the molding equipment to ride out the grenade blast. Fléchettes rattled against walls and equipment, and then Hawkins stepped into the open, aiming for the top of the stairs. He ducked back as automatic gunfire was returned.

"They've got good cover up there," Hawkins said.

"The last thing I want is for us to get stuck," McCarter said.

"We just might be," Encizo said. "If they're well-armed up there, they could hold the stairs for quite a long time."

"This is why we should always carry shoulder-fired rocket launchers," Hawkins said.

McCarter said, "Okay, bloody smart-ass, you, Rafe and Manning. Go back out the front, circle the building and see if you can find a way in the rear. James and I will keep our friends upstairs busy."

The three soldiers hurried away, and Calvin James stepped around the corner to deliver a burst to the top of the stairs. He saw a hand and an upper body sink down behind an eight-foot-wide window—the factory supervisor's office. James targeted the window. It shattered noisily. He waited for more signs of life, heard nothing at first, then came a clattering of feet upstairs. Another grenade came flying over the top rail and bonked on the concrete floor.

James hurried back to their cover. Another frag burst open behind him and filled the open factory floor with deadly shrapnel.

"We're making *some* progress, anyway," McCarter said.

"Such as what, exactly? Teasing out their supply of hand grenades?"

"That, and putting this factory out of commission. They are doing more damage to it themselves than we could possibly hope to."

THE EXTERIOR of the plant was deceptively peaceful. The night in Taiwan was quiet. The Phoenix Force warriors marched along the perimeter of the building and found nothing but blank brick wall. No windows or doors. The fire escapes were far above the ground.

"There's a loading bay in the rear," Manning noted. "We could make an entrance there."

"Wait," Hawkins said. "Look at this." He indicated the fire escape above them, its extendable ladder partially descended. It was still several feet above their heads.

"That's got to open up into the upper level, right?" Hawkins said.

"Can we get that ladder down?" Encizo asked.

Hawkins extracted a short length of utility cable and tossed the hook at the lowest rung. The hook grabbed the rung on the second try. He wrapped the end of the cable around his wrist and dragged on it. The ladder rattled, and Hawkins gave it another lunge with all of his body weight. The ladder began to descend, its corroded components protesting noisily. Encizo grabbed the line above Hawkins, and they both hauled against it, and the ladder moved four feet closer.

"Give me a hand, Rafe." Hawkins didn't wait for a response. He stepped up into Encizo's right hand, then onto his shoulder, using the brick wall for support, and finally onto Encizo's head, giving him the last few inches he needed. The bottom rung on the ladder fell into his grip. He held on, then swung his body and managed to drag the ladder a few feet closer to the ground.

Encizo leaped, snatched Hawkins by the ankles, and together their weight dragged the screeching, protesting ladder to its full extension.

Encizo followed Hawkins up the rungs, tousling gravel out of his hair as he did so.

Manning stayed below and quickly contacted McCarter via his new headset, updating him on their activity.

"I don't think we should ignore the rear loading bay," Manning said. "I'm going to go check that out myself."

There was a pause. "Do it," McCarter said.

Manning jogged in exactly the wrong direction— toward the front of the building.

"Gary—" Encizo called.

"I'm perfectly aware," Manning responded.

Manning headed for the parking lot, nearly empty, and ducked behind a parked truck at the rear, in an unlit corner of the lot.

"Maybe he needs to take a leak and wants some privacy," Hawkins suggested quietly.

In that moment they saw the outlines of an SUV,

running dark, veer off the street and stop behind the parked truck.

"I knew it," Hawkins said. "He's got a date with the CIA in the tight jeans."

They reached the top of the ladder and crept onto the steel-grate platform outside a tall window. The platform creaked under their weight, and Encizo couldn't help but notice that the bolts that held the platform into the brick wall were rusted and loose. A full inch of slack separated the wall from the landing.

They stayed clear of the window, just in case the dim light of the nighttime silhouetted them against the blinds. But the room seemed dark and quiet. Encizo pressed his ear to the glass, heard nothing and shook his head.

Then he put both hands against the glass and pushed up. The window moved, opening a few inches and squeaking slightly. He grabbed under it and muscled it all the way open, then poked through the blinds with his M-16.

The room was empty and dark, but a door stood ajar. They could hear activity outside the room. As Encizo stepped inside, a man scrambled down the hall, keeping low, and ducked into the room with them. He stopped cold, facing them. Encizo jammed the M-16 into the soft tissue under the man's chin and lifted his head high, while Hawkins relieved the man of his AK-47.

Hawkins checked the AK. Bone-dry.

"They may be running low on ammo up here," Hawkins noted.

"Where is Zordun?" Encizo demanded, pressing the gun barrel harder up under the man's chin, forcing him to rise up on his toes. The man had the look of an

Uyghur. He might have been one of Zordun's personal retinue and quite likely a relative.

The man was afraid, but he wasn't talking, either.

In fact, he made a break for it. He pulled away quickly and pushed himself through the door, shouting, only to collapse after just a few steps. Hawkins had shot the backs of his knees out.

Encizo and Hawkins took the offensive. They moved into the hall and cut down the gunners who appeared one after another from the room ahead. Another man attempted to leap to safety over their falling bodies but didn't make the distance. He landed on the head of a fallen friend and twisted his ankle savagely. The ankle stopped working. The gunner landed and twisted in the tight space with his dead friend and somehow managed to get his AK in front of him.

Hawkins had no intention of testing his theory that these men had used up all of their small-arms ammo. He stitched the man from crotch to throat with a burst from the M-16, and as the man died his finger jerked on the AK trigger. The gun coughed up a single round that buried itself in the wall.

Hawkins and Encizo advanced, swept the room that the three had emerged from and found it to be an empty media room. Across the hall were empty, filthy bedrooms. Up ahead the hallway ended at the railing looking out onto the manufacturing floor.

Hawkins was realizing just how large this upper-level residential structure actually was.

"Talk about dedication to work," Hawkins said. "They must've lived here."

Encizo touched his headset. "McCarter, T.J. and I are

in the upper level. We're going to be coming out onto the railing in a minute."

"Understood," McCarter replied.

Encizo emerged, finding himself at the far end of the landing at the top of the stairs. Hawkins stepped into the open and fired a burst at the other end of the upper level, which elicited return fire. It was another long burst of AK fire, which flew out into the open warehouse. The gunner had no line of sight on Hawkins.

But now Encizo and Hawkins knew exactly where he was. The wide picture window, where the supervisor could sit and watch the manufacturing activity below, was now obliterated. The glass had shattered in all directions. The gunner was inside that room—and essentially trapped.

Encizo and Hawkins hugged the wall and approached the open window, listening to the activity inside. Someone was panting, removed a magazine and replaced it. It sounded like a handgun.

Encizo was thinking that this gunner had also drained his AK-47 dry.

He could see McCarter down below, peering from his cover. McCarter spoke, and Encizo heard his voice through his headset.

"Would it help if I attracted his attention?"

Encizo gave McCarter a big, silent thumbs-up.

McCarter stepped into full view and triggered his weapon, aiming far to the right of the upper-level window, so as not to risk an errant round hitting Encizo or Hawkins. The man in the office saw his enemy emerge into plain view, completely exposed. Then for a heartbeat McCarter stopped firing and just stood there, looking at his gun with exaggerated confusion.

The man in the office was lured out. He came to the open window. McCarter bolted. The man fired a 9 mm handgun once—then Encizo chopped the hand off with a burst of autofire.

Encizo stepped in front of the window and swept the room, and found only bodies.

The one-handed man pushed himself to his feet, gripping his bloody wrist stump, and Encizo threatened him with a gunshot to the head.

"Where is Zordun?"

"Zordun left us!" the man snarled through bitterness and pain. "He betrayed his own family and left us to die."

"Where did he go?" Encizo demanded.

The man panted through his teeth and said, "You get him, you send him to hell with me. But now he's going to fly away."

"Where's the aircraft?" Encizo demanded—but all at once he knew.

The one-handed man confirmed it. "The loading bay." Zordun's relative jerked his head in that direction and then staggered out of the room and onto the landing outside. Very deliberately, he tipped himself over the rail. He fell thirty feet to the concrete floor below and landed with a crunch.

CELLO WAS POUNDING the steering wheel, barely able to contain herself as she watched the flashes of gunfire and a wisp of smoke rising from one of the windows of the Zordun plant. She couldn't stand not being a part of the insertion.

When she had gotten the call from Manning she'd

shouted and stomped on the gas. She'd driven dark to rendezvous with the big Canadian.

Manning pulled the rear hatch open and yanked their prisoner onto the asphalt.

"You stay with him," Manning said.

"No *fucking* way! I'm going with you."

"No way, CIA," Manning said. "You're official in this country. You get dirty and it could end your career."

"I'll risk it," Cello insisted.

"Sorry." Manning stepped behind the wheel and stomped on the gas, the lurch forward slamming the door for him. He sped across the asphalt and crossed the long, long acres of patchy grass. Up ahead he saw the double-wide delivery bay doors rise up and slot into the ceiling. Manning spun the wheel, maneuvering the Mercedes SUV until he could see what was parked inside.

He saw the nose of a small aircraft.

From this distance the stealth jet looked like an RC aircraft—but someone was preparing for takeoff.

Manning knew it was Ali Zordun.

And the isolated back road leading to the delivery bay could easily serve as a runway for one of those short-taxiing jets. In this isolated, industrial part of the country, a near-silent, unlit aircraft could make a landing or takeoff unnoticed.

Manning had little time to act. He chose his targets from a pair of vehicles parked in the grass near the bay doors. There was a tricked-out Hummer and an old Honda on blocks, no rubber on its rims.

Manning picked the Honda. He gave gas to the Mercedes SUV and plowed head-on into the little car. The front end of the SUV sent the Honda flying off its blocks, and it tumbled unsteadily over the ground.

Manning rolled down the windows. He could hear the distant burst of gunfire, and maybe he heard the hush of quiet engines—or maybe not.

He nudged the front end against the Honda and gave it a shove. The Honda rolled awkwardly. There were obviously more problems to the suspension and simply missing tires but Manning pushed it aggressively until it veered away and went broadside.

Manning reversed the SUV then drove into the Honda, shoving it toward the road-runway.

The nose of the aircraft emerged from the bay.

Manning couldn't risk losing the Honda again. If he kept the thing moving along steadily he would get it onto the road in time.

If he was too slow, then his only option would be to put the Mercedes SUV itself on the runway to stop that aircraft from taking off.

He wasn't sure if Cello's SUV was armored against .50-caliber machine-gun fire and he didn't want to find out.

Then the Honda veered off course yet again, just ten feet from the runway.

Manning saw the aircraft make a forty-five-degree turn to face down the runway, and he thought he could see the face of the man in the cockpit, lit by the glow of the cockpit controls.

Manning reversed the SUV as the small jet accelerated abruptly. The pilot knew Manning's intention and simply planned to outrace him.

Manning stomped on the gas and plowed hard into the broadside of the little Honda and pushed the little car at the road.

The two tail-mounted engines were already at full

thrust, and the rush of wind turned to a whine, and the aircraft sped over the pavement while Manning fought for every foot. The bare rims were plowing earth and the Honda was shuddering violently. The small jet was already just a few feet away. Manning took a gamble. He reversed a little and accelerated, hard, fast, and slammed the front end of the SUV into the junk Honda. And he didn't stop. One way or another there was going to be something there to stop that jet.

The Honda jarred against the pavement and rolled onto its side on the surface of the runway.

Manning for a fraction of a second could see the look of horror on the face of the pilot. Manning yanked the SUV into Reverse and gassed it hard. The SUV recoiled from the runway.

But suddenly the aircraft was steered into a sideways skid, and it crunched up broadside against the upturned Honda.

Fuel spilled from multiple penetration points. The hatch burst open. A man leaped from the cockpit as flame swept over the body of the jet.

But he left the aircraft seconds too late. Spilling fuel soaked his clothing, and the man danced while flames engulfed his body. He dropped and rolled on the grass desperately, slapping himself and shouting wordlessly, but the spilled fuel would not be quenched for many long seconds.

Then he got to his feet, clothing burned, his skin cooked across his chest and bare arms and shoulders and neck. His eyes were white with agony, but when he saw Gary Manning loping across the grass to intercept him, the man attempted to flee.

Manning sprinted after the figure and shoved him

between the shoulder blades. His hand came away with a crust of burned flesh. He shook it off and approached the fallen man.

The man's eyes rolled violently back and forth and he shook his head spasmodically. His violent actions broke open a crust of burned skin, and his blood flowed out by the pint.

Ali Zordun was drained and dead within seconds.

CHAPTER TWENTY-THREE

Manning was disgusted to realize that he had burned his hand on Zordun's cooked flesh. The charred crust wouldn't shake off.

He used his left hand to reach over his head and detach the lipstick cam from his headset. He touched the LED light on the cam and held it over the face of the dead man.

"Stony," he requested, "take a look at this."

Stony Man Farm, Virginia

BARBARA PRICE WAS NO stranger to violent death, but even she was shocked by the image that popped up, in brilliant color and vivid detail, on the huge plasma screen in the War Room. Carmen Delahunt gasped and put her hand over her mouth. Akira Tokaido stood and grinned from ear to ear.

"Got 'im!"

"Is this our man, Stony?" Manning asked.

Price examined the steaming, blackened corpse displayed on the screen, trying to concentrate on the relatively unscathed face.

She knew that face. It matched the photo in their files.

"That's him. Ali Zordun," Price said.

"Problem solved, Stony," Manning said.

If only it were that easy, Price thought.

"Stony," Manning said, "I could use a first-aid kit." Then he added, "And a hospital burn unit..."

THE NEWS NETWORKS worldwide were beside themselves. They didn't know what to make of the unexpected news coup staged by, of all things, a weather network. All over the world, people were turning to a dedicated live station established by Worldwide Weather News to view live video streams from around the world. Every time a stealth aircraft took to the air, its location could be viewed by millions of TV watchers worldwide.

Enthusiastic viewers helped raise alerts, and several of the planes were apprehended or destroyed. A cocaine shipment from Africa to France was met at an isolated landing site by a hundred French police officers and a thousand onlookers.

A cargo of heroin was forced down in a cornfield in southern Illinois and burned on the spot. The farmer who owned the field was on the news, describing how he was standing in his living room, watching the aircraft on his TV, then running to the porch to watch it land in his field.

There was even a sighting of an aircraft leaving the scene of the military buildup off Taiwan. The aircraft had put down quickly on mainland China. The government of China denied that such a plane had ever existed.

"THE TECHNOLOGY IS USELESS. China won't try to use it again. They'll be happy to forget the entire fiasco," Brognola reported from his office in D.C. "They're claiming that the activity in the South China Sea was a scheduled military exercise. The focus never was on

Taiwan. That's what they're saying. The buildup has been entirely dispersed as of today."

"Any recriminations coming out of Beijing?" Price asked.

"None. I don't know that they ever even suspected U.S. involvement."

"You can't ask for a better conclusion than that," Kurtzman said.

"What about their attack on Brezius?" Price said.

"The Chinese aren't going to say anything about *that*," Brognola said. "But the administration sure is. The President wants to know how a bunch of U.S. Special Forces, all with honorable discharges, ended up on the Chinese payroll."

Price said, "Is the administration surprised by it? We've seen this kind of thing before."

"The administration is—alarmed. By the way, Brezius got his immunity. On the condition he keeps his mouth shut. He's even been offered employment with a National Reconnaissance Office branch. He's going to accept the NRO position, whether he wants to or not. There's going to be a high degree of attention paid to his activities for the next decade."

"I'm glad he got a break. He was cooperative," Price said. "After we saved him from being killed."

"Yeah. A real trouper," Brognola growled. "What happened to the facilities in Pingtung? I assume the Taiwanese have taken care of it?"

Price nodded. "They did a very complete job. Our friend from the CIA made a drive-by. She reports both facilities were leveled. She thinks they're going to turn the sites into parks. Taiwan doesn't want China to have any suspicions that they tried to exploit that technology."

"And Phoenix?" Brognola asked.

"Gary burned his hand. Not much damage but a very serious risk from infection. He had pieces of Mr. Zordun heat-fused to his own skin."

Brognola grimaced.

"His hand was surgically scraped, and he'll be on an antibiotic IV for days. In fact, the rumor mill says he's got an extraspecial nurse taking care of him."

On the big plasma screen, Brognola raised an eyebrow. "Really?"

Antai Tain-Sheng Memorial Hospital

"TAIWAN HAS THE BEST hospitals I've ever been in," Gary Manning said. He was sitting in an easy chair, in civilian clothes, and the only sign of his infirmity was a bandaged right hand and an IV feeding into his arm.

In his left hand he had a remote for the flat-screen TV on the wall.

"They've got ESPN channels here that I've never even heard of. Ever hear of an ESPN curling channel? All curling, all the time, channel 678."

T. J. Hawkins glared at Manning, trying to figure out if he was lying.

A cafeteria tray rolled into the room, propelled by Cello Jiahua. She was all smiles for the men of Phoenix Force, but it was a bigger, better smile for Gary Manning.

"I found you a better tray," she announced. She lifted the cover from the cafeteria tray that was already positioned next to his chair, wrinkled her nose at the contents and moved it aside. She pushed her tray into its place and pulled a six-pack of cold Cokes from the bottom shelf. She put the six-pack in McCarter's hands.

"Mr. M."

"Thanks." McCarter began to break off Cokes and pass them around.

As they watched soccer out of Brunei, Manning ate his Cello-approved lunch happily, with Cello herself perched comfortably on the arm of his easy chair. Encizo inspected the lunch tray that had been deemed unsuitable for Manning and devoured it without complaint.

Calvin James leaned close to Encizo and said, "Ever heard the term *reverse jailbait?*"

Encizo chewed his rice and nodded. "Mena Suvari-type. She's thirty-three but looks sixteen."

"Yeah."

Cello cast a glare at Encizo and James. "Don't you guys have to get back to the United States or something?"

"Yeah," McCarter said, "this afternoon. You'll have to be on your own for a few days, Gary. Sure hope you'll be okay."

"I'll survive," Manning said. "This is the nicest hospital I've ever been in."

"So you've said."

The other four members of the Phoenix Force commando team left the hospital, on their way to the airport.

"What exactly is it that makes this such a fantastic hospital?" Cello asked.

"Cable TV." Manning waved at the flat-screen TV. "Recliner. These are all good things. Beds are way more comfortable than U.S. hospitals."

She folded her arms.

"But," Manning said, "I think the best part is definitely the reverse jailbait."

* * * * *